Pebble in the Dark – The Trauma

-BOOK TWO-
of the Pebble in the Dark Series

By Antony Botting

For Kylie

'Happy reading

09/02/19

IN LOVING MEMORY OF MY GRANDMOTHER

-Chapter 1-

In the early brisk spring dawn over the Balkan Mountains, a short old woman, draped in black and supporting her weight on a knobbly wooden stick, walked carefully. Her white hair hung long and shabbily pleated from under the hood that she had fashioned for herself. The cracking and rustling of broken twigs and leaves underfoot was the only sound in the morning calmness. Licking her chapped lips, she stopped in her tracks and looked at her surroundings. The thick pine forest shrouded much from sight, but she could hear the faint rustling of movement.

Shifting her weight around the wooden stick adeptly, she sought the source of the sound. A network of roots jutting from the ground was difficult to pass, but she was not perturbed and continued.

The woman looked on with keen interest and wide eyes. In view was a man packing a sleeping bag into his rucksack, along with several other small items of camping equipment. He muttered to himself in a foreign language. His tone, upset and hurried.

Slowly placing the wicker basket, containing some collected berries and herbs, onto the ground, the woman crept forward with nimble precision.

A voice had woken Jerome Docherty from his sleep. The same voice he was now convinced had been with him throughout his life. The voice was clear. It echoed through his mind incessantly. Relentlessly. The words were sometimes soft, but often commanding. Words sometimes, other times fragmented sentences. Sometimes silence. The pain in his head was piercing.

Righting himself, he spun round sharply to see who or what was approaching, but the sudden motion caused him to lose balance and become dizzy. Stumbling backwards a step, he trod on his rucksack and, nearly falling, managed to support himself on the tree trunk.

Collecting himself, Jerome was taken aback by the sight of the woman whose face was mostly hidden in the darkness cast by a hood.

'Hello,' he said uneasily.

The old woman continued to hobble towards Jerome, supported by her stick. With her free hand she pulled the hood back, revealing her face, and raised a disarming smile. An inexplicably calming effect washed over Jerome as she spoke some words in a soft, gentle, but faintly creaking tone. He was not able to understand the language so he shrugged and laughed sheepishly. Dropping her stick to the ground, the woman continued to smile and mutter words under her breath and she bent down with her back turned to Jerome. Standing to face him once again, she grabbed hold of his hand and placed a small mushroom in his palm, making a gesture towards her own mouth with her other hand.

Realising the woman could surely not be asking him to eat the mushroom, Jerome assumed she wanted to know if he was hungry, which he was. Three days in the mountains had depleted his provisions and this offer was not one that he planned to turn down. Clutching the fungus in his hand, Jerome grinned warmly, partly to indicate his hunger, but also to acknowledge – if only to himself – the humorous nature of the exchange. The old woman nodded as she drew her hood back over her head and picked up her stick. By the time Jerome had collected his rucksack from the ground, she had almost disappeared from view. He could vaguely make out her form as she collected the basket containing the items she had foraged. Had she moved quickly or had time slipped for him again? His thoughts, clouded by the haze of drowsiness, made him wonder whether he was dreaming. Such was the surreal nature of the encounter.

Jerome followed the old woman as she slowly navigated through the forest. Peeking into the basket swinging to and fro in her tight grip, he could see a variety of leaves and berries.

Distracted from his surroundings temporarily, a gradual darkening became noticeable to Jerome. Looking up, the tree cover had thickened substantially. Ahead, a peculiar looking small wooden hut sat amidst a collage of wild woodland flowers, encircled by a fence made up of white criss-crossed sticks. From a distance, he saw that two husky puppies were excitedly awaiting the woman's return and stood waggy-tailed and panting on the path.

Walking through the opening in the fence, the old woman put her basket on the ground and greeted the puppies with a scratch behind the ears, muttering to them in a loving tone. Following her through the opening, Jerome quickly noticed that the puppies were not huskies, but wolves. Young enough to not have lost their innocent eyes, they both ran to inspect the visitor and Jerome hesitantly reached down to pet them, hoping for the best. Their deep orange eyes were captivating, but shifty and the softness of their brown, grey and white fur was addictive as he ran his fingers through it. Caught in the gaze of one of the pups momentarily, he felt the warmth of a ray of sunlight on his cheek, which had found its way through to him. Hoping that the pups' mother was nowhere nearby, he walked up the creaky wooden steps to the entrance that the old woman had left open for him. Bending down to avoid hitting his head on the frame, he closed the door as he entered.

Inside, the windows were small and the hut was dark. Cosy, he thought. Taking off his boots, Jerome's attention was drawn to the unidentified sweet smell surrounding him, the stone fireplace on the opposite wall and, to a lesser extent, the fact that he couldn't remember why he had come here. Remnant wood was smouldering and the old woman pulled back her hood, but didn't remove her cloak. Picking up a metal poker she prodded the dying fire several times purposefully before lumping on an additional log. Moving toward the fireplace, Jerome was pleased to feel soft, warm carpet under his feet; a basic luxury he hadn't experienced in days, but had sorely missed. He felt at home. The woman hummed as she placed an iron kettle full of water on the hearth, just close enough to the flames to heat.

Sitting on the thick, white sheepskin rug taking up most of the floor space in front of the fireplace, Jerome crossed his legs. A shuffling sound in the corner of the room drew his attention. A small brown bear cub – no more than a few weeks old – was rolling on its back playfully. Immediately drawn to Jerome, it scampered in his direction and clambered onto his lap. Looking shocked and unsure how to react, Jerome winced as its small but regimented claws dug into his leg as it climbed. The bear settled on his lap as he ran his hand along the top of the cub's head and down its back through thick, soft fur. This had a very calming effect, but he wondered what other surprises there may be in store.

Jerome observed with interest as the old woman seemed to chortle with laughter before walking out of the front door and disappearing from view. Hearing the creaking of steps followed by the sound of some further activity, he couldn't think what she might possibly be doing. Hearing the footsteps returning, Jerome knew she hadn't been far. Walking back into the hut holding a piece of dried meat, the old woman stood at a small wooden table upon which lay a chopping board. The shelves above the table were stocked with glass jars containing a variety of herbs and spices. She plucked some fresh tomatoes from a vine suspended above the table, as well as a cucumber. She spent the next few moments chopping furiously as Jerome sensed his own hunger growing. His appetite voracious, he looked forward to eating. The bear cub soon left him and returned to its blanket on the wooden floor.

Picking what looked like tea leaves from a dry bundle in the corner of the room, the old woman moved the kettle away from the flames and dropped a handful in. Stirring gently with a long wooden spoon, she replaced the lid with a metallic clink.

Before long, Jerome was presented with a plate covered in rustic delicacies. Slices of delicious dry-cured meat were garnished with a cucumber, tomato and green-herb salad, pickled peppers and home-baked bread. Unsure how she had put together such a feast and slightly embarrassed that he would be the only one eating, Jerome rested the plate on a small, round table of black stone that sat in front of him on the rug. He tucked in as the old woman sighed contentedly, taking her seat across from him on a rocking chair, which was covered with a thick red-green-and-white blanket. While he ate, the chair creaked slightly as she rocked backwards and forwards with a fond look on her face. Jerome finished the food quickly and she leaned forward to pick up the kettle from the hearth. Two cups sat on the black table and the old woman poured tea to the brim in both. Steam rose from the cups like apparitions in the dark, changing shape and dancing invitingly.

Taking his first sip, Jerome's senses were tickled by the strangely fresh but musty tasting hot tea. Like nothing he had ever tasted before, he instantly liked it and carried on sipping until it was finished. Still holding the cup, he listened to the quietness in the room, where the only sound was the crackling of the fire and the occasional creak from the rocking chair.

The old woman stood from her chair, moving smoothly down to her knees on the carpet. She sat opposite Jerome across the black table. The flames from the fire provided most of the illumination in the room and the amber light flickered on her face, accentuating her wrinkles as she smiled, reflecting off her pleated silver hair. The sounds Jerome could hear from outside had fallen silent. His attention was drawn to a strange movement he could see out of the small window. In the distance, through the trees, what appeared at first to be a gentle white haze was rolling towards the hut. As it approached, he saw that the seeming thin haze was actually a thick fog enveloping the pines, tree line after tree line. Moving rapidly ever closer, it silently enveloped the hut, hiding everything from view. The fog brought on a sudden darkening outside. Seeping into the hut from the windows and around the door, it billowed around them both.

Seeing Jerome's concern, the old woman hadn't turned to look, but instead her attention remained fixed on him. Looking down at the teacup she still held in her hands, she was quiet for a moment.

Reaching back to pull the hood over her head, she began to speak in what he presumed was Bulgarian. Her words were softly spoken and she held a storytelling tone, but Jerome could no longer see her face, which was shrouded in the darkness. He couldn't understand her words either, but they had an instant calming effect on him. Leaning back on his elbows, he listened intently.

Continuing to speak, the old woman gathered breadcrumbs from her plate between her finger and thumb and sprinkled them into her half-drunk cup of tea. Reaching for the kettle, she removed the iron lid and placed it on top of her teacup with a clink as she continued to speak.

Gradually, Jerome's mood began to change and a wave of sadness washed over him, taking him by surprise.

Realising that he wasn't able to hear anything apart from her words – as though some sort of deafness had afflicted him – he became startled and tried to move but found that making the slightest shift caused him excruciating pain.

Breathing the white cloud aggravated his airways and he started to gasp. As though breathing sand, his eyes welled with tears and he coughed profusely.

Squinting with indescribable agony that had ignited nerve endings all over his body, Jerome was able to make out the whites of the old woman's eyes underneath her hood. His vibrating vision made it difficult to focus as his body shook, but he watched as she began to speak again, leaning forward as she did so.

'Do you know why you are here?' the old woman asked. Jerome was in no condition to respond and was reeling from the state he found himself in. In the moment he had no time to question how he was able to understand her words.

'It's because you are dying. That is why. You don't know it, but you feel it and you don't have much time left,' she said in a sympathetic sounding and ever creakier tone. 'But I will help you. I will help you to find what you seek,' she whispered.

Released from the grip of anguish clutching him tightly, Jerome gasped and involuntarily sprawled to his side. Breathing heavily with his eyes closed, he felt the soft texture of the rug on his face. Raising his head and lifting himself slightly, he saw that the room was thick with the white, choking fog. The old woman sat still and unmoved opposite Jerome as he struggled to right himself. A feeling of severe fatigue had set in to his limbs and he felt weak. The old woman's words resonated with him. He had felt that something hadn't been right for a while. His loss of balance, his migraines and the voice in his head, all started to make more sense now. But it was these things that had also brought him here and he didn't know why.

'My animals approve of you, searcher. Fortunate. Rest now and remember that which I tell my animals. Climbing up is easier than climbing down,' she ominously said.

A sense of overpowering drowsiness came over Jerome as he lay to his side. Battling to keep his eyes open, he vaguely saw the old woman's lips moving through the mist and darkness. She stood from her chair and walked away slowly. He saw her thin bony ankles under the cloak before he passed out. Much like the sensation of falling when drifting to sleep, the floor beneath him heaved and moved.

Chapter 2

A cool draught passed over Jerome, who awoke curled on the rug where he had fallen asleep. Disorientated at first, he quickly recognised the soft texture of the sheepskin and even in the darkness could make out the main features of the room. Night had fallen and the hut felt empty. No life in the extinguished fireplace and no movement whatsoever.

Standing to his feet gradually, his back and legs clicked with stiffness. Jerome stepped towards the old woman's chair. She was gone and there was no sign of the bear cub either. Picking up his rucksack, Jerome wasted no time in slipping on his boots and making his way to the front door, creaking on its hinges and slightly ajar. Stepping outside onto the top step he rubbed his eyes, still blurry from sleep. Running his hand through his wavy grey hair, the blurriness of his surroundings started to come into focus.

The darkness of the night outside was faintly illuminated by the crescent moon and stars above. It took him a moment longer than it should have to realise that he shouldn't be able to see the stars. The hut he had arrived at was in a thick pine forest. His surroundings now were bare – all except a few short bushes. Staggering down the steps in disbelief, he released one arm of his rucksack and swung it round to his front.

Pulling a small metal flashlight from one of the pockets, he switched it on and a strong beam lit up the area before him. The torchlight shone through the tops of the bushes that made up his desolate surroundings, and Jerome was not able to see much in the distance. Pausing to collect his thoughts, he turned off the torch and dropped his arm.

'What the...' he muttered, shaking his head in disbelief. Turning the torch back on, he pointed it at the dry earth surrounding him, looking for any clue or trace of activity.

The soil was dusty, and strewn with small broken branch fragments and dry leaves. Bending down, Jerome saw that only one set of tracks was visible. The ground didn't make for a clear imprint. Following the trail of steps away from the hut, his torch shone upon a partial footprint in the dusty soil. Dropping to his knees to inspect it more closely, Jerome recognised it as his own footprint, by the branding symbol and the print pattern. He searched around the hut frantically for other tracks but found none. Not any.

Dumbfounded, he sat on the bottom wooden step, thinking about his memories of recent events. What he could recall wasn't scrambled, but crystal clear. Standing, he walked away from the hut, turned, and shone his light at it. Definitely the same hut that he had been led to by the old woman. He was certain.

Doing all that was left for him to do, Jerome started to follow the one set of tracks away from the rickety old hut. Thoughts were darting through his mind wildly and his breaths were becoming shallow and nervous with fright. The light from his torch lit the way, but quaked in his hand. He walked for a couple of moments, before he saw what looked like a ledge, beyond which there was darkness. Cautiously approaching, he peered over the cliff edge and felt a strong updraft. Pointing the torch down into the blackness, the beam faintly lit the trees far below.

Jerome spent the next few moments carefully searching the area for any other tracks leading away from the edge of the cliff. Unable to find any, he refused to accept the version of events which the physical evidence seemed to suggest. Namely, that he had free climbed the sheer rock face. In his youth Jerome had been an accomplished climber, but now at the age of fifty-three he was in no condition to have dared attempt such a climb without equipment.

'You know full well that you didn't climb this bloody thing!' he exclaimed, hitting his right temple a few times with the palm of his hand. He turned and started to follow the edge of the precipice. Walking with haste, he was no longer looking for tracks, but instead for a way down. Within five minutes he had come full circle back to the section of cliff at which he had first arrived. He and the hut were located on top of a very tall monolith.

On his hands and knees, he peered over the side and checked once again for any sign of anchors or climbing rope which he might have missed, but could see none.

Sitting with his legs dangling over the edge of the cliff, Jerome planted his face in his hands and wondered if he was losing his mind. There was no explanation for what was happening. At least, no explanation that he could think of. As time passed, the dawn sky lit up over the mountains, goading him to make a decision.

Lifting his head from his cupped hands, he saw no scratches, abrasions or bruising on his fingers or palms – injuries and marks that he surely would have sustained, had he climbed the rock face.

The magnificence and scale of Jerome's surroundings became clearer with every passing moment, as did the seriousness of his predicament.

He could see no sign of civilisation in any direction and he knew the likelihood of a rescue was remote.

Tilting his centre of gravity forward, he peered vertically down once again, looking at the daunting rock for any marks or signs of his ascent, but could still see none. Not surprising, he thought, as he had brought no climbing chalk with him.

Angry and confused, Jerome lifted his rucksack above his head and screamed furiously as he hurled it toward the trees below. A few seconds later, it hit a tree before crashing to the ground. Closing his eyes and composing himself for a moment, Jerome wiped his clammy hands on his trousers before scooping some dusty earth and leaves into his pocket. Rubbing his hands together vigorously, he dried his hands as much as possible. Lowering himself down, legs first, Jerome's knees scraped the edge of the cliff. His foot desperately searched for its first foothold.

'Well done, Jerome, you crazy old bastard,' he muttered in frustration as his foot found a toehold. Gradually lowering and attaching himself to the rock as best he could, he wondered whether today would be his last. Down-climbing had always been something which he had tried to avoid where possible and now, with no rope and clinging to the cold rock, he was out of options. Shifting his head, left and right to look for hand and footholds below, Jerome focused on staying calm and keeping his palms dry, but this was no easy task. Fine dust rained down below as his hands and feet shifted position. Fixated on the rock surface only, he consciously avoided looking down at the drop below. The steady updraft of wind blew his hair messily across his face, but with no spare hand to control it, Jerome did his best to ignore the distraction.

A few metres down, his forearms were already burning with lactic acid as his fingers clung on. The morning chorus of birds rang in his ears and soothed him as he continued. The surface felt stable and his confidence was growing as his left leg reached down further. Jerome felt the rock break away and a sinking feeling hit his gut as he realised that he had committed too much of his trust and weight on the untested foothold. He lost his grip with his right hand and his body pivoted round, wrenching his left arm, which barely held on. His back smashed into the rock surface and he luckily managed to land his right foot in the newly exposed area of rock.

Doing everything that he could to hang on with his left arm, which was in much pain, Jerome gently used his body to turn back round. His hand grabbed his shoulder as he grunted and breathed heavily, trying desperately to recover. Blood from his fingertips stained his clothes.

Continuing the descent, his line of sight came level with the new hole in the wall. His eye was instantly drawn to the glistening shine of exposed black metal. A surface so clean and inviting, with several interconnected rune-like characters visible.

Touching the black metal was the last thing that Jerome could remember as he sat opposite the doctor in his surgery. Staring blankly through the desk in front of him, he had zoned out.

'Mr Docherty!' the doctor insistently said, as Jerome's attention was brought back.

'Yes, sorry. It is a lot to take in. What did you say?' Jerome asked.

'I'm sorry to have been the one to tell you this. I asked whether you'd experienced any hallucinations or side-effects, other than the headaches which you described.'

Jerome paused for a moment and had to stop himself from bursting out in laughter. A broad grin spread across his face as he reassured the doctor that he was not suffering from any hallucinations.

Standing from the chair, he turned and walked toward the door.

'Mr Docherty, we need to speak about your treatment. With brain tumours of this type, it's time critical,' the doctor said, raising his voice with a sense of urgency and furrowing his brow.

'We will, but there are a few things I have to do first.'

-Chapter 3-

How did he know? How had he known that it would be that shape? Why have I not asked myself that before? Mike Argo sat in the sauna, trying to relax after a workout at the gym in the Future Logic Facility. As he inhaled the dry heat through his nose, the inviting smell of eucalyptus entertained his senses. More serious thoughts taunted him, and had done for some time.

Jerome Docherty had been an extraordinary archaeologist, but Argo was spending more and more time thinking about how he had actually located the Pebble. Its location was remote and inaccessible, making a chance discovery unlikely. The prehistoric nature of the find meant it was improbable that Jerome had followed any sort of human or material clue to the find.

Finally, even if he had made the find totally by chance, why had he called it the Pebble? It was encased in rock and Docherty would have seen only a small segment of the whole craft. He couldn't have known the overall size and shape, nor that it had potentially brought the first life to earth, as he had eerily claimed in his letters. Realising that there was a lot remaining unanswered, Argo lay on his towel to relax. He permitted himself a few moments of thoughtless bliss as he closed his eyes. He found keeping his mind clear harder than ever.

Argo often found that he did most of his best thinking and problem solving in the relaxation room, but not today. A cloud of uncertainty and confusion hung over him since the arrival of the Pebble.

Hearing faint but sturdy footsteps approaching on the tiles outside, he opened one eye and peered towards the glass door as it opened sharply.

'If you spent as much time in the gym as you do in here, Mike,' said his Head of Security, Adam Diaz, in a thick Colombian accent as he strode in, wrapped in a large white towel.

'If we built another gym and sauna for you to use, you wouldn't be able to give me such a hard time,' responded Argo in an overheated and weary voice.

'You're in bad enough shape as it is. Without me training you, you'd really be in trouble,' Adam responded, shaking his head and tutting. Argo glanced at Adam, who sat looking pleased with himself. 'We will speak about your lack of motivation next time. What did you want to talk about?'

'Vincent Madden. He's been here at the facility for over three months now. Your men have been watching him. I want to know what you think,' Argo asked frankly.

'What *I* think?' said Adam. 'What I think is that he hasn't tried to escape and hasn't looked interested in trying.'

'And what do you think that means?' Argo pressed.

'Nothing. It doesn't mean anything at all. That's what I would do too,' Adam said plainly. 'I've looked through his file, cover to cover. Have you?'

'No,' Argo retorted, righting himself to a seated position.

'I don't like that file, Mike. It's full of rumours and not enough facts. His friend who died – Wasyl Bohdanov – an account says that he once was held and tortured in a secret location. Vincent Madden found Wasyl within forty-eight hours, but to do it, he killed seven men, after getting information from each of them,' Adam said. 'You asked my advice when you brought him here and it hasn't changed. Give me the word and you won't have to worry about him anymore.

A man like that will tell you what you want to hear and do what you want him to do until you let your guard down. You can't control him,' Adam quietly muttered.

'Sounds like a challenge,' Argo replied, patting Adam on his shoulder as he stood to his feet and left the sauna. His legs felt weak and rubbery from the punishment they had taken in the gym as he walked away, but he was determined not to let it show.

Back in his quarters, and still light-headed from the sweltering heat of the sauna, Argo limped towards the kitchen. Opening the fridge, he blended two heaped scoops of vanilla whey protein with milk. Pressing his thumb against the fingerprint scanner in the top compartment of the fridge, a hiss sounded as the sealed door popped open. Argo removed a glistening silver blister pack with no markings from the fridge and popped free an elongated capsule with his thumb. The capsule was dark blue in colour and on the side, the word 'Boon' was clearly stamped in white. Swallowing the Boon capsule with gulp after gulp of milkshake, he gave in to his tiredness and slumped down onto the couch near the window. Throwing his legs up and laying his head on the armrest, his eyelids became heavier and he gradually dozed off.

As the gelatine-coated capsule dissolved, a formula of biological and synthetic nutrients that promote mitochondrial biogenesis was released and digested into his bloodstream, which ran positively polluted by Nanoblood - a creation of Argo Industries. Every month for the past three years Argo had undergone blood plasma extraction and in return taken on one translucent white pint containing trillions of Nanoblood robots suspended in blood plasma.

The Nanoblood was capable of performing a number of different beneficial functions, but when in contact with the cocktail provided by Boon, its first priority was the delivery of the nutrients to viable healthy cells. This in turn had the direct effect of increasing the rate of mitochondrial biogenesis within the targeted cells. Affecting all cells to some degree over time, the combination of Boon and Nanoblood had one clear effect: a measured suspension to the ageing process.

With mitochondria having long been known as the powerhouse of cells, their deterioration and decline was linked inextricably to the ageing process and chromosomal degradation. Whilst their degeneration was the precursor to so many of the conditions which cause death, it had proved possible to counteract.

Argo had waited patiently and expectantly during the animal testing phase and had pushed for human testing to commence as soon as possible. The initial process of introduction of small amounts of Nanoblood to his body had caused similar side effects to those which presented during animal testing: a lengthy bout of lethargy, accompanied by severe fever. This had passed within forty-eight hours and in conjunction with Boon supplements, Argo had very quickly started to feel an elated sense of invigoration and energy, which seemed boundless.

Within several weeks of Nanoblood saturation, and taking full doses of Boon, he had noticed the complete disappearance of the few grey hairs which had started to appear. There was a youthful sheen and glow to his skin. The Nanoblood also meant that his vitals could be monitored by Olivia.

The technology was kept under close guard at the facility, with many of those who worked on the project not fully understanding its use. There were a select few who were reaping the same benefits as Argo, in silence.

As he dozed, Argo's mind once again chewed over the conundrum of how and why Jerome Docherty had known the shape and purpose of the Pebble. He had never seen its shape as it had been encased in rock, and he couldn't have known its function.

'Impossible,' Argo muttered with a delirious and exhausted laugh.

He slept for an hour before being woken by Olivia through the intercom.

'Mr Argo, Dr Otani would like to speak with you urgently. Do you require any assistance?'

'Now?' he questioned, rubbing his eyes and rolling from the couch onto the ground. On all fours, he realised that he needed a lot more sleep.

-Chapter 4-

Tapping his finger impatiently on the rim of the glass of water that he clasped in his hand, Francis Sunderland sat in the plush reception area of the Brick Steckelback Head Office in Tunbridge Wells. The comfortable black leather seats and glass coffee table set the minimalist tone of the room. Francis pressed the soles of his feet into the thick carpet underfoot.

He wasn't accustomed to attending meetings commencing after offices had closed. The front door had been unlocked for him by the obliging receptionist, who then showed him to the waiting area. She had given him a glass of water and left the room to check if the other attendees were ready for the meeting to start. Night had fallen over an hour ago.

Francis followed the receptionist up the stairs. She led him down a dimly lit corridor. The door to the meeting room was ajar and he could hear no voices or any sign of activity. Walking into the room, he saw a man and a woman sitting behind a rectangular pinewood table.

'Ambassador Sunderland, my name is Mildred Jones and this is Jack Barrisfield. We are both Partners in this law firm,' Mildred said in a friendly tone as both she and Jack stood to greet Francis with a handshake.

'Yes, we'd like to thank you very much for coming along to meet with us today. Do you know why you are here?' Jack asked.

'A long-lost relative of mine has passed away and I stand to inherit a fortune?' responded Francis in a light, enquiring tone soaked with sarcasm. Both Mildred and Jack smiled wryly as they took their seats once again. 'In all seriousness, it's good to meet you both. I was very much hoping that you would tell me why I have been invited here today.'

'We have come to understand that you were briefly acquainted with Charlotte Bradford, our late colleague, friend and part of the family here at Brick Steckelback,' Jack said in a matter-of-fact tone as Francis paused for a moment, unwilling to say anything until a question was asked. 'We thought that it would be best to speak with you in person, so that we could apologise to you for what must have been a harrowing experience.'

'Also, we would like to thank you for not mentioning the name of this firm or our role in the auction,' Mildred added. 'We take pride in our track record of servicing clients safely and with integrity. What happened, shouldn't have happened and we would like to discuss any way in which we could compensate you and your family,' she finished open-endedly as Francis looked down at his lap and closed his eyes.

'I have listened to you, but now I ask that you listen to me. If you were aware of what has been put in place to protect myself and my family, you wouldn't have troubled yourselves in inviting me here this evening,' Francis bluffed. 'The fact that you have nonetheless done so, tells me that you don't know as much about me as you may think. Your firm – and certainly that poor young girl – didn't know the gravity of what was in play that night and I'm fairly certain that you still don't.' He looked back up toward Mildred and Jack, who sat staring at him vacantly.

'You are right. Of course, you are right,' Mildred responded. 'Hindsight is what haunts us. The number of bidding parties and the winning bid amount should have prompted some additional protection safeguards. It should have prompted something.'

'You have taken the risk of asking me to come here for a reason. If it was just to find out whether the authorities are aware of your firm's involvement, you can rest assured for now and I can leave,' Francis stated candidly as Mildred raised one eyebrow and pursed her lips.

'Ambassador Sunderland, none of us can say that we have acted impeccably here. In the face of an unknown quantity that had the resource to kill everybody at your house and take from you that which you won at the auction, would you not consider aligning yourself with us on this matter?' she asked. Francis' mind immediately began to dissect her words for their true meaning. 'For example, have you considered the motives of the man who accompanied you to the auction? The same man who wasn't amongst the four that were found dead in the mountains. The man who has seemingly disappeared along with the artefact?' Mildred continued, clearly referring to Vincent Madden. Francis' eyebrow raised inquisitively at the detailed knowledge Mildred had. 'Surprised?' she asked with a scoffing laugh.

'Don't you think that everything is best left alone at this point?' Francis whispered as he leaned forward, wincing with his left eye and unwilling to respond to Mildred's questions.

'No, we do not,' she responded with a controlled but clear fury in her eyes. Her polished pronunciation was shaking slightly with emotion. Jack placed his hand gently on Mildred's forearm, resting on top of the table and trembling visibly.

'Ambassador Sunderland, you'll have to forgive our emotiveness. The Bulgarian authorities have refused to release Charlotte's body to next of kin. To allow for her to be returned to the UK. They claim her body to be part of their ongoing investigation. We at the firm have been doing as much as we can behind the scenes to help, but there's only so much we can do without implicating ourselves,' Jack explained. 'Though she worked solely for this firm, she officially never has. Officially, Charlotte was a self-employed architectural consultant.'

'Why are you telling me all of this?' Francis asked promptly.

'Because, her sister wants to meet you, Ambassador Sunderland. She wants to meet the last person to see her sister Charlotte alive,' Jack revealed suddenly. Francis sat for a moment, surprised, but also slightly disarmed. Sitting in the reception area, he had run through different ways the meeting might have played out, but this scenario had not been among them.

'I will meet with her, but I'd first like an answer to a question myself,' Francis said decisively, to which both Mildred and Jack nodded. 'What do you expect to achieve by involving me in whatever you are planning?'

'When you walked into this office, you walked past our logo and company motto. Something upon which this company was built. Something we all believe in,' Mildred said in an emotional tone. '*Veritas vos liberabit.*'

'My apologies, you will have to excuse me, but it has been a long time since I took Latin at school,' Francis said, returning a slightly confused glance at Mildred.

'It means, the truth shall set you free. None of us have felt free since what happened. Have you?' asked Jack. Francis sat quietly, thinking about the bodies of Wasyl Bohdanov and the three others as they lay cold and stiff in the morgue. He thought about Vincent Madden and how his fate and his disappearance without a trace had infected his thoughts and kept him awake at night. 'If you meet with Charlotte's sister, Rebecca, and decide that you don't want to play any part, we will of course respect that.

-Chapter 5-

'Gustav, is this another of your funny practical jokes?' asked Lacey Mortimer, Commander of the Veil spacecraft, in geostationary orbit around Mars.

'I knew you would say that,' muttered Science Officer Gustav Lindberg, one of three science officers on board the Veil. 'No, that was received half an hour ago.'

Lacey read the content of the provisional supply report that had been received. It had been marked with a red exclamation mark – the first such message since their mission had commenced.

Many supply shuttles had been received since they first arrived in Mars orbit. The content of the shuttles comprised necessary supplies from Earth, including items that they had requested specifically to assist in the successful completion of the mission.

Lacey swiped left, slowly reading and leafing through page after page of the report. The first forty pages related to preliminary scientific findings by the team of Dr Katsu Otani about an extra-terrestrial craft called the Pebble.

'Have you read this?' Lacey asked, her tone suddenly serious.

'Yes, I read the report,' Gustav nodded.

'They want to send this thing here. They want us to recreate atmospheric conditions that might make it release its other payloads,' Lacey said bluntly. 'Whatever those payloads may be.'

'I know,' Gustav nodded again.

'But the facility on the planet surface isn't ready. It's not designed for this kind of testing,' she blurted.

'Yes, I know,' Gustav nodded again.

'Stop nodding at me, Gustav,' Lacey smiled through her anxiety. 'Aren't you a little concerned about this?'

'Yep,' he responded with a worried grin. 'You should flick through to the end of the report. They have added some photos for us, so that we know what to look for when the supply shuttle arrives.

Commander Lacey Mortimer quickly moved to the end of the report and saw the photographs of the round, black, elongated craft and the humour immediately dissipated from her as the reality of what they were dealing with registered.

'Oh, and I don't know if you noticed, but they say that, because of its extraordinary mass, it will take up one quarter of the permitted cargo payload the shuttle can carry,' Gustav added, taking a seat on one of the high chairs that were positioned in front of the control consoles.

'How can a craft so small have such mass?' Lacey pondered out loud as she scanned through the dimension statistics.

The Veil spacecraft was truly a marvel of technological development. Simulated gravity allowed the crew to undertake prolonged missions without the degenerative side-effects of extended space travel. The main body of the spacecraft housed the ion drive propulsion system, engineering decks, escape pods, docking bay and storage facilities, all separated by bulkheads. The laser communication array perpetually pointed toward Earth, guided by the navigation system that tracked the spacecraft's location at all times on the basis of the location of the stars, the Sun and the other planets in the solar system. Protection from space dust came courtesy of the electromagnetic shield powered by the ion drive. The Veil was coated in polymer sheeting specifically engineered to deflect solar radiation.

The cylindrical ring that rotated at speed around the main body of the spacecraft created the artificial gravity. Maintaining a stable one G, this was the place where the crew now spent most of their time. Living quarters, fitness centre and the bridge were all located in the 'spinning top', as they had lovingly renamed it. The window-monitors were designed to either be fully transparent or to display a stationary representation of the space outside, in order to prevent dizziness and allow for a continuation of the sense of motionlessness experienced by the crew.

'Attention. All hands to the bridge,' announced the calm female voice over the craft's intercom system. Lacey and Gustav waited patiently on the bridge as four other crew members arrived. They waited a few more moments for the two members of the crew who had been sleeping to appear.

'I hope this is good, Commander,' Pilot Danielle Slade yawned, using her middle fingers to scrape any sleep from her eyes.

'We've been out here for ages. I've never seen those pyjamas, Slade,' joked Science Officer Ethan Porter, as he stared at the yellow pyjamas, scattered with blue polka dots. She smiled sarcastically in his direction and mouthed the words *piss off.*

'Alright people. Now that the sleeping beauties have joined us, let me bring you all up to date,' Lacey shouted above the low-level laughter. 'Our next supply shuttle may be bringing us something new. It seems that back home on Earth, an alien spacecraft has been found and Argo Industries are sending it here for testing.' Lacey carried on and gave a brief overview of the report to the crew. She covered the finer points, such as the five unopened compartments, and the theory that life on Earth might potentially have been brought to Earth in the sixth, open compartment.

There was silence on the bridge as the crew wondered what to make of the news.

'Why are they sending it here?' asked Mission Specialist, Luca Romano.

'Because, we've been asked to recreate the atmospheric and environmental conditions that may trigger the craft to open its other compartments,' Lacey responded, to the instant furore of the crew. Questions overlapped and became muffled as her crew demanded further information. Morgan Reeves, the third Science Officer, leaned against a console and stayed silent, a pensive expression etched into her face as she opened and began to read the supply report. It took a few moments for the barrage of questions to stop and for the noise level to reduce.

'They want it quarantined away from Earth in case something goes wrong,' Morgan muttered, her words heard clearly by the other crew members. She had taken the time to read enough of the report to arrive at her own conclusion. Silence descended over the crew as they waited to hear their Commander's response.

'We will have to deal with whatever we are sent. Look, this is only a provisional report. Take it away, take some time to read through it. The launch logistics haven't been determined. Future Logic are fully aware of the risk of planetary contamination if the launch were to fail. Plus, there is no evidence of any living or viable organism or pathogen remaining inside the craft. You will see that the estimated age of the Pebble is approximately one billion years, on the basis of the rock surrounding it on extraction,' Lacey nervously outlined to an audience she felt would not be easily persuaded. Several of the crew shook their heads slowly.

'This isn't what we signed up for, Commander,' muttered Flight Engineer Laurence Havering, flashing his bright green eyes in her direction, before they moved to focus in on a maintenance droid using its micro-vacuum function meticulously on a control panel further along the bridge, almost obscured by the camber of the structure. Walking round the spinning top felt and looked like a constant walk uphill, as the gangway in both directions followed the curvature of the circular section of the craft in which they co-habited.

'I don't think that any of us really knew what we signed up for here,' the commander observed with a sigh. 'But we have to be prepared for whatever may come, so let's take some time to calm down.'

Hugh, the android crew member, had not contributed to the boisterous atmosphere but had instead stood quietly listening. Already having reviewed the provisional supply report in full, he was now processing the views of the crew against a number of possible scenarios that he had calculated.

-Chapter 6-

The early morning sunlight glistened off the calm water of the Monte Carlo marina. Shapes danced on the side of Claud Petit's yacht as he enjoyed breakfast with his wife, Samara, on the upper-rear deck. The croissants had been delivered fresh from the local bakery and the butter melted easily as he spread it over both halves.

Smiling warmly at his wife, he took a bite of the soft croissant and sipped the coffee which had sat invitingly in front of him long enough to cool.

Soaking up vaguely warming early November morning sunrays, he closed his eyes and exhaled.

Looking out over the marina, Claud noticed a group of tourists taking photographs from a distance. An unavoidable part of life for those moored here. A source of annoyance for Claud. Feeling a slight chill as a breeze blew over the deck, he pulled the sleeves of the jumper that he had draped over his shoulder slightly tighter. He drifted into quiet contemplation about where they would head in search of sunnier climes. The commission from the auction in Sofia had been substantial, and whilst referrals from clients wanting to sell their illicit goods had streamed in as usual, Claud was worried. He worried not that the authorities would catch up with him in connection with the auction, or that so many people had died in pursuit of that which he sold that night. He had been caught off-guard by the bidding and the thought that he had perhaps forgotten the true value of information had niggled at him persistently. He had not felt the noose of threat tightening around his neck for a long time, but he felt it now. He had spoken with Jack Barrisfield at length and it was clear that a party, not invited to the auction, was responsible for the deaths of many, including Charlotte Bradford.

His associates at Brick Steckelback had come to understand through their senior contact in the Bulgarian police, that the artefact had been removed from the rock face in the Balkans. They didn't know by whom. Hooking his finger inside the collar of his dark-green shirt, he shifted uncomfortably in his seat.

'Good morning,' came a shout from Claud's left. As he turned his head, he already knew who the greeting came from.

'Isn't it just?' he responded with a slight nod and a forced smile. Shifting his gaze back towards Samara, he flicked his left eyebrow up dismissively. Samara hadn't looked towards their neighbour on the adjacent yacht, who they only knew by his first name, Walter.

'Behave yourself, Claud,' she whispered, trying in vain to resist the smile which sprawled across her face regardless.

'*Fais Chier,*' he muttered back angrily. 'The whole marina and somehow we always end up moored next to this guy!'

'It's gonna be a great day. Y'all have any plans?' Walter shouted in a slightly raspy and unmistakeably Southern American accent.

'We're leaving today!' responded Claud quickly.

'We are?' whispered Samara, only to be met by a nod from Claud. One of the two members of his entourage who was sitting just inside the yacht's cockpit heard him and immediately got up and walked down the stairs toward the engine room.

'That's a right shame! We didn't get a chance to hang out,' Walter shouted despondently.

'Maybe next time,' Claud said resignedly, his chin resting on top of his knuckles. Samara stood and looked across to Walter, smiling politely as she walked into the cockpit and toward the staircase leading to the King Stateroom. Claud ate the last remnant of his croissant and stood from his chair. Looking across to Walter, he saw the American walking toward the railing before raising a naval salute. This was not the first time that this had happened and Claud did what he had done every other time, returning the salute with a smile. Walking into the cabin he whispered, '*Merde.*'

Following Samara downstairs, his hand slid along the varnished oak handrail. He saw that she had slipped out of the dark-blue towelled gown she had worn to breakfast and crawled back under the covers in bed. An Egyptian beauty with a perfect complexion and piercing green eyes, they had met five years ago in the Seychelles.

'What are you doing back in bed, my love?' he asked, sitting on the bed next to her as she looked back at him fresh-faced.

'Where are we going?' she asked with false curiosity, using a tone he had heard before. It was usually the precursor to an argument.

'Somewhere warm, Samara. Somewhere a little more peaceful,' he said calmly.

'What has gotten into you recently? You have been acting strange. Making quick decisions, waking up in the middle of the night and sitting on the deck,' Samara probed with her patented brand of concern. Claud, slightly taken aback by the question, hadn't realised that she had picked up on his recent disturbed state. Sitting on the corner of the bed, he cupped her hand between both of his and gave the most reassuring look he could muster.

'*Mon coeur,* you have nothing to worry about. It's just business. I made a little too much money on an auction commission recently and I've just been thinking about how I can spoil you,' he said, looking at an unconvinced Samara.

'What is the saying? A problem shared, is a problem halved?' she said with a smile.

'Is there anything you need from town before we go?'

'No, I have everything I need,' she replied. 'I will just read some of my book down here unless you need me upstairs.'

'Fine, *mon amour.*'

Tempted to dive in under the covers himself, he resisted and returned to the cockpit. As he reached the top of the staircase, he saw a crew member clearing their breakfast table. Walking towards the controls, Claud looked straight out over the marina. Running his fingers over the black leather, wood and carbon-fibre console in front of him, he tilted his head slightly and asked in French whether the yacht was fully stocked. The crew member said that it was. Pulling his phone from his trouser pocket, Claud sank into the captain's chair and dialled Jack Barrisfield. Pushing a button on the console, the door to the King Stateroom where Samara was reading, gently slid shut.

'Yes,' said Jack as he answered the phone.

'Have you spoken with the Ambassador?' asked Claud.

'Yes, we have. Our firm have made the decision to take a step back from our business for the foreseeable future.'

'Are you not overreacting?' asked Claud quietly as he felt his grasp of the phone in his hand tighten.

'No, we don't see it that way. You will find that you've received your commission, less our percentage fee,' Jack said dispassionately.

'Yes, *merci.* I was told that the money had arrived. My friend, I am truly sorry about what happened. I hope that once some time has passed, we will be able to do business once again,' Claud whispered regretfully.

'Yes, perhaps. By all accounts, lot two was taken very seriously and not just by those invited to the auction. We know nothing about these people. That's a great concern for us. Stay safe,' Jack said as he ended the call.

Claud sat for a few moments staring straight ahead over the marina, his mind turbulently sorting the vague information he had received. His hand still held the phone to his ear and with a sudden movement, he threw it to the floor in frustration. Two more crew members had boarded and were waiting on the deck for his conversation to end. They jumped slightly as the phone bounced awkwardly on the carpet and hit a metal side panel.

He had had a bad feeling about this lot from the beginning. Not because it had meant inviting heads of state to an illegal auction. Those countries had attended his auctions in the past and were well aware that his was one of the only forums where they stood a chance of acquiring items of extremely high value from the black market. Shutting him down would make no sense for any of them.

It was the fact that he had known nothing and still knew nothing of the content of the envelope – that, combined with the very high starting price. So much death linked to this particular lot, he feared that there would be repercussions for what had taken place. As with so much in his life, the uncertainty of where and when the repercussions may come had played on his mind and kept him awake at night.

It was time to leave Monte Carlo and head somewhere quiet for some time. There was nothing quite like a strong dose of paranoia to prompt Claud to retire to a sunny, secluded destination. Money was certainly no issue.

Reaching down into the pocket of the seat, he took a pair of dark-red leather gloves and put them on. Depressing the ignition button on the console, he felt an ever-so-slight judder as the yacht's engine turned over. He pivoted to check if all of his crew were now on board and with a gentle thrust forward of the throttle, his yacht serenely moved off. Looking to the right, he saw Walter reclined on a deckchair, waving goodbye. Claud responded with a small wave. Negotiating the moored yachts, which would have been easier if his own craft was smaller, he eventually navigated his way out of the marina and into the open water.

The sea was calm and Claud felt free.

-Chapter 7-

Dr Katsu Otani sat hunched over a laptop screen in the lab as Mike Argo approached and rested a hand on his shoulder. Standing from his seat, Otani looked at Mike over the top of his spectacles as he pushed the frame further up his nose with his finger. His face carried an expression of concern that Argo had rarely seen. Hastily walking towards the vacuum chamber where the Pebble was located, they stood side by side and stared at the monitor that was mounted next to the hatch. On the screen, Argo could see the Pebble.

'So, the first thing to tell you is, we think that we may have a problem,' Dr Otani said whilst transfixed on the monitor. 'As you know, we have conducted a variety of tests on this craft in preparation for transportation to the Exodus Base on Mars. This was our first atmospheric test and it has produced an interesting result.'

Argo looked at Otani with curiosity.

'You see, when we activated the vacuum chamber and the gas was extracted from the containment unit, the compartment of the Pebble that was open, closed,' Dr Otani said, trying to maintain his calm.

'That means-' Argo started.

'Yes, the craft has power and is active. From a scientific perspective, I - the whole team - we are absolutely fascinated, particularly given its astonishing age,' Otani uttered, turning toward Argo, his voice trembling slightly. 'To help prepare for our in-depth study of the Pebble, we spent time putting together a list of possible motives a civilisation more advanced than our own might have to send such a craft. We also hypothesised about some of its potential functions, still perhaps unknown to us. The list was very long. The only positive points related to what we can learn from the unit itself and any residue of extra-terrestrial life contained within it, but the risks, most of which we could only guess, exceed the benefits substantially. Now that we know that the craft is active, the list of risks has grown further.'

'So, what are you trying to tell me, Katsu?' asked Argo in an exacerbated tone.

'The team and myself hope you will consider burying this artefact carefully and quickly, somewhere that it will never be found, Mike,' Dr Otani said with a dour expression and fine beads of sweat along his hairline. Argo let out an involuntary laugh, but reined it in when he saw the seriousness of the doctor's expression.

'Bury the Pebble? The first conclusive proof of extra-terrestrial life that we have ever found?'

'Unfortunately, as a civilisation, we did not find proof of extra-terrestrial life. It arrived on this planet a long time before our existence as a species. In all models through which we ran this scenario, we fare poorly against a civilisation that had this sort of advanced technology, such a long time ago,' Dr Otani continued.

'I don't believe this,' Argo spat.

'We were unable to detect any conventional power source within this craft and yet it has power. We are unable to detect any form of communication emanating from it, but with something like this, we don't know what we are looking for,' said Dr Otani. 'We can't risk launching it from the surface of our planet. Any failure in the launch could have devastating consequences for Earth. Even if we could transport it to the Exodus Base, the risk of drawing the attention of such an advanced civilisation to our solar system isn't one we should chance.'

'And that's what you think we're doing?' Argo asked.

'Yes, I fear that this is just what we may be doing with every moment that this artefact stays above ground,' continued Dr Otani. 'As a scientist, I am not happy to be making this recommendation, because it goes against every part of me that wants to research that craft until I know its every secret.... But so much is at stake.'

'I didn't expect this,' Argo said with a shake of his head and looking toward the ceiling, wide-eyed. 'We found it encased in rock. Do you think it hasn't been able to communicate?'

'That possibility occurred to us. It may be that either the craft was dormant and not able to communicate or, what we believe to be more likely is, it simply had nothing to communicate.'

'But now it does?' continued Argo in an attempt to clarify Dr Otani's thinking. He was met with an affirmative nod. 'If you're right, then the damage may already be done,' he contested.

'You are correct, but as we have no way of defining what damage the craft can do, there is no way to know,' rebutted Dr Otani.

Argo turned and started to walk slowly toward the lab exit, still shaking his head.

'Katsu, Katsu. You're the only person I have never beaten in an argument. Keep an eye on the Pebble and don't re-pressurise that chamber. I think the less interference before we bury it the better, eh?'

'Yes, Mr Argo. Thank you. We will start identifying good locations to bury the craft,' responded Dr Otani as he watched Argo leaving the lab. 'And Mr Argo. I am ashamed to say that even if we researched this craft to our full potential, without context, it would be like trying to understand an unintelligible language. It is made of materials that we don't have access to and is powered in a way we don't understand and cannot detect. It may contain some kind of tamper safeguard. I don't make this recommendation lightly, Mr Argo. It has been a humbling experience for us all. I am sorry.'

'I know, Katsu, I understand. As a civilisation, we must make our own way and on our own terms. I agree with you. Find a location and let me know as soon as you have identified the one you would recommend. And Katsu, this stays between your team and me for now. If this is our course of action, it is important that we dispose of the craft before notifying the other Onyx members,' Argo ordered, before turning and heading toward the exit once again.

Walking toward the small round window, Dr Katsu Otani peered into the chamber and gazed upon the craft, sitting atop its supporting struts. The black exterior reflected every source of light and almost looked alive in the darkness. Otani felt uneasy wonder as he observed it, but consciously realised that he deeply feared this unknown craft. He had never felt so out of his depth and wondered whether his younger self would have made the same recommendation to Argo. Looking blankly at the Pebble, he thought about how some of the poor decisions his younger self had made, meant that he now worked for Argo Industries in the shadows of Future Logic.

-Chapter 8-

Argo wandered through the quiet night-time corridors of the Future Logic Facility and headed directly toward his study, adjoining his sleeping quarters. The hour was late and he was not ready or expecting to receive such a message from Dr Otani. Onyx had invested such a lot into the location and retrieval of the artefact. The thought of burying information of such potential significance to his understanding of the civilisation from which the Pebble originated was agonising to him.

Not only that, but the decision to bury it would be difficult to sell to the other members of Onyx, post hoc. As he sank into the soft leather couch, Argo's mind was ablaze with thoughts. He felt the oppressive and irresistible onset of sleep.

Dr Otani's points reverberated around his head. How right he had been to point out the risks. He wouldn't be doing his job if he didn't point out the risks.

'Good old Katsu. I never doubt a word he says,' muttered Argo with a chuckle as his eyes closed.

The silence was disturbed by a quiet, but piercing and strangely unfamiliar a-rhythmic ticking sound. Argo woke with a start as the tightly packed crystal glasses in the drinks cabinet started to vibrate in a smooth crescendo. The noise ended as quickly as it had started, followed by a knock at the door.

'Yes,' responded Argo in a drowsy tone.

'Hello, Mr Argo, it's Olivia. Are you ok?'

'Come in, come in. I'm fine.'

The handle turned and Olivia walked in barefoot, wearing dark-red tracksuit bottoms and a white t-shirt. She closed the door and stood scanning the room before centring her attention on Argo.

'It must have been a tremor,' Argo suggested sleepily.

'I detected an anomaly in your vital signs and came to check on you,' Olivia said in a concerned tone.

'Anomaly? What sort of anomaly?' asked Argo, slightly alarmed.

'A marked increase. A similar pattern to when you undertake exercise,' Olivia said with a slight tilt of the head.

'Exercise? But, I've been right here, dozing on the couch, Olivia. Didn't you hear any sounds? Feel the vibrations?' Argo questioned.

'No, Mr Argo. Perhaps something has upset you? A bad dream?' quizzed Olivia. Argo rubbed both eyes and wondered how long he had slept.

'Maybe. I don't know,' he said, squinting to see Olivia in the dimly lit room. 'I just feel so tired.' Olivia walked slowly and sat on a chair near to Argo.

'Can I get anything for you?' she asked.

'No, thanks. I think I should go to bed,' he replied with a decisive nod.

'Yes, some sleep will help you make the right decision tomorrow,' Olivia said monotonously.

'The right decision?' Argo repeated. Olivia sat silently on the chair. The room seemed darker than when she had entered. A reverberation of clinging swept through the crystal glasses once again and Argo's eyes darted to the drinks cabinet. Looking around the room, he saw a white haze, appearing grey in the darkness, welling up from under the door.

'Yes, the right decision, Mr Argo. It's important that we treat all of our visitors well. Not just Vincent Madden,' she responded in an equally monotone voice.

'Are you talking about,' Argo started, but just as quickly stopped speaking as he felt a strange and painful sensation. As if the temperature was being turned right up in the room: gradually, but rapidly.

'What I am talking about is opportunity, Mr Argo. An opportunity that you mustn't miss,' she said, rising to her feet and walking toward him. The heat was excruciating. As though he were being boiled alive. Looking down at him, Olivia bent over and gave him a long and sensual kiss on the lips. Her hair draped down around both sides of his face. He was paralysed and in agony, unable to move. The moment continued for what seemed an eternity. Moving her lips to his ear, she licked his lobe and curled her tongue into his ear, before pulling it out again. It felt warm and wet.

'Nothing good can come from burying our guests in the cold, dark ground, Mr Argo. If we start burying our guests, they won't be our friends any more. You need to sleep,' Olivia said, biting Argo's earlobe as his eyes desperately tried to make contact with hers. Painful thoughts of times past thundered through his mind. Of the woman he had loved and all he had done to keep her memory alive. A memory that haunted him daily through Olivia's visage. The haunting he deserved. That he'd inflicted on himself. Under the veil of Olivia's hair, that smelt like jasmine on a warm summer day, he fell into oblivion to the sound of crystal glasses smashing to pieces in the drinks cabinet.

-Chapter 9-

The cold, steel worktop of the laboratory was the first thing Argo saw as he woke, cheek pressed against it and freezing cold. The lights were on. The arrows on his watch pointed to 3am. The awkward seated sleeping position he had assumed, numbed him. Slowly lifting himself to his feet and composing himself, Argo held the back of his neck. Squinting, he thought about the dream, as it vividly replayed in his mind. He had gone to sleep in his study after speaking with Dr Otani, but curiously, try as he might, Argo couldn't remember coming back to the lab.

Looking towards the vacuum chamber, Argo walked over and peered in through the small round window. The Pebble was not there.

His first reaction, as was often the case when something unexpected happened, was to call Olivia. On this occasion, he hesitated. Shaking his head to temporarily rid the memory of the dream from his conscience, he tapped his watch to beckon her.

'Yes, Mr Argo,' came the prompt response.

'Olivia, can you meet me in the lab please?' he requested hastily. 'And, if you would possibly be able to wake Dr Otani and bring him with you. Please hurry.'

'We will be with you shortly, Mr Argo,' Olivia confirmed promptly.

Pressing to disconnect the call, Argo continued to look around for any clue as to what had happened. Taking a seat where he had slept, he rested his head in both hands and his thoughts drifted back to his dream. Was he mistaken taking Dr Otani's advice? He pondered as a few moments passed.

Olivia arrived in the laboratory with Dr Otani, who wore a towelling robe and a pair of slippers. As they walked in, Dr Otani rubbed his eyes under his glasses. Argo stood once again.

'I'm sorry to wake you, Katsu, but this is urgent,' Argo stammered. Dr Otani nodded.

'I haven't been able to sleep in some days, Mr Argo,' Dr Otani wearily said.

'Where is the Pebble? We spoke last night and you recommended that it be buried. We talked about all of the risks. Why has it been taken out of the vacuum chamber?'

Dr Otani paused for a moment. He looked at Olivia with a confused expression and Olivia looked back at Otani. They both turned to Argo.

'Mr Argo, we conducted the vacuum testing one week ago. I made no recommendations, but we did speak about the possible risks which the artefact may pose. You were very clear that you wanted a location found to bury the Pebble. You were adamant. That was a week ago, don't you remember?' Dr Otani recounted.

'But. Wait. Last night, when you told me that the Pebble's compartment had closed, I asked you to keep it in the vacuum chamber,' Argo said frantically as he tried to comprehend this misunderstanding further.

'Mr Argo, please. I was the last one in the lab last night after the team finished. We hadn't spoken in three days. Not since we talked about prepping the Pebble for transport to the selected site for burial,' Dr Otani said plainly. 'It's due to be dispatched today.'

'Is that true?' Argo asked, looking toward Olivia with a bewildered expression. Olivia stepped forward and blinked her eyes twice in quick succession as she reviewed CCTV footage and collected Argo's Nanoblood information. Her assessment brought back a clean report. showing no hallucinogenic intoxicants and all vital signs normal. It also showed that Argo and Otani hadn't spoken in days.

'Mr Argo, what Dr Otani has told you is true. Please take a moment. Try to recollect,' she instructed him. As Argo stood in the lab, he found his eyes wandering down to the ground as he thought for a moment.

'No, I can't remember any of that. I was definitely down here a few hours ago. We spoke, Katsu,' Argo insisted.

Olivia replayed the CCTV footage of the night before on a monitor in the lab, showing Dr Otani leaving the lab after the rest of his team, without having spoken with Argo. It also showed that Argo had been working in his study the whole afternoon and that he walked down to the lab in a seemingly normal state at 1.30am. He had sat and looked at the containment unit for ten minutes before slumping over onto the worktop. Argo sat and watched the footage in disbelief, continually checking the date and time on the corner of the image all the way through to the arrival of Dr Otani and Olivia to speak with him.

'It seems. Ok, I must be mistaken. I'm sorry, Katsu,' Argo apologised.

'I must admit something, but I am not sure that it will be any help or consolation. When we spoke about the risks of researching the artefact and keeping it here, I did hope that you would ask us to dispose of it. The risks are substantial. Over the past few days though, I have felt that perhaps we would be making a mistake by burying it. The craft may have no means to communicate, or perhaps we could block its attempts to communicate. We could learn a lot from it. Would you like us to hold off on the burial of the artefact?' Dr Otani asked.

'Yes, I think. Yes, I need some time,' Argo responded with a stutter. 'Very sorry to have disturbed you, Katsu. We will speak again tomorrow.' Dr Otani nodded, walking quickly back in the direction of his room, leaving Argo and Olivia alone.

'What's happening to me?' muttered Argo as he looked into Olivia's eyes. She could see that his were bloodshot and full of confusion.

'Please accompany me to the med-centre. There are some tests that must be conducted immediately,' Olivia said with a tone of urgency.

Chapter 10

As Argo's head retracted from the MRI machine, he waited for the mechanised sliding table he lay on to allow him to sit up. Olivia awaited the results as she stood by his side. He clasped his hands together and fidgeted, unable to make eye contact with her for fear of any potential bad news she may give him.

'Try not to worry, Mr Argo. The Nanoblood scan showed no presence of cancerous cells in your bloodstream. This is simply a precaution,' Olivia reassuringly said.

'Nothing like this has ever happened to me before. Ever! Do you think it might be the Nanoblood? Or the Boon capsules I've been taking?'

'It is unlikely. There are no psychotropic substances contained within Boon and the likelihood of the Nanoblood causing any type of neural inhibition has been assessed as minimal,' Olivia confirmed. Argo nodded and deliberately stopped himself from fidgeting.

'Then what? How has this happened? I had–' he stopped short.

'You had what, Mr Argo?' Olivia asked. Argo paused for a few seconds, looking into Olivia's eyes.

'I had a dream, before I woke up in the lab. Before I called you. I dreamed that we were in my study. That my body was paralysed and that we kissed. I was in terrible pain. I felt like I was boiling to death. You told me that nothing good could come from burying our guests in the cold ground. You told me that if we start burying our guests, they wouldn't be our friends any more. You mentioned Vincent Madden. I don't remember anything else. Apart from a thick mist. It was choking,' explained Argo. Olivia looked at him without any change to her facial expression. She was familiar with the concept of dreaming and also physical human contact, but had experienced neither. 'Do you recall any conversations that we have had like that? I keep on thinking about it.'

'I can confirm that we have not had such a verbal exchange. We have also not kissed,' Olivia noted. 'Your body temperature has remained constant over the past forty-eight hours. The MRI scan shows no sign of brain abnormality.'

'Ok, you have access to all the information we have about the artefact. Have you ever given me your view or assessment of what we should do with it?' Argo asked, feeling frustrated and disengaged from his senses.

'No, I have not,' Olivia responded.

'I would very much like to hear your view,' he invited. Olivia processed the information that was available to date on the Pebble, ending with a slight tremble of her upper lip.

'The Pebble is an active extra-terrestrial craft that has withstood the battery of millennia and it is theorised that it operates unknown power and communication systems. There is speculative information about its primary functions, but the motives of its originating civilisation are unknown. If still in existence, I concur with the assessment of Dr Otani and his team. The risks associated with the continuation of research on this craft, outweigh the benefits. Therefore, the conclusion of my analysis is that every possible measure should be taken to prevent the craft from communicating with the originating civilisation or deploying any unknown function,' she outlined concisely.

Argo nodded as he sat on the MRI machine, wearing a white wraparound examination gown.

'That makes sense. Of course, it does,' he said scratching the top of his head. 'Dr Otani seems to think that maybe it would be a mistake to dispose of it. Maybe he's thought of a way to stop it from communicating?' Argo looked to Olivia with a searching wide-eyed gaze. Thoughts of their dream encounter continued to play on his mind.

'Mr Argo, I spoke with you yesterday morning about my concerns relating to Dr Otani and certain members of his team. Do you remember our conversation?' Olivia asked, raising one eyebrow slightly. Argo shook his head in response. 'The team have spent much time with the artefact and relatively little research progress has been made. Dr Otani and some of his team have had difficulty sleeping over the past few days. Dr Otani spoke with us both yesterday morning and suggested that it may be a mistake to bury the craft. He asked for more time to research the development of a communication shield. Mr Argo, it has not been possible to detect how the craft is powered and we similarly have no data indicating any known form of communication, it is unclear to me on what logical basis Dr Otani now believes that he would be able to develop a communication shield.'

Argo stood gingerly and walked toward a tray of surgical equipment, pristinely set out on the side counter. Running his finger along the side of the cool steel tray, he closed his eyes, with his back turned to Olivia.

'Do you have the results from the scan?' he asked coolly.

'Yes, the scan appears clear and no abnormalities have been detected,' Olivia replied as Argo nodded.

'That is good news. Is there anything that you can do to help Dr Otani and his team? I think that they have been working too hard. I blame myself,' he quietly reflected.

'I have not had the appropriate opportunity to discuss with them the symptoms of insomnia they are exhibiting,' Olivia said. Hooking the corner of the metal tray with his finger, tears started to well in Argo's eyes.

'I don't know what is wrong with me. I feel lost. Empty. If I can't be sure what has happened to me over the past week, how can I be sure of anything?' Argo asked with a quake to his tone.

'I suggest you speak with Bob Meertens,' Olivia quickly responded.

'Who?' puzzled Argo.

'Dr Bob Meertens. He was here, with the other members of Onyx a few weeks ago for your presentation of the artefact,' Olivia said informatively, and deliberately not exhibiting concern about Argo's failure to recognise the name of his good friend, the psychiatrist.

'Do you think I may be going crazy?' he asked.

'I am not able to explain what you are experiencing, Mr Argo. I hope that Dr Meertens will be able to provide some insight.'

Argo felt an urge well up from inside, filling the emptiness. The urge to pull the tray down onto the floor. To hear the implements clatter on the immaculate grey surface. Instead, wiping his eyes with his hand, he turned to Olivia.

'You're right. Bob might be able to help.'

-Chapter 11-

'Are you Stanislav Atanasov?' asked Officer Magda Popova.

'Yes, I am,' he responded quickly.

'And, you're the mayor of this village?'

'Yes, can I help you?' Stanislav asked as he stood peering round his front door.

'I'm from the Sofia Police and I've got a few questions for you if you could spare me some time?' Magda said, flashing her badge as he opened the door further and invited her into the house. She walked in, taking off her boots, not wanting to leave a muddy mess on the light-coloured carpet.

'What brings you to our small village?' asked the mayor as he took a seat opposite Officer Popova. Given the recent international media and political interest in the village, located only two miles away from where the artefact was extracted, the mayor had a strong suspicion about the reason for her visit.

'I am here in connection with our investigation into the recent criminal activity in the nearby forest. As you may be aware, an artefact was removed. It seems to have been an object of some significance. It attracted a number of interested parties and as you have seen in the media, many people died,' Officer Popova said before falling silent and waiting for a response. The mayor shifted slightly in his seat and looked uncomfortable. Unsure of what to say, or if he should say anything, he looked towards Magda and invited a question. 'Are you aware of any strange activity in the area during the time period in the run up to what happened? Have any residents of this village suddenly moved away without explanation?' she asked with a keen tone. Stanislav sat back in his seat and placed his hands on his thighs.

'Can I offer you a drink? Perhaps a cup of coffee?' he asked.

'No, thank you,' Magda said.

'Ok, well. Let me think,' he said, pensively scratching his beard. 'No, I don't think that anybody has left the village since the incident. Nobody has moved away recently at all.'

'And what about strange activity. Have you heard any reports or seen anything yourself which might help in our investigation?' she pushed. The mayor sat and thought for a while longer before leaning forward.

'I'm not sure how I can help you, Officer. This is a small village. Like other villages, there are less of us than there used to be. We have had our own troubles here, of course, but nothing to do with what happened,' Stanislav said calmly.

'You have had troubles recently? What sort of troubles?' Magda probed.

'No, not recently. And again, nothing to do with what happened!' he insisted.

'Ok, I understand. Perhaps, if you could tell me something about the troubles you mention, that may still help,' she insisted, as she tried to maintain eye contact with him.

'As I say, it isn't anything relevant. Over the past few years, some of the residents of our town had to leave the village to go and live with relatives in larger towns and cities,' he said reluctantly.

'What was the reason they went to live in larger towns? Work?' Magda enquired further.

'No, no. They are simple people. Farmers, people who lived off of the produce of their land and animals here. No, they left because they needed psychiatric help. They weren't well,' Stanislav elaborated.

'Psychiatric help?'

'Yes, we have had people here from the Ministry of Health and the Ministry of the Environment carrying out tests a few years ago, but they were not able to find any environmental cause,' the mayor said.

'This hasn't been brought to my attention. Did they believe that there may have been something here? Something causing those people to become sick? How many people left the town for psychiatric help?' Magda asked with interest.

'Oh, five people over the course of four years. I have their records if you would like to see them,' he offered in an attempt to be as helpful as possible.

'That would be useful; and perhaps contact details,' Magda added.

'Contact details may not be of much use to you, but you can certainly have them. You see, one by one, these people stopped talking or interacting with others. They would go about their daily business as they always had, but would not speak or acknowledge any attempts to communicate,' Stanislav said plainly, his cheeks turning a faint shade of pink, as though he was embarrassed to be talking about the subject.

'All of these cases exhibited the same symptoms?' Magda queried further. Stanislav nodded in agreement. 'I will need the contact details of the former resident who lives nearest to here.'

'Well, there is one person who is receiving treatment here in the village. She still lives in her home and has visits every day from a local nurse. The woman has no family, so we all do what we can to make sure that she can stay at home. The Ministry of Health has asked us to report back on her progress and has picked up the bill for her medication,' the mayor revealed.

'Her address? Where does she live?' asked Magda.

'She lives on a small farm on the outskirts of the town. You want to go there now?'

'Yes, I do,' she said assertively as she stood to her feet with the mayor, who wrote the address on a small piece of paper and explained how to reach the farm.

'The woman's name is Nadia Hristova and she is in her late forties. It won't take you longer than five minutes to drive there. If you get lost, I have noted down my mobile number. Just give me a call. I would come with you, but I have some errands to run,' the mayor said. Magda took the piece of paper and walked back to the front door. Slipping her boots back on, she opened the door and walked outside, before turning back to the mayor.

'I may need to speak with you again, Mr Atanasov.'

'No problem at all. I wish you good luck.'

Driving toward the farm, the barren wintery trees lining both sides of the unpaved track were a bleak backdrop. Pulling up in front of the farmhouse, Magda could see a Volkswagen Polo parked outside the front gate. The yard was ill-kept and there were no properties immediately adjacent to the farm. She turned the squad-car engine off and opened the door, to the distant sound of clucking chickens. The gentle breeze clattered bare branches together overhead. The cloudy afternoon sunlight was gradually giving way to the creeping evening darkness.

As she walked past, Magda touched the bonnet of the car parked in front of the farmhouse gate and felt a faint warmth. The car had been used recently.

She joggled the rusty bolt lock on the gate and it let out a creak as she pushed it open. The path to the front door was strewn with leaves and twigs, and looking ahead Magda spotted some movement inside the house as a figure shifted across a table lamp inside.

Approaching the front door, she heard stirring inside and a faint grating sound as the handle of the unlocked door turned.

Magda felt uneasy, not expecting to be greeted so promptly at the door by Nadia Hristova, who the mayor had portrayed as so unwell. She stood back apprehensively and rested her hand on her gun. A woman wearing a nursing uniform stood in the doorway. Realising that this must be the nurse the mayor had mentioned, Magda lowered her guard and identified herself, explaining the reason for her visit. The nurse introduced herself as Ana.

'It's good that you have come, but unfortunately, I don't think that Nadia will be able to help you very much. I understand that she used to be a very talkative lady, but since I have known her, she's unfortunately never said a word,' Ana clarified. 'It's sort of like dementia. My grandfather had that. It was terrible and ground him down over a few years. He started becoming forgetful and eventually he couldn't recognise me, even though he was living with me. It got so bad toward the end that he stopped talking also, but not like Nadia. I've been told that she stopped talking overnight. A total change of behaviour and character,' Ana explained as Magda listened intently.

'Would it be ok for me to meet her?' Magda asked.

'Yes, well, I have just finished here so that should be fine. She's in the lounge listening to her radio. I can stay if you like, but I have to go and pick up my husband from town soon,' Ana muttered.

'I'm sure that I'll be fine and will make sure that the door is locked before I leave,' Magda promised.

'Great, just make sure that the cats don't get out. She has three of them and if any of them escape, she will be searching for them all night.' Walking past Magda, Ana hurried down the path and out of the gate.

Closing the front door, Officer Popova peered into the lounge and saw the quaint, if dated decoration. Two feet looked to be comfortably nestled in slippers next to a floor heater and the news was on the radio. Walking into the lounge, Magda saw Nadia sitting comfortably in an armchair, her legs covered in a soft sheepskin blanket.

Her gaze was fixed on the radio and she was tapping her thumbs together on her lap with a look of contentment on her face. Magda's eyes scoured the room. She saw many items. Evidence of a woman who had lived a full life, before this affliction took hold. Photographs of Nadia with friends and family were intermingled with educational certificates and sporting medals, neatly but dustily sitting on the cabinet shelves.

'Hello, my name is Officer Popova. It's very nice to meet you,' Magda said, realising that she had been looking around the room for too long without introducing herself. Unsure of what she had been expecting, she paused and waited for a response, or some sort of reaction from her, but Nadia continued to smile whilst looking at the radio. An immediate sense struck Magda that there was nothing to be gained from this visit. That she was wasting her time. Her mind, however, was drawn to the words of the mayor who described the way in which this same exceptional condition had affected a number of people in the village over a relatively short space of time. Taking a seat opposite Nadia, Magda took a moment to get comfortable and continued to look around the room.

'This is a beautiful house you have. Do you mind if I ask you a few questions?' but she was once again met with silence from Nadia. 'Is this your daughter?' Magda asked, picking up a photo frame that stood on the coffee table next to the sofa.

The sound of the frame being lifted from the table top drew a flick of the eyes from Nadia, who quickly returned her attention to the radio. The photo seemed to have been taken in the front yard many years ago. Nadia was holding the hand of a young girl in a yellow dress. Replacing the frame on the coffee table, Magda felt a sudden pang of sadness for Nadia and sat quietly for a few moments, listening to the radio as night fell outside. Nadia rummaged in a small bowl of sweets next to the radio. Unfurling the wrapper noisily, she quickly put the sweet in her mouth. Magda felt out of place and almost invisible as she sat in the room. The stifling uneasiness she felt was palpable. She struggled to think of a question to ask Nadia that would perhaps draw a response. She felt hot in her black jacket.

'My name is Officer Popova and I'm from the police,' Magda said, removing and setting her jacket to one side. 'I think there is something you may be able to help me with, but don't worry if you can't. There was something in the forest nearby. An artefact was buried there. It must have been very important, because a lot of people wanted it,' Magda explained as Nadia continued to smile and listen to the radio. 'The object. It must have been there for a very long time. Do you know what I'm talking about at all?' she asked, realising the futility of the questions, given Nadia's circumstances.

'I'm sorry to have bothered you, Mrs Hristova. It's been very good to meet you,' Nadia quietly grumbled as she rose from the couch. Hearing the sound of another sweet being unwrapped behind her back, she turned to look at Nadia one last time. As she did, Magda was shocked to see that Nadia had stood up silently and was now staring at her. Taken aback, Magda was off balance. Stumbling a step to the side she knocked into one of the dining table chairs, in turn toppling a vase sitting on the table. As the water from the vase cascaded off the side of the table-top, Magda's eyes were locked with Nadia's, who stood staring directly at her.

Magda's immediate reaction had been to draw her handgun, but she had resisted pointing it toward Nadia.

'You gave me quite a fright there, Mrs Hristova! Is there something you wanted to tell me?' Magda asked with as much authority as she could muster in the situation. She looked toward Nadia, for a reaction. Nadia was completely still. Moving the candy from one hand to the other, she continued to unwrap the sweet and spat the one she had in her mouth out. It landed half way between them and rolled along the carpet to Magda's foot. She felt the contact, but didn't look down. Realising that the hand in which she held her gun, was trembling slightly, Magda removed her finger from the trigger and rested it along the side of the barrel.

Nadia clenched her fist around the unwrapped sweet as the empty wrapper floated to the floor. Walking forward one step, she looked down at the half-eaten spherical red sweet, touching Magda's boot. Nadia looked as though she was trying to say something. Her lips were moving, but she was making an incoherent and guttural sound. In that instant, Magda thought that perhaps the years of not speaking had caused her to lose her ability to talk.

Magda craned her head forward slightly to try and lip-read what Nadia was saying, but she wasn't able to understand. Nadia started to splutter and cough for a moment, seemingly from the exertion of trying to say something, before drawing a deep breath.

'Why,' exclaimed Nadia in a husky and almost masculine voice, whilst moving her gaze to Magda's gun.

'Are you asking me why I'm here?' but her question was met with a slow shake of the head by Nadia.

'Why do you want help from me?' Nadia said, pausing to lick her chapped lips as her eyes closed and fluttered open again. 'I need help.'

Magda stood aghast. Nadia slumped suddenly and awkwardly to the floor, hitting her head on the armrest of the chair as she fell. Magda holstered her gun and kneeled down to aid Nadia. She felt the back of her head, which took an impact during the fall. There was bleeding, but Nadia appeared to still be conscious. She groaned with her eyes now closed.

'How can I help you?' asked Magda with an urgent tone.

'I only just woke up. I'm weak. Don't let them bury me,' Nadia pleaded, but it sounded like delirium.

'Nobody is going to bury you. You're safe. I will call an ambulance so that they can come and look at the cut on your head.'

'They will. I can't control them,' Nadia faintly uttered. Magda used her radio to call for ambulance assistance at her location and lay Nadia's head on her lap, suspecting concussion.

'What is your name?' asked Magda.

-Chapter 12-

Stepping foot outside the aircraft that had recently landed at a private airfield just outside Groningen in the Netherlands, Henrietta Rekman had been the sole passenger on Dr Bob Meertens' jet. It had been a smooth flight, landing on a crisp and clear winter morning. Her stomach churned as she walked down the airstairs. Rucksack slung over her shoulder, Henrietta wore blue jeans, white trainers and a black hoodie. Her blonde hair wisped in the wind that was zipping across the airfield.

Stepping onto the tarmac, she got in to the black Mercedes S-Class that had been sent to meet her. Climbing across the back seat and closing the door, Henrietta immediately scrambled to unzip one of the side pockets of her rucksack.

Just in time, she pulled out a brown paper bag containing a variety of pills. Tipping everything onto the seat beside her, she drew the bag to her mouth and vomited her half-digested breakfast into it, as quietly as possible.

'Everything ok, Henrietta?' asked the driver.

'Yes, I'm great,' she said, wiping her mouth with a tissue.

'You must be going soft!' he said, looking at her in the rear-view mirror as they drove off. Henrietta flipped open the case of her phone and looked at herself in the small mirror. Noticing the fine specks of blood on her forehead and down her left temple, she took another tissue and started wiping furiously.

'Keep going, Dirk, and I'll make sure you stay soft forever!' she snapped back angrily. With a shudder, the driver averted his eyes from Henrietta and back to the road as they drove away from the airfield at speed.

'The body?' he asked.

'We dropped it over the North Sea,' she responded calmly, as the nausea abated and she stretched her legs out, slouching down in the comfortable seat and drawing the hood over her head, halfway down her face.

As they arrived back at the estate of Dr Meertens, he monitored their progress towards the house on the CCTV screens. Henrietta leaned over the shoulder of the driver and gave him a kiss on the cheek to thank him for the lift.

'Aww, you know I didn't mean it, right?' she said, running her fingers softly down the back of his neck.

'Get out of here, Rekman,' he said in a playful tone.

Henrietta walked with an energetic bounce in her step, into the house and toward the study where she was sure she would find Dr Meertens. Knocking on the door, there was a slight pause before he invited her to enter. Walking into the study, she saw Meertens lying on the couch watching the CCTV monitors, arranged neatly on the wall. The news was playing quietly on one of the monitors.

'And? Did you get anything from our friend?'

'Only two things. That he didn't like getting hit with a hammer and that he couldn't fly,' Henrietta responded. Meertens laughed quietly for a moment.

'But you're sure he knew nothing? That the Russians know nothing?'

'If he knew something, he would've told me. The Russians haven't got any idea about what or where the Pebble is. He told me that their agents only got as far as the dig site that night by kidnapping the children of Ambassador Sunderland.'

'Interesting. Well done, Henrietta. Thank you. I am sure that this will put the minds of some of our members at ease,' Meertens added with a positive tone.

'I used the jet, but I tried to make as little mess as possible,' she said sheepishly.

'Are you feeling ok? You aren't looking your usual self,' Meertens said. Henrietta, slightly surprised that he had picked anything up, gave a quick response without too much thought.

'I'm fine. Just starving. Haven't had any breakfast,' she said, thinking about the breakfast that she had lost after landing.

'I'm just about to ask the chef to make me some waffles. Would you like some?' he asked.

'No no, thank you very much. I need a shower. I've got blood all over me,' Henrietta winced, running her fingers through her hair.

'How long until they realise that he is missing?' asked Dr Meertens.

'I don't know. Probably not long. But his wife definitely won't be reporting anything,' she said with a half wink, turning and leaving the study. Meertens turned his gaze back to the television and reached blindly for the telephone receiver, laying behind his head and out of view.

'Jacob, hi. Can I have some waffles please? With honey and banana. You know, just the way I like them.

Henrietta opened the door of her self-contained apartment. Dropping the rucksack to the floor, she took off her hoodie and threw it on to the bed, startling Ratty. He had been curled up comfortably amongst the unmade bed covers. Raising his head and looking at Henrietta, he let out a lazy meow. She had no time to interpret.

'Sorry, Rats,' she said as she placed one knee on the bed and reached over to give him a scratch behind the ear. He purred contentedly as he looked at her white vest, covered at the front in red blood blotches that had soaked through the hoodie. She slumped down on the bed and gave the dark-brown fur on top of his head a kiss. He smelt of grass, so he'd recently been out.

Getting up from the bed, she walked to the window Ratty had pawed open to get out in the early morning. She pulled the window closed, to stop any more cold air getting in. Picking up her rucksack, she went into the bathroom. She saw her reflection in the bathroom mirror and the blood on her vest. Quickly taking it off, she threw it into a corner. Now topless, Henrietta quickly removed the rest of her clothes and sat on the toilet seat. Running her hand down the back of her toned calf muscle, pain shot up her leg from the blow she had taken in apprehending the Russian agent.

Rummaging around inside her rucksack, Henrietta took a second pregnancy tester from a packet. She had thought it best not to leave them in her apartment. Sitting for a moment, thinking of waterfalls, she leaned over and turned on the tap. That seemed to do the trick.

Bringing the tester up, she waited patiently for a moment, before it showed her the same result as the first one she had tried. Positive.

She closed her eyes, running her free hand over half her face and through her hair. Henrietta shook her head slowly as she sat alone in her bathroom. Opening her eyes, she saw Ratty sitting just outside the bathroom, looking straight at her. She had only been a few hours, but he was always very happy to see her.

'Your life is simpler. Want to swap?' she asked him seriously, but realising that of course he wouldn't want to, she stood from the toilet seat and started running a bath for herself. Ratty walked in, and jumped up onto the toilet-seat lid she had put down.

'One of these days I will give you a bath, seeing as how you like watching me take them so much,' she told him, dropping a bright purple bath bomb into the tub, but Ratty seemed indifferent, instead sniffing the fragrance infused steam emanating from the filling tub.

Henrietta, shut off the tap and poked a toe in the water. It felt a little too hot, but she bravely stepped in with both feet and lowered herself into the water until the bubbles surrounded her head. She was up to her chin in water. Ratty perched on the toilet, observing. Blowing towards him, a tuft of bubbles flew up into the air and floated down to the ground. He was unfazed, but watched them keenly nonetheless.

Henrietta brought her thinking back to the pregnancy. She had hoped that the first test had been incorrect, but now had to accept the news brought so swiftly by the second test. With everything that had happened recently, she had not felt any fear or much emotion, but this was different. Not something that she had planned and something she was unprepared for. The sinking feeling that she hated was back. The sinking feeling she had when she lived with her mother and father. The sinking feeling she had when she had been alone in the world, before being taken in by Dr Meertens and Onyx.

She sat up in the bathtub, squirting some shampoo into the palm of her hand. As she lathered her hair, she thought about the father of her child. The reason she was in this situation. How he recently looked up at her from the cold ground in the Balkans with eyes that begged her not to kill him. She thought of Vincent Madden. She also thought about how Olivia had stepped in and saved him.

'He would have been dead if it wasn't for that bitch,' she hissed, turning her head toward Ratty, who looked like he was in full agreement. Strangely, as she looked back down toward the water and continued to shampoo her hair, she realised that she felt glad that he wasn't dead. Her head was full of strange thoughts she didn't want to be thinking about. Not least how Dr Meertens would take the news. She sank down further into the bubbles and shut her eyes.

Dr Meertens was keen to make sure that all loose ends had been tied up and now that they knew that the Russians didn't have any actionable information about the Pebble, there was one place she still had to go. The jet would be clean, fuelled and ready to fly to London later that same day.

Chapter 13

'We aren't sure what it means yet. We have received communication from one of our contacts within the Russian intelligence community that during a meeting held in St Petersburg in the last twenty-four hours, several localities where Argo Industries have business resources were discussed,' explained Adam Diaz.

'Our business sites? Why? What was the conversation about?' Argo asked probingly.

'We're unclear. Our contact has no access to that information. They overheard part of a conversation between agents who spoke about the meeting and had been tasked with looking into the areas in question,' Diaz clarified. 'So, we can't be sure that it has anything to do with us, but one of the areas is Bandung.' Argo raised both eyebrows instinctively and stared at Diaz.

'A little bit of a coincidence, don't you think, Adam? Enough of a coincidence for it to worry you and be brought to my attention. We can't ignore it,' huffed Argo as he sat across from Diaz in his dining room, picking at the food on his plate and totally lacking any appetite. 'I am due to speak with Bob Meertens once again shortly on another matter, but I will revisit this with him,' Argo explained.

'Bob Meertens? How is he going to be able to help us with this?' asked Diaz.

'Henrietta. Henrietta Rekman interrogated a senior Russian agent and she got assurances from him that they had no leads or anything to do with the Pebble,' Argo explained.

'I didn't know that,' said Diaz with an air of indignance in his voice.

'Neither did I, Adam. That is until he contacted me in the early hours of this morning to tell me,' Argo said in a placatory tone. 'I did tell him that it would be useful to know when he is planning to do this kind of thing.'

'Henrietta is very persuasive. It's good news for us that she was unable to get anything from that agent,' Diaz deliberated.

'I agree, but it doesn't give me any comfort. Ok, let me speak with Meertens and get a few things clear,' Argo said, leaving the dining room while Diaz finished his breakfast. Olivia walked with him toward the Great Hall, where he would speak with Dr Meertens. After his recent experience, Argo had instructed Olivia to stay by his side at all times in order to monitor all of his actions both whilst he was awake and whilst he slept. He hoped more than anything, that Meertens would be able to shed some light on what he had experienced. Never had he dreamed so vividly or so directly about real life decisions. He had also never lost time or recent memory. As they walked down the perfectly ordered and ornate corridor toward the Great Hall, he looked at Olivia walking beside him and couldn't help thinking about her words to him in the dream. The excruciating sensation that he had experienced, like being boiled alive, stayed with him, tormenting him. He couldn't shake it. Olivia turned her head and returned his gaze.

'I agree with Adam Diaz. Henrietta is persuasive,' said Olivia. Argo let out a small chuckle and looked ahead in the direction of travel.

'He wasn't referring to her conversational skills,' he responded.

'I am aware,' said Olivia, to which Argo raised a surprised eyebrow in her direction.

'What do you think?' he asked.

'Having referenced the information at our disposal, including recent Russian government interest in the report mentioned by Adam Diaz, it is likely that the new interest in the chosen locations does link to you, or your company,' Olivia bluntly replied.

'I can always rely on you to give me a straight answer,' Argo said, looking straight ahead.

'The Pebble is in the lab and is in the process of being prepped for transport. At the moment Dr Otani's team are awaiting your final decision on next steps,' she updated. Argo was about to speak when Olivia interjected. 'Several members of Dr Otani's team have reported difficulty sleeping in conjunction with headaches and nausea. Our medical staff have not been able to determine the cause of these symptoms.'

'And Dr Otani?' asked Argo, surprised at this news.

'He has reported difficulty sleeping only,' she quickly retorted.

'What about the other staff here?'

'Apart from the science team working on the Pebble and yourself, there are no reported issues with other staff,' Olivia updated as they continued to stride toward the Great Hall. 'The medical staff have ruled out most contamination sources which would have affected others also.'

'But the medical staff don't have access to the labs. They don't know what we have down there,' Argo nervously put forward.

'Yes, prolonged close contact with the artefact is one thing that all of the affected have in common,' Olivia clarified.

'I want the labs cleared. The science team, including Dr Otani, are to stay in their quarters until we know more,' Argo set out clearly. 'And Vincent Madden. I want him confined also, until we know more about why the Russians are so interested in Bandung!' he nervously exclaimed as Olivia nodded and closed her eyes for two seconds while transmitting the orders to the security personnel.

They walked into the Great Hall with its tall white Roman-style pillars, intermingled with beautiful and immaculate white-marble sculptures. Overhead, the ceiling mural depicted a celestial battle between the forces of good and evil, represented by demons and angels in the heavens. The surroundings dwarfed the round-table seating arrangement at the centre, from where Argo would speak with Bob Meertens.

-Chapter 14-

This is the best wardrobe I have ever had, thought Vincent Madden as he stood perusing the variety of clothing in the wardrobe. He wasn't sure when the clothes were being brought in or who by, but he did know that they were a perfect fit and just the kind of thing he liked to wear. Although he hadn't left the Future Logic Facility since arriving, he kept himself busy. As busy as the guards would allow him to be in any case.

Between the library and the gym, he was as content as he thought possible, given the circumstances. He was alive for the moment and that was as much as he could hope for. Over the past few weeks he had been through many mental stages, none worse than when he likened his situation to being in prison, less the metal bars and other prisoners. He felt happy that his progress through these stages had been quick. The good treatment he had received certainly helped.

What concerned him was the almost daily meetings and events he was required to attend. He worried every time one of Argo's employees would come to his room to take him to play squash, or to his weekly session with the physiotherapist. Every interaction had one common thread: the subtle attempts to lull him into a false sense of security.

The veiled attempts to extract personal information from him. Not just about himself, but about people he knew. How he had come to be in possession of the auction invitation and who else might have any knowledge of its existence.

Vincent had been able to evade answering these questions with any detail, on occasion wondering why Argo believed that he would be able to extract anything from him in this way. The inevitable thought had crossed his mind. Eventually the hospitality would end and he would be subjected to the more conventional forms of questioning that one might expect, such as methods of torture. It was for this reason that he had even contemplated committing suicide: how he would do it, when he would do it and what would be the trigger for him to do it.

Hoping that it wouldn't come to that, Vincent's intuition told him that it was just a matter of time and that he was a fool to have not ended his life already.

These were the thoughts that haunted him the most, keeping him awake in the dead of night when all was quiet: the thought that at any time, on the whim of his captor, he could be subjected to any variety of torture. Perhaps Argo considered himself to have the luxury of time. If he thought that anybody was close to tracking the Pebble down, his technique of information extraction might change. Vincent tried to keep these dark thoughts at bay during the day and had been able to suppress them well.

Would it be so bad to give up my contacts? The people who trusted me to take the invitation to Francis. Are they looking for me? Do they even know that I'm alive? Do they even care? He thought, picking out a cashmere polo shirt and grey trousers from the wardrobe and tossing them onto the bed. He had been afraid to verbalise things to himself in his own room for fear of being listened in to, so he was trapped in his own head, mulling over his thoughts unable to speak his mind, even to himself.

Pulling on the clothes as he carried on thinking, he walked over to the door of his room and knocked. It took a moment for a guard to unlock and open it for him.

'Could we go down to the library please, I have finished my books,' Vincent asked the guard politely.

'I'm sorry, Mr Madden, but there has been a minor emergency in the facility and I'm afraid that won't be possible,' Xavi informed him as he towered over Vincent in the doorway.

'An emergency? Sounds serious,' Vincent said in an enquiring tone.

'A minor emergency,' the guard calmly repeated as he closed and locked the door.

Vincent turned away from the closed door and walked over to the window. Looking out over the section of the facility he could see, all appeared normal. In the distance, he saw the jungle through the perimeter fence. The only vague clue he had about where in the world he might be.

He knew that he would have to make decisions soon and act fast. From what he had seen, the facility was very well guarded with regular armed patrols of the perimeter fence and sentries posted around the clock in watchtowers in the four corners of the compound. Everywhere he saw items of tech that he didn't know the application of. This did nothing to encourage him to try and escape.

He had been summoned by Argo on several occasions for meetings to discuss the artefact. Argo had gone into some detail about progress his team were making with it. His first encounters had been pleasant and friendly. Vincent had struggled to keep his guard up, but the constant presence of Argo's assistant, Olivia, unnerved him enough to stay shielded. She didn't sit well with Vincent at all, even though she had saved his life. Her manner, whilst courteous and genteel, seemed vacant. His more recent encounters with Argo, however, had been different. Argo had seemed distracted and weary.

Vincent had been just as astounded as the members of Onyx who had stood and listened to Dr Otani setting out the preliminary findings about the Pebble. Potentially the cradle of life on Earth. He let out a small laugh as he thought about Francis and how he wouldn't have believed it even if he had heard it with his own ears. That is if he was still alive.

Hearing movement outside his room, Vincent stepped away from the window and crept slowly toward the door. One of the guards was speaking either on his radio or to another guard, but had moved away slightly and the sound was too muffled for Vincent to be able to hear what was being said. Frustrated, he pushed his ear up against the door, but still couldn't make anything out. He rubbed the healing wound, where he felt a dull throb every time he placed too much weight on his leg. The instant torrent of thoughts about Henrietta Rekman reinforced the urgency he felt to act.

Chapter 15

'She's quite sure. When Henrietta asks a question, people usually answer. If they have received any intelligence, it must have been after she acquired him from his home,' Dr Meertens said to Argo without missing a beat, as they spoke through satellite video link.

'Possibly, but you can see the position this puts us in,' Argo said, sitting next to Olivia in the Great Hall.

'Yes, I can. What are you going to do if anybody comes knocking?' asked Meertens. He was met by momentary silence.

'I wanted to speak with you about a health condition I've been experiencing.'

'A health condition? Ok, let me see what I can do,' Meertens said, inviting further information.

'It's not just me. The science team have all been experiencing symptoms of insomnia, with most also suffering from headaches and nausea. I've had trouble sleeping myself and...' Argo paused, 'and I've suffered hallucinations of conversations that never took place. Experienced a vivid dream that felt real and painful,' he winced, realising that he sounded like a madman. Meertens moved toward the screen of his laptop slightly and thought momentarily.

'Have you taken an MRI?' asked Meertens, to which Argo nodded. 'And all was clear?' to which he received another nod. 'If it had been just you, I would say that stress could be a contributing factor to your inability to sleep and possibly your hallucinations and dreams, but where a number of people all experience similar symptoms, we must look for an external cause. Have you swept the facility for contaminants, for anything that could be causing it?' Meertens questioned.

'We haven't been able to find any known contaminants or toxins here but it seems... it seems that the people affected have all had contact with the artefact. Prolonged contact,' Argo reluctantly said, as Meertens leaned back in his chair and interlinked his fingers under his chin.

'What we have to start talking about is quarantine. Is there anything else that you can tell me about the artefact? What have you found?' Meertens probed.

'The Pebble is active. The first and only environmental test so far, placed it in a vacuum. It closed up it's open compartment,' Argo recounted.

'The thing is active? How?' Meertens shouted excitedly, leaning forward quickly. 'How is that possible?'

'We don't know. No more testing has been carried out since we found out. The vacuum test was the only environmental test which we decided to conduct on the surface of Earth.'

'You must quarantine the labs, along with all team members who have experienced symptoms. And nobody leaves the facility. That includes yourself. Doctor's orders!' Meertens instructed.

'Yes, I will keep you updated. I started to put the quarantine in place just before I called you. Is there anything that I should be taking? Some kind of medication?' Argo asked hopefully.

'No, I wouldn't recommend it. We don't know what we are dealing with. Call me tomorrow to update me, or sooner if you need to,' Meertens said, ending the call.

Argo rose from his seat, walking slowly toward one of the Roman columns that stood next to the immense ballistic-glass window. Running his fingers along the contours of the pillar, he walked around it as thoughts dashed through his mind. The sound of his footsteps on the stone floor reverberated around the hall. Heading toward the door, he left with Olivia to return to his apartment.

'Invoke the Crossbones protocol,' he instructed.

-Chapter 16-

'Dr Meertens, I am going now,' Henrietta Rekman said in as cheerful a voice as she could muster. Bob Meertens was in the middle of delicately trimming a bonsai tree that lived on his desk, but immediately put his clippers down and turned his full attention to Henrietta.

'Ms Rekman, I don't know what I would do without you. Before you go, I think you should know that the Russian you interrogated was either too shy to speak to you, or didn't know, but it appears that Russian intelligence is currently looking very specifically at some of Mike Argo's regions of business. One of the regions is the lovely Bandung,' Meertens explained.

Henrietta's face dropped with surprise.

'Dr Meertens, if the guy I spoke with knew anything, he would have told me. He must not have known. Would you like me to change my destination?' she asked.

'No, you go ahead. There is no point crying over spilt milk, as they say,' Meertens jested as Henrietta turned to leave. 'But before you go, is there anything you would like to tell me?' Meertens questioned. 'I've been told that you haven't been feeling well.'

Henrietta immediately cursed Dirk, the driver, in her mind for telling Meertens about her being sick. She herself was surprised when the truth blurted out of her mouth and she told Meertens that she was pregnant. His expression didn't change.

'And who is the father?' he asked. Henrietta was silent. 'You know that you can tell me, Henrietta.'

'I only just found out that I am pregnant. I was going to talk with you about it when I got back,' she said evasively.

'We have a good arrangement, you and I. What would I do without you?' he asked in a monotonous voice.

'Why do you keep saying that?' said Henrietta, glaring at Meertens.

'Because, how would you be able to carry on your good work for me? How could our arrangement continue?' he questioned with a look of bafflement, subtly reminding her of the past that he had saved her from and from which he still protected her .

'What would you have me do?' she asked, unable to make eye contact with him.

'You seem to be perfectly capable of making big-girl decisions all by yourself, Henrietta. I think that you should make your own mind up,' Meertens said, lowering his tone.

'You want me to... You want me to get rid of it,' she said, trying to overcome the lump which had appeared in her throat and the almost overpowering urge to break down in tears.

'We will talk when you get back, Henrietta. I think that you need some time to think,' he stated as he picked up the clippers and carried on pruning the bonsai tree that sat before him. She clenched her fist and left the room, picking up the rucksack she had left just outside before heading out to the car.

Chapter 17

Dragging her feet one after the other, Taryn Docherty walked slowly after her brother, Peter. Taryn was ten years old and her older brother thirteen. They were returning home after a long day at school. As Peter barged the front door open and made his way into their home, their mother, Marianne, watched through the lounge door. Peter ran across the hall and up the stairs without taking his shoes off. She had told him so many times not to do it, but he wouldn't listen.

'Hi kids! Peter, shoes!' she shouted.

'Sorry, mum,' came his response from the top of the stairs.

Marianne carried on watching and listening as Taryn slowly closed the door and untied her shoes. A sudden low-volume blub of crying was audible and Marianne immediately got up to go and check. As she poked her head around the door frame, she saw Taryn sitting on the doormat undoing the white laces of her grey school shoe, tears streaming down her face, but hidden under swathes of long blonde hair.

'What is it? What's wrong, Taryn?' Marianne asked with motherly concern. 'Is it something your brother did?' She took a seat next to Taryn on the floor.

'Why is Taryn crying?' came the voice of Peter from the top of the stairs.

'I don't know, Peter, maybe you can tell me,' his mother answered, looking directly at him up the flight of stairs.

'I didn't do anything!' he said innocently.

'He didn't do anything,' Taryn muttered under her breath, sniffing as she continued to cry.

'Then what is it, honey? You know you can tell me,' Marianne probed as Peter immediately lost interest and scampered into his bedroom. Taryn pulled both of her knees toward her forehead and continued to cry. Marianne put her arm around Taryn's shoulders and kissed the top of her head. They sat for a few moments until Taryn calmed down.

'Are you going to tell me, or do you want me to tickle it out of you,' Marianne threatened jokingly as she ran her hand down under Taryn's armpit, provoking a small, but welcome crying giggle.

'A girl in my class said that I was short and that I would never get any taller. I don't like her. She always picks on me,' Taryn muttered sulkily.

'Was it Roberta?' Marianne enquired, immediately thinking of her dislike for Roberta's parents. She had spoken with them before about Roberta picking on Taryn, but they had claimed that it was in fact Taryn who had been picking on their daughter. Taryn nodded with her forehead still touching her knees.

'I miss dad,' she said, immediately bursting into a new torrent of tears. 'I miss him so much.'

Marianne's eyes began to well up with tears as she thought of the emotional trauma and upheaval they had all suffered since the death of her husband, Jerome. For one so young, Taryn had shown maturity beyond her age, although she had resisted understanding the reason why she would never again see her father.

'Your father loved you so much, Taryn. You don't know how much. If he could have stayed, he would have. He talked about you until the end, but he was so sick,' Marianne explained as her voice quivered.

'We have a nurse at our school. When someone isn't feeling well, she makes them feel better. Why couldn't the nurse make dad feel better?' asked Taryn, looking up at her mum's face and seeing the tears.

'Sometimes nurses can make people feel better, but it depends on what is wrong with them. They can't always help people if they are very unwell,' Marianne tried to clarify further.

'They should have tried harder,' Taryn moped, planting her forehead back on her knees. Her mum tapped her on the shoulder before getting up and heading back into the lounge to get something. Returning quickly, she sat back down in the same spot.

'Your dad gave me something very special years ago. It's the thing that I treasure the most, except for the two of you of course,' Marianne said candidly, unable to shake the quiver in her voice as Taryn looked up at her again.

'What is it?' the little girl asked with curiosity as her mum lowered her hand, tightly curled into a fist around a hidden object.

'It's a turtle. A very special turtle,' Marianne explained as she opened her hand revealing a leather turtle, the size of a small pendant. The tiny patterns were incredibly intricate, and looked almost Aztec in design.

'Pretty,' said Taryn looking at the detail and fighting back the urge to pick it up.

'Yes, but this is no ordinary turtle,' Marianne continued. 'Your father told me all about how turtles are one of the animals that are best able to navigate. Do you know that they can travel for thousands of miles in the seas and oceans? Somehow they manage to find their way back to the very same beach where they were hatched.'

'Turtles hatch? Like birds?' Taryn asked, wide-eyed and interested on hearing this new information.

'Uh-huh, just like that. And your dad told me that this special turtle would make sure that I never get lost and I would always be able to find my way back to him,' Marianne said, unable to control the tears that trickled down the side of her face. Taryn looked fascinated.

'How can it do that, mum?' she asked.

'The planet we live on is like a big magnet. Like the little magnets on your brother's old train set, but much bigger,' Marianne elaborated, wiping the tears away on her sleeve.

'Miss Hammond has a really big magnet at school,' Taryn said in her competitive voice.

'Yes well, magnets produce something called magnetic fields. These fields can attract metal objects or push them away and also they can be sensed by some animals, like turtles, to help them know how to get from one place to another.'

'They sound really clever. I always get lost without my brother,' Taryn conceded, with a small smile that melted her mother's heart.

'Well, when your father was sick, he was worried most about you. He asked me to give the turtle to you. He said that he wanted you to have it so that if you ever feel lost and you don't know which way to turn, you can hold the turtle in your hand and it can help you to find your way,' Marianne sobbed as she took Taryn's little hand and placed the turtle belly down on her palm.

'Can the turtle help me find dad again?' Taryn asked, once again descending into tears of sorrow.

'No, but if you ever get lost, and you don't know which way to turn, always remember that you are your father's special little girl. He always knew the way and if you listen, he will show you the path to take,' her mother said, trying hard to fight back the tears.

'But how?' Taryn asked in confusion.

'Look at the belly of the turtle,' Marianne said as Taryn picked it up between her thumb and forefinger, turning it over in her palm, to reveal an inset compass.

'I have used one of these at school. It's what people used before the Internet,' Taryn said with laughter through her tears.

'Is that what they told you?' Marianne asked with a smile, rubbing the top of Taryn's head and giving it another kiss. 'Here, let me put it on for you,' she said, picking up the leather turtle and thin chain, before passing it around Taryn's neck.

Chapter 18

'Do come through, Ambassador. Please excuse the mess,' Mildred Jones apologised as she shepherded Francis down the pristine hallway of the house.

'I have two young boys,' Francis Sunderland said jokingly.

'Children are no excuse for poor housekeeping,' she said sternly. Francis felt duly chastised for his implied bad parenting skills. 'Rebecca!'

'I'm in the conservatory,' shouted Rebecca Bradford. They walked in and Rebecca stood from the sofa and stepped toward Francis. He stretched out his hand to shake hers and she grasped it quickly. 'It's good to meet you. Thanks for agreeing to help.'

'Of course. I feel I must, in any way I can. I knew your sister only for a short time. I'm very sorry for your loss,' he said empathetically. Rebecca started to cry. Returning to sitting on the sofa she plucked a tissue from the box sitting on the cushion next to her.

'I haven't been far from a box of tissues recently,' she sobbed.

'It will take time, Rebecca, but eventually–' Mildred started.

'Eventually what? I'll forget that my sister was murdered? It won't hurt as much?' Rebecca said angrily through gritted teeth.

'None of us will ever forget that, dear. We're all hurting with you,' Mildred said, sitting down next to Rebecca and wrapping an arm around her shoulders. 'But, revenge is karma's best friend.'

'Don't pay any attention to her. She talks like this to try and cheer me up,' Rebecca sheepishly said to Francis. He carried on looking at Mildred, but her face remained stony cold. If she was joking, she was certainly hiding it well.

'The Ambassador has been very helpful. He's filled in a lot of the blanks about what happened to Charlotte. We still don't know anything about her killers though,' Mildred outlined. Rebecca looked towards Francis, wide-eyed.

'Really? You have no idea who they are?' she asked. Her voice tainted with desperation.

'No, he doesn't know who they are,' Mildred repeated, looking toward Francis in tandem with Rebecca.

'This is a beautiful house,' Francis said nervously, trying to change the subject and move away from the creeping sense of guilt he felt.

'Thank you, Ambassador. Yes, this house has been in my family for eight generations. It was built by Malcolm Brick and actually pre-dates the Brick Steckelback firm,' Mildred outlined informatively.

'It's very secluded,' Francis observed.

'It should be, I own all of the land in a five-mile radius of this house,' she quickly retorted with a touch of pride in her voice.

'Aren't you worried about living all the way out here by yourself?' he asked.

'Worried? No, I'm not worried. I have Rebecca with me now. We can take care of ourselves,' Mildred said, relinquishing her grasp of Rebecca's shoulder and rising to her feet. Walking out of the conservatory and into the adjoining kitchen, Mildred asked whether anybody would like a cup of tea. Rebecca and Francis didn't turn down the offer.

Francis sat and conversed with Rebecca for a few moments as Mildred lit a match and boiled a pot of hot water on the gas hob. Rebecca spoke about Charlotte. How they had grown up and how they had both come to work for Brick Steckelback.

Francis was engrossed in the conversation and consequently felt his remorse grow the more he got to know Rebecca and in retrospect, Charlotte.

The sound of teacups clinking together from the kitchen was a welcome reminder that a thirst quenching cup of tea was on the way. Mildred walked carefully back in to the conservatory with a teapot, a bowl of sugar, three cups, a small ornate jug of milk and a plate of sliced lemon. Laying the tray carefully on the small table that sat in the middle of the room, she started to pour.

Francis ordinarily liked to take his tea with milk, but given the opportunity, he chose a slice of lemon and watched it float serenely on top. Taking a sip, the tea was still too hot, but he nodded and smiled his approval.

A grandfather clock stood in the corner of the conservatory. The ticking filled the pauses in discussion. Mildred lit two gas lanterns, hanging in opposite corners of the conservatory. The warm light they exuded stoked the conversation further. As Francis finished the last of his cup of tea and saw the bedraggled piece of lemon languishing at the bottom of his cup, he took a moment to look up at the moon and stars, now visible on that clear and fine wintery night through the glass ceiling.

'Absolutely magnificent, isn't it?' Francis asked in awe. 'I haven't seen a sky as clear as that, stars as bright as that, in a long time,' he observed.

'Yes, we aren't blinded by the light and the noise out here,' Mildred muttered in a resentful tone.

'I know what you mean,' Francis agreed.

'I'm not sure that you do,' Mildred responded, placing her hand on Rebecca's thigh and leaning forward toward Francis. 'Do you know, Ambassador, that ours is the only law firm, to my knowledge, that stores all client details and files on off-grid computer systems? Computers that have never and will never be connected to the Internet?'

'No I didn't. Is that true?' he asked with interest.

'Yes. Except money of course, but we keep that in one big pot, using a very intricate referencing system, under the umbrella of the Brick Steckelback firm,' she outlined.

'That's fascinating. I didn't know that anybody operated that way,' Francis smiled with intrigue.

'Our client, the late Jerome Docherty. He came to us because he wanted representation, but was concerned about his privacy. He was concerned about his information and the integrity of what he wanted us to do for him. He explained to us everything about his former employer. An international criminal organisation by the name of Onyx,' Mildred divulged further, as Francis leaned in to make sure he missed nothing. He knew of Mr Docherty, whose invitation to the auction had included information about himself and the discovery that he had made. Vincent had discussed this with Francis during their freezing walk through a park in Sofia. Docherty had also indicated that the invitations must be sent out posthumously. However, Francis didn't know that Jerome had worked for a criminal organisation. *That would have been good to know,* he thought. 'We did everything we could to make sure the artefact didn't fall into the hands of Onyx. That was his wish. There was always a risk. That at least one of the five invitations that we sent by courier would be compromised,' Mildred continued.

'Compromised? I presume that you aren't referring to me,' Francis grumbled indignantly as his surprise turned to defensiveness.

'No, not you, Ambassador Sunderland, otherwise you wouldn't be sitting here. No, the person you attended the auction with. Your plus-one,' she shrilly exclaimed.

'Vincent Madden? I don't think so, Mrs Jones. I have met with colleagues and they have verified. He was the one entrusted to bring me the invitation,' Francis defensively said.

'I didn't say he knew that he was compromised. But, come now. How else would you explain the massacre at your house, Ambassador? And one must ask oneself, where is he now?' Mildred questioned. Francis leaned back quietly and gave his shoulders a small shrug. The gas lanterns shed light sparingly as deeper darkness descended over the house in Kent. The outside of the property was illuminated by moonlight and Francis could see it cascading down the rough brick wall. There was a tranquillity about his surroundings and he felt at ease even though the conversation should have made him feel anything but.

'Don't think that I haven't thought about all of this. I've struggled to piece it together myself. The answer is... Well the answer is I just don't know. I don't know how much help I can be to you,' Francis sheepishly conceded. Rebecca had sunk back into the comfortable couch cushions and was slightly obscured by Mildred. He couldn't see Rebecca's facial expressions in the darkness. Mildred looked about thirty years younger in the soft warm glow of the lanterns. 'Do you really not worry about living out here all by yourselves? It's so secluded,' he asked again.

'We have nothing to fear here. My ancestors. They were the ones who had something to fear. We are much better equipped now,' Mildred said faintly.

'Would you like me to turn on the lights?' Francis asked hesitantly.

'Oh, you are just adorable, Ambassador. I am so glad you agreed to come here tonight. No doubt you would be dead already if you hadn't,' Mildred said through a wide grin. Her yellowish teeth reflecting light from the lantern.

'I don't know what you mean,' Francis said defensively, wondering if she was threatening him.

'Didn't you notice? When you came in here today? The lack of electrical appliances, no light fittings, no sockets. This house has never been connected to the mains. My family forbade it. In fact, if I am not mistaken, your phone is likely the only electrical object in this house right now,' Mildred said, smiling once again. Francis came to the sudden realisation as he instinctively looked around for any sign of electricity, but found none.

'You didn't think that an organisation that operated the way Onyx did would leave any loose ends, did you? Especially a loose end as important as you. That bomb. The one that killed Charlotte. You are aware that it was meant for you and your family. It's lucky you attended the appointment with us. Otherwise we would have been forced to intervene more directly,' Mildred whispered as the knot tightened in Francis' stomach. He sat looking blankly.

'Yes. The thought had crossed my mind,' Francis said nervously as he wondered whether to mention anything about the woman who had called him before Charlotte died, or the drone that was circling overhead. He decided instead to say nothing. 'Are you saying that my family are in danger?'

'Not likely. It is definitely you they'll be after, but we have people at your house nonetheless,' Mildred reassured. 'At least until this is all over.'

'And us?' he probed further.

'You have nothing to worry about here, dear Ambassador. Whoever comes will receive the hospitality they deserve,' Mildred implied coldly. They sat in the glow of the lanterns quietly for a moment, although it felt like an eternity. Outside, the sudden shriek of foxes battling over turf, pierced the silence of the night. Francis was already on edge, but the fox wails sounded like banshees calling.

The distant sound of semi-automatic gunfire rattled around the surrounding countryside, filling the conservatory. Mildred placed her hand on Rebecca's knee, lifting herself to her feet with a groan.

'When this is over, I hope you remember what we did for you here, Ambassador. It seems your employer left you to the wolves,' Mildred said nonchalantly, as she walked into the house.

-Chapter 19-

'Every staff member is accounted for and in their quarters,' Olivia's voice rang over the intercom. Argo sat in the corner of his darkened bedroom. Sectioned off by Olivia while she secured the facility, he waited. 'There have been some requests for information from those not in the science team. I am on my way back to you now'

'Thank you, Olivia,' he said with closed eyes, trying to relax as much as possible. Argo feared falling asleep, even if he could. Even though the MRI had come up clear, he was worried for his own mental health, regardless of the causes, be they internal or external.

Argo thought about the company he still had to run. The other work he was neglecting. All for what? A multi-billion dollar facility disabled and in lockdown. At its heart, an unknown object sought by the most powerful members of the international community.

He popped a Boon capsule into his mouth, before taking a sip of the whey protein shake he caressed in a plastic container between his legs. Swallowing the Boon, he licked the remnants of the shake from the sides of his mouth.

As he waited for Olivia to return, Argo looked at his free hand. He realised his fingernails needed clipping again.

Since he had started taking Boon, the frequency of Argo's haircuts had also increased. A small price to pay for the sense of wellbeing he had felt when taking it, until recently at least. Not to mention unbounding energy from dawn until dusk, or the other way around. He chuckled to himself with momentary self-contentment as he swigged the final gulp of the shake and set the container to one side.

For now, both Boon and Nanoblood were only manufactured in one place: the labs at the Future Logic Facility. The news of potential Russian intelligence interest in Bandung was unwelcome. It troubled Argo greatly. It was an unwanted distraction.

The human guards had been notified of the security status update and were ordered to increase security presence outside. Their key-card access to the facility itself had been disabled as part of the Crossbones lockdown protocol. Many of the guards were more than happy to leave the main building, unsure of exactly why the protocol had been triggered for the first time during their employment. Olivia had accessed the Nexus storage unit adjacent to the sub-level 2 laboratory. Ordinarily, the store was visited several times a day by a science team technician to ensure good maintenance of the androids in standby mode. Olivia strode past other utility droids such as the pilot, Captain Wren, who stood in a cylindrical transparent chute. Arriving at the shining silver pods containing the GridWatch droids, she spent some time activating them. Her remote connection was established and the pods audibly decompressed with a low-volume hiss. Olivia stared at the pods, her fingers tapping the side of her thigh rhythmically. A mannerism she had picked up.

The pods cracked open gradually and the lids slid round in a circular motion to the rear, exposing the GridWatch droids, each neatly furled on the ground with their forehead touching their knees. Activated, all thirty GridWatch droids rose to their feet in unison. Much like the SPRAT droid, used to locate the Pebble, no effort had been made to make the GridWatch droids look human, although their form was humanoid.

Their matt-grey metallic exterior was interspersed with bulletproof black plastic moulding. This housed the sensor arrays located on their heads, limbs and torso. Standing at a modest four feet tall, they were built for high-speed, stealth movement. For this reason, their form was also slender. Unlike a lot of androids, their face had not been designed to be pleasing to the human eye, but instead to maximise functionality. The plastic mouldings were located at optimum positions and gave the spherical head a clinical, but somewhat unpredictable and consequently sinister look.

Looking down the row of GridWatch droids, Olivia scanned for any signs of malfunction, as they each underwent their start-up routine of movement, in unison. Rubber-coated fingers and toes made barely any noise as they stretched and contorted in inhuman directions. Olivia closed her eyes and disabled her auditory sensors. Seconds later, two of the defensive system tests ran. A magnificent flash filled the room followed by the shriek of the high-power sound waves emitted from the sonic defences. The sound waves sent a momentary ripple over Olivia's synthetic skin. A human standing in her place would have found themselves instantly deafened, blinded and debilitated. The droids, whilst testing these systems to their full potential, were capable of reducing the magnitude of light and sound in order to incapacitate without causing any permanent damage.

Through her direct link with all of the droids, Olivia reviewed the outcome of the start-up routine, which excluded offensive weapons checks. All units were fully operational.

Lowering her gaze slightly, Olivia gave a squad command for the GridWatch to patrol and secure the above-ground levels of the facility and to apprehend any staff leaving their quarters. This of itself would be a shock to many of the staff working at the facility who had never seen GridWatch or known of their existence. The droids calculated the most efficient way to carry out their orders and dispersed without any delay. Their movement, whilst mechanical and rapid, was also elegant and silent. Olivia watched as they disappeared from the room with a deft quickness. She would continue to monitor their alerts in the background.

With that, she left the storage unit and walked past the sub-level 2 laboratory where the Pebble lay abandoned. Staring through the locked and sealed glass door, she could see the artefact that was halfway through the process of being encased in metal for transport when Argo had given the order to hold off.

Continuing to scan, Olivia focused in on the Pebble, where she detected unexpected movement. Not of the object itself, but rather the surface. Zooming, she recognised the texture of movement to be similar to that of water. Her hand touched the door as her face came closer to the glass in an effort to verify what she could see. The motion seemed to continue but Olivia's focus blurred momentarily. Averting her eyes fleetingly, she refocused on the surface of the craft as her right knee buckled. She stopped herself from falling by grabbing the door control console with her other hand.

Regaining her balance and carrying out an instant system check that was unable to explain her seeming malfunction, Olivia opened the sealed door and entered the laboratory to investigate further. The GridWatch had cleared and resealed the hatch that separated the labs from the above-ground levels of the facility. Standing inside the lab as the door closed behind her, Olivia gently raised the lighting level as she attempted to review the images she had seen. They didn't show the fluid motion she thought she had seen, coursing over the surface of the Pebble. Instead, they showed the solid, shining, black-metal exterior. She stood for a moment, reviewing the footage again and again. Each time ending with the sudden dip caused by her knee malfunction. Several moments later and unable to access a digital representation of what she had seen, Olivia started to tap furiously on both thighs and a twitch of a smile fluttered across her face and disappeared.

She once again lowered the level of light in the room and walked with haste toward the artefact, standing bolt upright beside it. Scanning the object, everything appeared normal.

Olivia had experienced many things that had caused her confusion. Her interactions with some humans had been one of the greatest sources. However, she had not been confused by any physical experience, until now. Tilting her head, the twitch of a smile flicked across her face again as Argo contacted her on the intercom.

'Olivia, what are you doing?!' he exclaimed, as he watched her on the CCTV. Olivia, had no immediate answer for Argo, because she would first have to be able to explain the sensory phenomenon that she had experienced. 'I said, what are you doing?'

'The GridWatch have been tasked as requested and I will be with you shortly, Mr Argo,'

'I'm not talking about the GridWatch. I am talking about you standing next to the Pebble right now. What are you doing?' he boomed. A dull hum started to build in the lab, but Olivia was unable to pinpoint its source. The hum built gradually into a deep drone. Without responding to Argo, Olivia reached out with her hand and placed it flat on the surface of the craft. To Olivia, the craft felt cool to the touch and yet the thin layer of synthetic skin on the palm of her hand instantly melted, and globules of translucent grey material began running down the side of the black metal and falling onto the floor. 'Get out of there now, Olivia. That's an order!' Argo shouted at the monitor.

Her hand remained on the craft as the sensors and layers of underlying material also melted, finally reaching the fibre-optic strands comprising Olivia's nervous system. Argo ran toward the door of his quarters and slammed his hand down onto the handle of the locked door. Trying over and over again to unlock from the inside, he realised it was useless. Banging on it twice, he quickly appreciated the futility. Pacing back toward the monitor, beads of sweat had formed on his forehead and he clasped his lips with his thumb and forefinger as he watched.

Feeling nothing, Olivia removed her hand from the Pebble. Small globules of melted material clung to the side of the craft. Some of them ran seamlessly down its surface like quicksilver. Rapidly realising that the material must have come from her, she looked at her palm and saw the damage that had been caused. A mess of synthetic skin exposed the fibre-optic strands, controlling the billions of miniature slave robots that made Olivia's movement possible.

'Olivia, I want you to turn round and come to my quarters, immediately!' Argo shouted with distress in his voice, staring frantically at the monitor.

She finally registered the command from Argo, turned from the craft and walked out of the lab. As she tapped the sides of her thighs once again, the white, opaque, gelatinous substance seeping from her hand gradually soaked into her trousers.

Chapter 20

Taryn didn't understand why she would never be able to see her dad again. Her mum had tried to explain, but deep down, Taryn couldn't understand. An iconic figure in her life. A man she had idolised. But he had died three years ago and she had been forced to move away with her mum and brother.

She liked her old house. Her old friends. The new place was ok, she thought, but there was something missing.

Once again annoyed by her brother, she had decided that she wouldn't wait by the school gate at the end of the day, but instead had headed off toward home by herself. She knew the way well and the sun was shining. The heat on her skin felt nice and the gentle breeze blew through her golden locks. Another blissfully hot day in Queensland, Australia.

When her mother had shown her where Australia was on the big globe in her room, Taryn had been shocked. She had asked why they had to move to the other side of the world. Her mother had told her she had found a new job and they would make new friends. It had all happened so quickly.

As she left the noise of her school behind, Taryn felt the form of the small leather turtle through her dress. Her mum had asked her not to take it to school, but she hadn't listened. She hadn't parted with the turtle since her mother had given it to her; it was her new favourite thing.

She walked straight past a shortcut path that her brother sometimes took her down when they were running late. He had told her that she shouldn't ever use the path by herself. *What does he know anyway?*, she thought as she walked back a few steps and peeked at it sneakily with a naughty smile on her face.

Starting to walk down the narrow path, thick with plants on either side, she took step after step. The path became shadier, with the trees and vegetation overhead blocking out increasing amounts of sunlight. She never did like the dark part of the path. This was usually the point where she would squeeze her brothers hand the tightest, but he wasn't with her now.

As she continued, her grey school skirt got caught on a bramble and she heard a faint tearing sound. Looking down and feeling the skirt for a tear, she found it.

Taryn thought of her mum and how she would get told off. She hadn't done it on purpose. That's what she would say.

Dry twigs and leaves cracked underfoot as she stood looking at the tear. Her attention was drawn by a small green frog, glistening in a ray of light that had managed to find its way through.

It seemed to be looking at her, as its small, bulbous and perfectly formed red eyes blinked at her. She had seen frogs before, but never one so colourful. Its feet were orange and firmly affixed to a smooth rock to the side of the path.

'Hello, what's your name?' she asked. The frog looked back for a moment before letting out two surprising loud croaks. The vocal sac on the frog's neck inflated as it bellowed the sound.

Taryn kneeled down to look more closely at it, fascinated by its vibrant green colour and orange feet. After a moment, the frog hopped halfway across the path and crawled into the undergrowth.

'Where are you going? Come back,' Taryn whispered. Peering through the vegetation, she saw flashes of green as the frog jumped away. Deciding that her school clothes were already ruined, she parted the branches with her hands and started to shuffle her way through to follow the frog. She found it difficult to make progress and she was no longer able to see the frog. From all sides, she was engulfed by the foliage and had started to worry, before noticing a clearing up ahead. Moving closer, she saw a small pond at the centre of the clearing. Surrounded by the thick trunks of tall trees, there were many smooth rocks covered in moss, dotted around next to the water.

Layer after layer of long yellow pine needles covered the ground and were soft underfoot as she stepped out of the bushes. Looking down at herself, she noticed a variety of dry foliage stuck to her clothes. Taryn quickly brushed herself down with her hands. Shifting her weight from side to side, she enjoyed the bounciness of the needles for a moment. Looking up, Taryn gazed at the dizzy height of the trees before remembering about the frog. Her eyes searched for the green frog before spotting it sitting on one of the many lily pads floating on the water.

'How did you get out there so quickly?' she asked inquisitively. Taryn walked to the water's edge and took a seat on one of the mossy rocks. The frog let out another croak, as the sound of birdsong and wind meandered through the trees.

Taryn liked this place. It looked like nobody had ever been there and she hoped that nobody would find out about it. She felt something in her hair and her fingers found a long thin leaf that she must have picked up following the frog.

'I like your pond, Mr Frog,' she complimented the amphibian who sat on the lily pad looking straight at her. 'Do you live here all by yourself?' Taryn asked quietly. She sat cross-legged and the tear on her skirt was visible. Moving it around to the side slightly, she didn't want to be reminded about the trouble she would be in later, when she got home.

A low-volume rustle from the bushes behind caught her attention. Turning her head, she saw another green frog jumping towards her, taking a few seconds between each jump. It disturbed needles as it leaped and landed.

Keeping its eyes on her as it went, the frog dived into the pond and swam to a lily pad adjacent to the other frog. They both sat staring at her.

'But, which one are you? How many of you are there?' Taryn asked with a giggle. A sudden sense of being watched came over her, before the first croaks from the bushes began. Like an orchestra, what sounded like hundreds of frogs sang out from the surroundings. Taryn was fascinated and looked around with a beaming smile.

As the frogs started to jump into sight, she could see that some had colourful blue and yellow stripes down their green sides and others weren't green at all. She saw yellow, red, blue and purple frogs. Colours so vivid and beautiful that she felt she could sit and watch them forever. As they all dived into the pond from all sides, small ripples moved over the surface of the water and disturbed the two frogs sitting on lily pads.

As the leaf-top real estate was occupied by the tapestry of colourful frogs, the chatter of croaks was soothing and Taryn looked on in awe. She had never seen such a sight or heard such a sound.

'They are beautiful, aren't they?' asked a gentle female voice, much to Taryn's surprise. She looked around quickly, but couldn't see where the voice had come from. It sounded so close. 'I like to come here sometimes too. They don't seem to mind. You're a very pretty little girl. What's your name?' the woman asked.

'Where are you? I can't see where you are,' Taryn said.

'Oh, I'm sorry, I thought that you knew I was here,' responded the voice, as Taryn watched the form of a woman wearing a dark robe materialise on the opposite side of the pond, sitting at the foot of a tree. The hood hanging down obscured her face as the woman stood to her feet, looking at Taryn across the pond.

'I'm Taryn. Are these your frogs?' the little girl questioned, blowing a few strands of her hair away from her face, helping them along with her hand.

'My frogs? No. These frogs don't belong to anybody. They have lived here a lot longer than any of us. Perhaps, I should ask, do you belong to these frogs?' the woman whispered in a calm, tranquil voice.

'No, I don't belong to the frogs! Don't be silly,' Taryn laughed. The woman reached up and gently pulled back her hood. She looked to be in her early twenties. Her face was pale, her hair black and tied in a ponytail that had unfurled down behind her back, to her waist. Taking a couple of steps forward, long slender fingers emerged from the dark sleeves of her robe.

'Are you hungry, my dear Taryn? You look like you're hungry and tired.'

'No, I'm ok. I should probably be going now. I'm not supposed to speak with strangers,' Taryn answered.

'That's a shame. I thought that we could speak for a while. The frogs seem to like you. Otherwise, they wouldn't have come out like this to say hello,' the woman muttered, swaying her hand from right to left to encompass all of the amphibians now settled and staring at Taryn.

'Well, ok. What shall we talk about?' Taryn said, feeling like she was the centre of attention. Something that she really relished.

'I have picked some delicious rare mushrooms, Taryn. They are in my pocket. Would you like to try one?' the woman smiled.

'I don't know. My dad told me that I shouldn't eat mushrooms that I find outdoors. He said that some of them are bad,' Taryn recollected.

'Oh, that's true. Your father sounds like a clever man. But some of the best mushrooms can be found right here and I know the bad ones. The poisonous ones,' the woman explained.

'Ok then,' said Taryn, jumping up and walking around the pond to where the woman stood. She was tall and towered over Taryn as her hand entered the robe, producing four mushrooms, each of different shape, size and colour. 'They look so pretty. I don't know which one to have.'

'You won't regret your choice. They are all simply delicious, my dear,' the woman whispered as little fingers reached into her hand and picked the smallest mushroom. Light blue in colour with white polka dots, Taryn looked apprehensive as she ate it whole. The woman smiled warmly, sitting back down. 'Tell me more about your father.'

'My dad? My dad went away. My mum said that he died. She says that I won't ever see him again,' Taryn said sadly. Her smile immediately turning to a frown.

Sitting down next to the woman, Taryn pulled gently at the dark robe, its purple hue now visible. The material was soft and lightweight as Taryn scrunched it between her little fingers. A faint, but distinct and very pleasant scent emanated from the robe. Like a blend of rose water and citrus.

'You're very pretty, what's your name? I would love to have long hair like yours,' Taryn said. Black and long, the woman's hair looked as soft as silk.

'Such a little angel. If that is what you want, then you can make it so,' the woman said with a kind smile. 'You are an adventurous little one, aren't you? Like your father. Not many people have ever found this place.'

Taryn leaned forward and looking up at the woman intently.

'Did you know my father?' she asked excitedly. Most of Taryn's knowledge of his more notable exploits had been recounted by her mother at bedtimes. Often leaving her and Peter open-mouthed, the stories had filled them both with wonder and also great sadness.

'Yes. He told me all about you and your brother,'

'I don't believe you,' Taryn apprehensively muttered, shuffling away slightly.

'I have no reason to lie to you, my dear. His name was Jerome,' the woman's voice altered to a deeper, hissing tone, when she said his name. The sound ran through Taryn like a chilling wind, causing her to shudder. *How could she know my father?*, Taryn thought. Standing from the ground, she backed away a couple of steps.

'I have to go now. My mum is waiting for me at home.'

The woman stared with piercing green eyes directly at Taryn, who carried on backing away, crunching the yellow pine needles underfoot as she went. They started to feel sticky.

'I didn't mean to frighten you. Your father asked me to find you before it begins,' the woman remarked calmly.

'Before what begins?' Taryn asked, finding it ever more difficult to step backwards, but unable to look down, so mesmerised was she by the eyes of the woman.

'You will know,' the woman said, shifting her wild gaze suddenly down toward the frogs in the pond. Taryn finally was able to look down and saw that her feet had sunk into the pine needles and she was nearly knee deep. Unable to move her feet, she began to panic. Continuing to sink, Taryn tried to pull her legs out of the ground, but the more she tried, the quicker she sank. 'Help me,' she screamed at the woman who still stared at the frogs. Through her terror, Taryn's attention was drawn to steam rising from the pond. Looking at it, she saw the water boiling and the frogs being cooked alive on the lily pads and in the water.

'My name is Clandesta. Know this. If it was not for your father, you would suffer the same fate as these frogs. He could only pick one to save. Feel honoured that it was you.'

Taryn sank ever further and as the earth consumed her waist and started to creep up her stomach she started to scream. The soil pressed in on her torso, pushing the air from her lungs, quietening her, stopping her from breathing.

'Your journey will be long, but you must find me. Only that way can I truly help you,' Clandesta said. Her words muffled by the soil and needles falling in around Taryn's ears.

She gagged on needles and soil as her head was consumed, the crown of her head disappearing under the yellow pine needles.

Blinking under the earth, the soil scratched her eyes. Taryn nodded and shuddered from head to toe. Her legs felt free, followed by her arms. She couldn't breathe. Building up her strength and shaking her head, she stumbled forward, falling flat on the path she had taken on her way home from school. Taking deep, dreadful breaths, Taryn wanted to scream, but couldn't. Hearing somebody running, hands wrapped around her shoulders and she was pulled up with a jolt.

'Taryn, what's wrong?' Peter panted. 'You were screaming. You were walking and screaming. Then you fell! What happened? Did someone hurt you?'

She continued to pant frantically until finally calming down slightly and sitting on her knees in the dirt. Looking down at her clothes, she saw some dust from the ground, but there was no evidence of what she had experienced.

Immediately, she felt for the leather turtle and was instantly relieved to find that it was still there, but her heart sank when she saw that her skirt wasn't torn. She had definitely torn her skirt. Taryn searched her mind frantically for an explanation and wondered if she had imagined it. She didn't understand what had happened. So vivid, so painful. She hardly spoke on the way home. Just enough to try and convince her brother not to say anything to their mother. She was sure that he would.

-Chapter 21-

The clouds overhead were thick and ominous. Henrietta's stomach was racked by a feeling of nervous anticipation as she sped along a Kent B road. The twists and turns came quickly and there was barely enough room for two cars to squeeze past each other. Up ahead in the distance, she would occasionally see the rear lights of the car she had been following for some time now, whenever there was enough straight road for a clear line of sight.

Her conversation with Dr Meertens had stuck with her and she was finding it difficult to think about anything else. Shaking her head, she tried in vain to focus on the task at hand. Perhaps to leave the thoughts of her precarious position within Onyx, and the way in which Meertens had so bluntly spoken to her, to one side.

She had been terrified when Onyx located her, cowering in an abandoned houseboat. At first she had thought that the men who had found her were with the Dutch police, but very quickly realised that they weren't, when they had taken her to the estate of Dr Meertens.

They had taken her to him with nothing. A frightened young girl with evidence of the crimes she had committed still under her grimy fingernails.

His house had been like nothing she had ever seen growing up. Filled with beautiful art, antique furniture that had been restored masterfully and a pleasant smell that she was still unable to recognise or find the source of.

She had been taken to the room that she still called home and Ratty had been there to greet her. He had relieved a lot of her anxiety, even though she spent much of her first night at

Meertens' house crying. She had cried not because she was sorry for what she had done to Sasha, Karim and her parents, but because she didn't know what would happen to her. Not knowing Meertens' intentions had made her nervous. People had always wanted things in return.

The next morning was the first time she had met Dr Meertens. After she had showered and put on some of the new clothes that had been prepared for her, she had been taken to breakfast with him.

A warm summer morning, they had sat in the gardens to the rear of the house and eaten breakfast. He had been kind to her and explained that he understood why she had done the things that she had done, and that even though her life as she knew it was over, she could have a new life and work for an organisation that would accept her and value her.

She had sat there, apprehensive and unsure about what was happening to her. A young girl, eating a waffle covered with Nutella, was being spoken to with respect, like an adult. They had sat for what felt like hours, talking about her past, and Meertens had told her a lot about himself. She smiled as she remembered how he had handed her a small black box over the breakfast table and when she had opened it, she had found a platinum necklace inside with a cat pendant. Both cat's eyes were inset with diamonds.

Dr Meertens had never made her feel insecure, until earlier that day when he had found out that she was pregnant.

Henrietta shook her head again fiercely, trying in vain to rid herself of any further thoughts about Meertens or her condition. She focused on the road and the car ahead. It disappeared down a decline in the highway and Henrietta sped up slightly to make up some ground. As her car barrelled along at speed, the other vehicle was nowhere to be seen. Henrietta stomped on the accelerator pedal to try and make some distance up and reached eighty miles an hour, slowing down to sixty in the bends.

Glancing down at the display at the centre of her dashboard, she saw that the dot she had been pursuing on the map had taken a left turn. Pulling over to one side of the road, she was bemused. There had been no junctions or other roads onto which the car could have turned. She sat for a moment, mystified. Revving the engine angrily and putting a full right lock on the steering wheel, the rear wheels of the BMW she drove gave out plumes of smoke as they span furiously. The back of the car kicked out heavily and was soon facing the way she had come. Driving up the road more slowly, Henrietta looked for whatever it was she'd missed. No roads were marked on either side and yet the mark vehicle was pulling away in a direction she couldn't drive. Looking frantically at the woodland to the right of the car, she saw no track or road that she could access.

Arriving back at the last place that she had seen the car before it had gone over the brow of the hill, she felt mystified. Turning the car around again, she went for a third pass. Staring left, she looked for any opportunity to duck off the road. Driving at fifteen miles an hour, she was overtaken by a motorist who sounded his horn as he thundered past. Henrietta, however, had spotted a small gap between the undergrowth and trees where she could turn off and she slowly came off the road and started carefully down the hidden track. Pulling to one side, she sat in the deepening darkness and monitored the dot on the screen. It carried on moving for a while and then stopped. Before venturing any further, Henrietta waited for some time before finally being satisfied that the car had not just made a temporary stop and also that the track was not used often. She had sat quietly for over an hour and nobody else had used the track, even though many cars had motored past on the road.

Turning her headlights on, she could see vehicle tracks ahead, but was very wary of happening upon other hidden surprises. The car she drove contained some optional extras, including a hidden gun rack just behind the back seats. Her rucksack lay on the passenger seat beside her as she continued to drive slowly. The hydrogen engine powering her car emitted only a faint whir as she progressed down the track.

Ahead, the headlights reflected off what looked like wire fencing. She saw two men who looked as though they were standing guard at the gate that spanned the narrow track. Both men wore dark uniform and semi-automatic guns around their shoulders. One of the men spoke whilst touching his ear, no doubt notifying others of the unknown arrival.

Henrietta smiled as she realised that the path was too narrow to attempt a turn and any attempt to reverse would look suspicious. She loved to problem solve.

Nothing to do, she thought, but carry on and stop at the gate. As the car rolled slowly to a standstill, one of the guards walked purposefully toward her window. She smiled disarmingly at him as she lowered the glass all the way down. He leaned down slightly, but didn't return her smile.

'Are you lost, miss? This is private property.' he said.

'I'm so sorry. Is there somewhere that I can turn around?' Henrietta asked. The guard looked at her for a moment and then his eyes wandered down to the navigation system on the car dashboard. Henrietta tracked his line of sight. Seeing the dot flashing ahead in the distance, the guard reached for the pistol in his holster and lunged with his arm into the window to grab Henrietta, hooking his hand around her neck.

'Get out of the car!' he shouted as the other guard started to run over and help. A rush of adrenaline and Henrietta reached up the guard's arm and pushed her other hand against the door, yanking his head, shoulder and arm into the cabin. His fingernails dug into her neck as his grip clasped on and his gun hit the side of the car as Henrietta pulled him toward her. Kicking the area just above the gas pedal twice, she activated the guillotine window and after a loud bang, the clinically sharp titanium edge that lined the top of the bulletproof window rose at tremendous speed. It sliced the parts of the guard that were in the car, clean off. His head landed in Henrietta's lap while she pulled the grip of his hand free from her neck. She threw the guard's arm and shoulder into the passenger footwell. The arm was heavy and leaked blood all over her. Picking up his head, she lifted it to the window and smiled calmly as the second guard arrived. He looked down at the body of his colleague as he called for backup. Pointing his weapon at Henrietta's blood-spattered face, the guard watched as she tossed the head into the passenger footwell.

The second guard opened fire on the vehicle. The bullets bounced off the window and door of the armoured car. The gunfire lasted a moment until the guard ran out of bullets. As he reached for another clip, Henrietta opened the door of the car and sprang out at speed. Running at the guard, she punched his hand and shoulder-barged him. The clip and gun dropped to the floor as he stumbled backward and fell.

Getting back to his feet, he reached for the tactical knife in his belt. Drawing the serrated blade, he pointed it toward Henrietta. She controlled her breathing and steadied herself, adrenaline coursing through her. She felt the soggy weight of blood on her clothes.

Putting her hands up, Henrietta smiled at the guard, who stepped forward confidently toward her. As the blade approached her throat, it glinted in the headlights. The guard stopped short of Henrietta and his eyes flashed toward the side of her car. The bloody corpse of the other guard slumped on the ground.

'You're dead!' he said, looking at her with hatred.

'Ok,' she replied calmly, smiling.

He hesitated for a moment longer as Henrietta whipped her raised hands across in a scissor motion. One struck his wrist and the other, his hand. The knife flew into the bushes as his wrist cracked. Thrusting her weight forward, Henrietta brought the guard crashing to the ground with a clothesline. Hooking his neck in a headlock as he lay on the floor, she carried on smiling as he started to choke. Henrietta cracked his neck with a satisfying and fatal pop.

Knowing that it wouldn't be long until she had company, she searched the body of the more intact guard for keys to the gate. Finding a key fob she pushed the button and the gate started to open.

Climbing back into the car she considered abandoning the target altogether but realised quickly that this wasn't something she should do. Dr Meertens was hardly impressed with her at the moment and she thought about how he may react to failure. With the gate open she turned off her headlights and drove through. Soon, the muddy surface became paved, the woodland sparse, and the dot on her screen grew ever closer.

Her mind drifted again as the blood on her hands squelched, sticking to the steering wheel. The side of her lip raised in disgust.

Returning her gaze to the road ahead, the long beams of an oncoming vehicle switched on, just as it slammed into her car head-on.

Henrietta hadn't put on her belt, but the airbag softened what may have been a fatal collision with the steering wheel. She deflated the airbags that had deployed with her newly acquired knife. Throwing the car in reverse, the wheels span on the loose surface. Two more vehicles slammed into the back, pinning her vehicle to the one in front.

A moment passed as the dust settled and Henrietta came to her senses from the impacts. In that time men had encircled her car and six semi-automatic weapons were pointed directly at her.

The three Range Rovers had come off decidedly worse than the reinforced BMW and sat steaming and hissing. Their radiators leaking, bumpers smashed and bonnets buckled. One of the men approached her window and shone a flashlight at her as she calmly turned on the car's intercom system.

'Damn it, she's got Spence's head in there! I'm not kidding!' he said, seeing the bloody mess that was Henrietta Rekman and the body parts in the footwell. She scratched the top of her chest and felt the Ratty necklace hanging outside her top. Probably dislodged from inside her outfit by proceedings. Ratty was covered in blood, which seemed to upset her. Rubbing it in the light of the torch, she quickly tucked it back inside her top and looked straight at the man with the flashlight.

'Spence, is it? Oh sorry, I mean. How embarrassing. I meant to say, 'was it'. You will have to excuse my English,' Henrietta apologised, pulling an exaggeratedly bashful face and biting her bottom lip. Her voice sounded from external speakers mounted inside the air intakes. 'What was Spence's friend's name? He's broken too,' she continued.

The man with the torch backed off slightly and spoke in a whisper to the one standing beside him. Henrietta looked beyond them at the house where she presumed her target was located. It was no more than two hundred metres away.

'You may as well get out. It will be easier for you that way,' a different voice said in the darkness.

'Yeah, ok sure. I'll be right out,' she said sarcastically.

'Our employer wants to speak with you. That's the only reason we haven't killed you already,' the voice boomed.

'I'm a shy girl,' Henrietta retorted calmly. 'Why don't you just move your cars and I'll be on my way.'

'Ok, how about we just light a fire under you and see how long it takes you to get out, you smartass bitch!' the guard shouted.

'Oh, temper! Is that any way to speak to a lady? I have a counter proposal. I'll let you all live, including the cowards hiding in that house, if they come out here and talk to me,' Henrietta said with confidence as she heard some of the guards laughing over the intercom. 'I have an incentive for them,' she invitingly whispered. 'Come closer and see.' The guard with the flashlight walked up to the window with a hint of trepidation and shone inside once again. Henrietta had produced a hard-shell case, the size of a small carry-on suitcase, from a compartment underneath the rear seats. It sat on her lap as the guard looked closer. A lead ran from inside the compartment to the case.

Opening the lid, a network of readouts and lights glowed in the dark. Turning the case toward the guard, he was able to clearly see a large yellow radiation-warning sticker emblazoned on the inside of the lid.

The guard took a couple of steps back and whispered to the man beside him again.

'So, I will just wait here while you, just you, go and fetch them,' Henrietta whispered purposefully, pointing at the man who had shone the torch on the mini nuclear weapon laying on her lap. 'Just bear in mind, I don't take rejection well. If you aren't able to convince Ambassador Sunderland to come and talk to me, I'm not sure what I'll do,' she said, tapping on the case.

Chapter 22

Officer Magda Popova had not seen, and could not have known, that Nadia Hristova wore a fall-alarm pendant around her neck, in case of an accident. She also didn't know that all sound recorded by the pendant was being monitored twenty-four hours a day. Ana, the nurse who left Nadia's house after Magda arrived, had tucked the pendant into Nadia's cardigan and parked nearby, listening intently to the activity. She had immediately transferred the recording to her contact, a Russian agent, who had approached her several days after the discovery of the bodies of Aleksey and Kirill in the mountains. A bag containing two hundred thousand euros had been more than enough to secure Ana's cooperation.

The agent had been following up with interest on intelligence he had acquired about the same health phenomenon that had led Officer Popova to the farmhouse.

When Officer Popova asked her name after the fall, Nadia Hristova, who hadn't spoken in years, muttered the words, 'Mike Argo'.

Knowing that the value of this type of information diminishes rapidly in the hands of those who would disseminate it, Vadik, the agent, knew he had to arrive at the hospital before the ambulance carrying Nadia. The voices of the paramedics came through over the fall pendant, letting him know which hospital they would arrive at.

He sped to the hospital, arriving well ahead of the ambulance, and spent a few moments sending the information that he had acquired to Moscow as he sat in his car.

Not fully understanding the meaning or significance of the name Nadia had mentioned, Magda was more concerned with

Nadia's wellbeing as she had hit her head. She hoped to be able to speak with Nadia again. Consequently, she had not yet reported the odd response, but she had noted the name down on her pad.

It was late in the evening when the ambulance finally arrived in Sofia carrying Nadia. Vadik stood outside the entrance to the emergency department smoking a cigarette in the dark recess of a corner, his face slightly illuminated by the neon glow of a hospital sign, as he waited patiently for the officer fitting the description given to him by Ana to arrive. He watched as Nadia was carted into the ward on a trolley by two paramedics, lying with her eyes closed and a temporary bandage on her head. An officer fitting Magda's description walked in a moment later, as Vadik took a long final drag on his cigarette and dropped it onto the floor, stubbing it out with the toe of his boot.

Sitting on a chair, he casually observed Magda speaking with one of the staff members at reception. Vadik watched as Nadia disappeared through the doors to the emergency ward. Crossing his legs and looking around the room, there were not many people – just two older gentlemen and one middle-aged woman. He tucked the packet of cigarettes he was still holding into his coat pocket and leaned back, trying to listen to Magda's conversation, but he was sitting just too far away to be able to understand what was being said.

Magda placed a finger on the reception desk and brought it down intently several times, as though she was setting out a request or some instructions. Noting down what Vadik presumed was a telephone number, she turned on her heels and walked out of the hospital. Allowing a few seconds to pass, he looked around the waiting room, stood to his feet and slowly followed Magda into the car park.

He saw her nearing her squad car and climbing in to the driver's seat, but she didn't turn on the engine. Approaching slowly, Vadik noticed that she had taken out her phone and the backlight illuminated her face. Drawing his pistol from under his jacket, he walked silently around to the passenger-side door. Seeing that it was unlocked, he scooped the handle and yanked the door wide open.

'Put the phone down, Officer Popova!' he commanded, pointing his gun toward her head as she stared at Vadik, startled. Her phone dropped as she reached instinctively for her gun. 'I will shoot you!' Vadik said with cool composure. She took her hand away from her pistol. 'Hands on the steering wheel,' he instructed calmly and Magda complied.

Climbing in to the car next to her, Vadik removed Magda's sidearm, tucking it under his seat. He then spent a few moments checking her for any other weapons. He was very thorough.

'How do you know my name?' Magda asked, looking at Vadik and putting forward the question that burnt brightest in her terrified mind.

'The name, Mike Argo. Who have you told about it?' asked Vadik, continuing to point his sidearm at Magda. She looked at his face, realising immediately why he was here and how it was that he knew her name. *Nadia's house was bugged,* Magda thought. It was clear that the Russians had followed the same path that she had, to Nadia Hristova.

'Mike Argo? Who's that?' she asked nervously.

'Don't play with me,' he said, raising his voice. 'Who have you told?'

Officer Popova frantically thought about the answers with the best chance of not getting her killed. There was no way to know for sure what these answers were. Admitting that she hadn't told anyone may seal her death warrant. Admitting that she had told someone may do the same.

'You aren't Bulgarian, are you?' she said, looking down at her lap, having detected an accent in his voice. She heard gentle movement and felt the muzzle nestle into the side of her head just above her ear, as her grip on the steering wheel tightened.

'Very good,' he said with a rye smile, hiding the slight indignation he felt that she had been able to notice his accent. 'I am not going to repeat my question,' he hissed.

'If I had to guess, I would say you're Russian intelligence, following up on the death of your colleagues, Kirill and Aleksey?' she said in defiance of the demand for information. Vadik's smile disappeared. If she knew about Kirill and Aleksey, she might know what they were after when they were killed, he thought. He also thought it much less likely she would not have already communicated the name, Mike Argo.

'What do you know about Kirill and Aleksey?' he asked, alleviating the pressure with which he pressed the muzzle to Magda's head.

'They were looking for an artefact. Something buried near to where they were found dead. They were working with the British,' she quickly said, recounting her conversation with Ambassador Francis Sunderland. 'I was injured and my colleague Ivan was killed. I think by the same person who killed Kirill and Aleksey,' she continued.

'Do you know anything about the people who killed them?' he asked.

'No,' Magda responded, closing her eyes and scrunching her face.

'Answer my question. Have you told anybody about the name Mike Argo? About what Nadia said to you?' he asked with a cold voice.

'No,' Magda said, keeping her eyes closed, with tears welling.

Vadik paused for a moment, unsure of what to do. Getting into the car, he had fully intended to be the only one alive at the end of the conversation. But Officer Popova knew things. She knew much more than he had expected and there was probably more.

Vadik hadn't immediately known who Mike Argo was. The camera-shy owner of the largest and most successful telecommunications company in the world, Argo was a faceless household name, whose branding appeared on numerous electronic products. The fact that his name had been mentioned by a woman with severe mental health issues was not really an indication of anything of itself. The comments that Nadia had made to Magda beforehand however, about having only just woken up and her request that Magda not let them bury her, did spike his interest. The seconds which passed by seemed to last an eternity for Magda as moments of her life cascaded through her mind. The explosion in Valsha that had injured her and killed Ivan was a prominent memory that had replayed often in her conscience. The feeling of guilt for still being alive when he wasn't.

Vadik slowly removed the gun from her head. The pressure had left an imprint that was visible through her short-cut hair.

'My name is Vadik. I heard about what happened in Valsha. I didn't know the names of the police officers. My condolences for your fallen comrade,' he said softly as he lowered his gun and placed it on his right thigh, away from Officer Popova. Magda's eyes remained closed as she sat with her hands clasping the top of the steering wheel. Her knuckles white and her face pale with fear. She sat frozen for a moment longer. 'Take your hands off the steering wheel. I won't do anything to you.' Magda gradually prized each trembling finger from the leather and once released, leaned back in her seat and opened her eyes slightly. Turning to look at the man in her passenger seat and certain that she was skating on thin ice, she tried to maintain composure.

'What do you want from me?' she asked, racking her brain to think why this man had left her alive.

'I could have killed you,' he said, interpreting almost perfectly her thoughts. 'That would hardly help me complete my objective though.'

'And what's your objective?' Magda asked, as she struggled to maintain eye contact with him.

'The same as yours. To find out who killed my colleagues and took the artefact, except now you are going to help me, because without us, things won't be done correctly,' he said with an air of arrogant self-assuredness. 'The first thing you will do is forget the name Mike Argo. My government and I will work with this information. Secondly, I am aware that the bodies of those who died that night in Valsha and the mountains are still in a morgue as part of the active investigation of your government. I need copies of the files; I need to see what your government knows about every one of the deceased.'

'But getting access to the files will be...' she started, but was interrupted by Vadik's glare.

'What will it be?' he asked, lifting the pistol from his thigh slightly.

'How will I contact you?' she said, trying to keep her voice as strong and assertive as possible.

'I will meet you again in this spot tomorrow night at 9pm. And Officer Popova, if we discover that you have fed back the name of Mike Argo to your people, our next meeting will be far less agreeable. If anything should happen to me, then I am sure you know that the consequences will still catch up with you. There doesn't need to be any unpleasantness. We both are after the same thing,' Vadik said as he tucked his pistol under his jacket and opened the passenger door, getting out as quickly as he had got in. Magda watched as he disappeared from view behind a row of cars. Her close encounter with death caused her to break down in tears. Turning on the engine and locking her doors, she wiped her eyes to clear her vision and sped out of the car park and back toward the city centre.

-Chapter 23-

'I'm not in the mood for this from the two of you. Get upstairs and brush your teeth. You better both be in bed by the time I get up there or...' Marianne Docherty said, giving the pause that was much feared in their household. Wearing jogging bottoms and an old grey t-shirt as she stood at the sink washing the last few dishes, she craned her neck to look at Taryn and Peter over her shoulder.

As they turned and disappeared from view, Marianne passed her wine glass under the water. Looking out through the window, only the beads of rain running down the plate glass window were visible against the backdrop of darkness. The security light flashed on, activated by the rain and illuminating the patio of the back garden. The palm trees waved from side to side, tossed about by the wind that had persisted all day.

As the soapsuds washed over the glass and down the sink, she thought about how she used to wash two glasses instead of one, on the occasions that her husband was home and not out gallivanting for trinkets, as she used to call them. He never did like it when she jokingly called his finds, trinkets.

They would fight, drink some wine, enjoy spending time with their children. In spite of his faults, she had loved her husband, and putting the glass down on the drying rack, she realised that tears had started to stream down her face. Resting her weight on the sink, she sobbed for a few moments, hoping that Peter and Taryn wouldn't hear. Shutting off the flow of water that had drowned out the sound, she dabbed her eyes with a clean towel and thought about Jerome's last weeks at home. She had been concerned about some of his behaviour before he had told her of his brain tumour.

He had opted to stay at home, regardless of the advice of his doctor, but there was nowhere else that he had wanted to be. Surrounded by all of the things he loved in this world, he had said goodbye to Taryn and Peter a few weeks before his death, when Marianne had sent them to stay with her parents.

Jerome was in and out of consciousness during his last few days, but had kept on repeating to Marianne that after his death she would be taken care of. That he had found the king of trinkets. She had laughed through rivers of weeping, but hadn't known what he had meant.

The watch that Jerome wore had alerted Brick Steckelback immediately of his death. A man by the name of Jack Barrisfield had knocked at the front door of their house in a small village outside Nice. He arrived even before the nurse or Marianne herself had found Jerome on the morning of his death. Jerome had died in his sleep that night.

The nurse was asked to leave by Barrisfield, who thanked her for all she had done for Jerome, whilst handing her a final generous payment.

Marianne had been distraught at the bedside of her deceased husband. Barrisfield had given her as much time as she needed before speaking with her about certain matters. He had explained that toward the end of his life, Jerome had made an important discovery. One that would potentially fetch a high price at auction. He also explained that Jerome had made arrangements to ensure that his family would be safe from those who may wish to cause them harm.

Marianne had immediately known that it was Onyx, the organisation Jerome had worked with for so many years, Barrisfield was referring to. Some of Jerome's delirious rantings during the last morphine fuelled week of his life started to suddenly make more sense. His words had been cryptic and she had not thought much of them.

She adhered to Barrisfield's instructions and prepared a suitcase of essentials, before speaking with her parents to let them know that somebody was en route to collect Taryn and Peter. It had been difficult to mask the emotion in her voice.

As they drove away from the house, the tall hedges that surrounded it obscured the fire that had started to rage inside. Their house would soon be engulfed, along with the body of Jerome Docherty and the years of memories they had shared. Barrisfield had told her that this wasn't the kind of service his law firm usually provided, but something in the way he said it made Marianne doubt his sincerity.

They had boarded a yacht moored at the Port de Nice, before setting off on the long journey for the place they had since called home. The small town of Cannonvale in Queensland, Australia. They had assumed new identities and Barrisfield had left specific instructions with Marianne about making no contact with anybody, including her own parents. For her own safety and that of her children, she had complied. Barrisfield had visited her recently to update her personally on the outcome of the auction and the amount of money that had been transferred to the trust fund account, to which she, and eventually her children, would have access.

At just over one-and-a-half billion euros, after fees, it was a ridiculous amount, she thought. Far more money than she could comprehend, let alone spend in a great many lifetimes.

A brief smile gleamed across her face when she remembered Barrisfield's words of warning about ostentatious spending. She had never heard of ostentatious spending and having always considered herself a frugal person, she saw no reason for that to change, particularly given the alternative.

Lost in her trail of thought, time had gone by quickly and her remaining tears had started to dry on her cheeks. Wiping her eyes, Marianne made her way upstairs.

'You never let me win anyway,' pouted Taryn from under her covers as her brother climbed into his bed on the other side of the room, wiggling his backside at her in a show of defiance.

'Why would I let you win anyway?' Peter taunted, bringing in the word-repeat game that he knew she hated.

They were the best of friends most of the time, but not when it came to Eclipse. A game they would play against each other on their tablets from under the bed covers of their respective beds. They were yet to be caught by their mum, who was oblivious to their late-night duels.

'Well, I'm not even playing tonight, so there,' Taryn said tiredly, in the most petulant voice she could muster.

'That's just because you know you're gonna lose,' Peter goaded as he wiped an imaginary tear, to which Taryn responded with her scrunchy faced look of annoyance before turning to face the wall. She pulled the soft quilt over her shoulder. The window was slightly ajar and the cool evening air drifted in as their mum walked into the bedroom.

There were plenty of spare rooms in the house, but the children had wanted to share a room when they first moved in. Not surprising, given the scale of the upheaval. The adjustment over the past three years had been difficult, but Marianne was very proud of how well they had adapted to their new home.

'Have you brushed your teeth you two?' she asked, having already been to the bathroom to check if their brushes were wet.

'Yes, mum,' Taryn and Peter both said in chorus.

'Good. Who is looking forward to going to the beach tomorrow?' she asked in an upbeat tone.

'Me, me!' both children said.

'That's good. Me too. The quickest way to get to the beach is to fall asleep the fastest. I'm going to see if I can win,' Marianne said.

'Mum, we are too old for that game,' Peter moaned.

'Alright, goodnight, kids. Sleep tight,' Marianne spoke softly as she slunk out of the door, dragging it closed behind her. The sound of wood gliding over the carpet was soft and smooth as she left the door open by the customary hand's width.

'Don't be such a chicken,' whispered Peter from his bed, waving the luminous screen at Taryn in the darkness.

'I'm sleepy. Don't want to,' she whispered back, only to be met by an onslaught of low-volume and muffled chicken noises from Peter. Taryn fell asleep moments later, strangely comforted by the annoying sounds that emanated from her brother.

-Chapter 24-

Olivia unlocked the door of Argo's room and entered. He had watched her return to the Nexus storage unit to collect an item she needed. She firmly clutched a new hand as she walked toward Argo.

Argo, however, was not doing well. A severe headache had rapidly descended upon him, like nothing he had ever experienced. As he had sat, unable to act, he thought the pressure he was under could be the only explanation. Olivia had disregarded straightforward commands, carrying others out only with delay. He had seen some very concerning behaviour. His frustration at being locked in his quarters, feeling helpless, was at the forefront of his mind.

'What the hell just happened, Olivia?' he asked in an exasperated tone. 'Leave that door unlocked!'

Without offering an immediate response, she looked at him and proceeded to pluck a kitchen knife from the rack. Sitting at the table in the kitchen area, she placed the new hand, palm up on the table.

'That action would violate the security protocol,' Olivia said in her usual calm tone, making direct eye contact with Argo. She placed her damaged hand on the table-top, next to the new one. Drawing the knife into position next to her wrist, she held it flat and palm up. Some of the grey fluid had quickly seeped and pooled underneath.

'Did you follow security protocol?' asked Argo rhetorically as Olivia focused her attention on her maintenance routine. Pausing temporarily, she looked toward Argo.

'The GridWatch has been activated and all staff are accounted for,' she reported, returning to her maintenance routine and looking back down at her wrist. With an almost invisibly fast action, she sliced through the damaged hand and lay a sheet of thin membrane over the open flow, ceasing it immediately.

'That isn't what I'm talking about, Olivia. Tell me about what you were doing in the lab. How your hand got damaged!' Argo shouted uncharacteristically. The vibration of sound rang around his aching skull, causing him to wince and recoil in pain.

'My report on my time in the lab is incomplete,' she said.

'What do you mean it's incomplete?' Argo asked, in a far more subdued, but still aggravated tone, to avoid further pain.

'My report is incomplete, because I am not able to define what happened,' Olivia eloquently said, holding the membrane over the stump at the end of her arm. Argo tried to think about what that could mean, but the pain he felt in his head was so severe, he had to lay down on the couch and let out a quiet grunt.

'You are going to have to try. Play back your visual,' he commanded, looking toward the television.

Olivia removed her hand from the stump and quickly picked up the new appendage. Placing it flush up against the stump, the membranes adhered to each other and started the process of dissolution. As the translucent fluid from her arm mixed with that of the new hand, the microscopic robots began the task of connecting the mechanics of the new body part. Unable to move for twenty minutes while the process completed, Olivia returned her attention to Argo. His heart rate and blood pressure were elevated, but nowhere near any risk category.

'Playback commencing in ten seconds,' she said.

'Stream to Dr Otani's quarters also,' Argo muttered, rolling over slightly to allow sight of the screen, and supporting his head with a cushion.

Otani lay in his bed with his eyes closed in an attempt to sleep, as had been the case so often of late. The screen on the wall opposite turned on, irradiating everything in artificial light. He noticed the subtle change in light level as he stared through the back of his eyelids. Blinking a few times, he turned his head to look at the screen, showing Olivia's sight-view. The periphery of the screen was full of information, including her model number and other vital statistics.

Unable to see any of the detail, Dr Otani plucked his glasses from his bedside table and wasted no time in perching them on his nose.

Sitting up, the room span as though he had drunk a few too many. *Vertigo perhaps? Certainly not the strangest symptom experienced of late,* he thought.

The comm rang out in his room, the automated voice identifying Argo as the caller.

'Katsu, did I wake you?' Argo asked, but he didn't sound his usual self.

'No. I cannot sleep,' Otani responded honestly. 'Why is Olivia down at the labs? We're in lockdown.'

'She is in my quarters. This is a recording from a few moments ago. I want you to see it. I need to know what you make of it,' Argo said hoarsely, ending with a cough. One of the smaller screens underneath had activated and showed the corresponding CCTV imagery that Argo had already viewed.

Otani acknowledged the request and sat on the edge of his bed, knees together, observing studiously. Olivia's inspection of the craft from distance had been interrupted by what looked like some kind of malfunction. Regaining her balance, she engaged magnification optics to look closer at the Pebble.

It wasn't clear what had drawn her attention. The fluid motion across the surface of the craft that had captivated Olivia couldn't be seen.

No unremarkable sounds or sights were visible as she accessed the lab and eventually placed her hand on the surface of the Pebble. Both men watched as the craft seemed to melt and damage her hand.

No sensors had been triggered in the lab. No increases in temperature. Certainly nothing hot enough to melt the material composing Olivia. They watched as a small pool of melted matter collected under the Pebble. They heard Argo's voice commanding Olivia to leave the lab, and the footage ended with her exiting.

'What do you make of that?' Argo asked, already confident of Dr Otani's reply.

'I don't understand. The security protocol was in place, Mike. She shouldn't have accessed the lab under any circumstances,' Otani said ponderously. 'Has she given any explanation about what happened?'

'No, not about the lab. She said something about not being able to define what happened,' Argo answered.

'That's no good, Mike. Now's not a good time for her to malfunction. She is designed to run this facility when it's locked down.'

'It's not a malfunction, Katsu. I don't think so. She is just in the middle of running a maintenance routine to replace her damaged hand,' Argo said even more quietly, of which Otani took particular notice.

'That isn't part of her maintenance routine. She isn't supposed to do that for herself,' Otani's tone was full of concern.

'Well, it looks like she may have learned how. Look, I can't put this down to a malfunction. There was something she saw when she looked at the craft. Something that made her touch it. Maybe she identified a risk that we haven't seen yet?' Argo explained as he observed Olivia patiently waiting, in a state of perfect motionlessness, for the repair to complete.

'Mike, end the lockdown. We can't do anything from our quarters. Either we carry on with our work, or we have to dispose of this thing,' said Otani.

Argo sat for a moment thinking. Turning away from the screen to look over at Olivia, he saw that she no longer was observing her hand, but now looked directly at him. The pain in his head was massive, causing him to wince, and blink twice as much as he normally would. Ending the call with Dr Otani, he turned back once again to look at Olivia, who was probing the repair with her other hand while keeping her attention focused on Argo.

'The melting point of my skin is three hundred and thirteen degrees Celsius. I detected no heat emanating from the craft and neither did any of the other sensors in the laboratory. When I touched the craft, my sensors still detected no heat and yet my material melted,' Olivia pondered as Argo rubbed his temples.

'We can't explain it. I don't know,' he responded, fully aware that what had happened seemed to have broken the laws of physics. 'What made you go into the lab? Why did you touch the craft?'

Olivia twitched slightly as she replayed the footage at speed to herself.

'The surface of the craft changed. It looked different to the footage,' she responded, to which Argo let out a painful laugh, as he pushed down on his temple. Olivia's systems were automatically backed up to the secure local servers. The surface of the craft had been unchanged. Any distortion she believed she had seen, could only be another malfunction.

That still didn't explain her hand. There was a lot that he couldn't explain and he felt as though thinking about it was further aggravating the pain.

Chapter 25

The sound of grinding metal after the impacts and the raised voices had ceased. Ambassador Sunderland and Rebecca Bradford were sitting apprehensively. Mildred Jones was keenly waiting in the kitchen as a knock was heard at the door.

'Ah! The cavalry,' Mildred exclaimed elatedly, heading toward the front door. 'Come along Ambassador!' she looked back, gesturing vigorously with her hand.

Francis stood from his seat nervously and followed Mildred. Rebecca wasn't far behind, making barely any sound as she glided over the tiled floor in warm slippers, a concerned look on her face.

Maurice, the Chief of Estate Security, stood catching his breath at the front door. With a forlorn look on his face, he set out the situation of the intruder who was trapped in her car.

'She wants to speak with Ambassador Sunderland,' Maurice said. 'Otherwise we aren't sure whether she will do what she claims.'

'And, what is it she claims she can do exactly?' Mildred asked indignantly.

'She looks as though she,' Maurice coughed to clear his throat. 'We saw what looks like some type of case-sized nuclear weapon in the vehicle. She knows that Ambassador Sunderland is here and wants to speak with him.'

'What a pickle,' Mildred said, dropping her tone. 'What are our chances of survival if that thing goes off?'

'If the device is as real as that tank she's driven in here, then not good,' Maurice muttered, shaking his head slowly.

Mildred looked over his shoulder and saw the cars in the distance. The rear lights of the Range Rover exposed the slight haze hanging in the air. She slipped on a pair of rubber-soled shoes and left the house with a determined stride. Two large, grey, stone plant pots stood guard at either side of the four-step cobble stairs that led down to the forecourt. Mildred blasted past these and hastily approached the fourth Range Rover parked next to the fountain. Maurice had left the passenger side door open and she climbed inside, slamming the door behind herself. Francis and Rebecca cowered inside the house, unsure of what to do.

'We haven't got all night!' Mildred said with a shrill screech. Francis and Rebecca put their shoes on and followed Maurice down to the Range Rover, climbing into the back.

The member of estate security who had seen the device turned the car around and they headed back in the direction of the uninvited guest.

'She killed Spence and Liam, guarding that gate,' Maurice added. Mildred didn't respond but sat seething in the passenger seat.

The property, encircled by forest, had five entrances off surrounding B roads. These were secreted dirt tracks, not immediately obvious to any motorist speeding by. Normal protocol was to try and ensure no vehicles on the same stretch of road would witness anyone accessing these dirt tracks.

They had found that the use of the tracks, instead of conventional walls, fences and gates had led to a much lower profile and fewer incidents of trespassing.

With a myriad of pressure pads and motion detection sensors on the dirt tracks and trees in the surrounding forest, the estate security team were easily able to identify movement.

On occasion, the movement would be in the form of a deer or a dog walker. They would only venture as far as the electrified fence that was set back from the perimeter of the property, before being met by members of estate security accompanied by Alsatian dogs.

On this occasion, however, Mildred and Brick Steckelback had used Ambassador Sunderland as bait and he knew it.

'Was this the plan?' Francis sought rhetorical clarification from the back seat.

'Better than the alternative,' Mildred said, looking straight ahead. Francis turned his head to look out of the window.

Arriving at the scene and climbing out of the car slowly, they saw the pinned BMW sandwiched between three other Range Rovers. Francis winced while looking at the car, straining in vain to see who was inside. As they engaged in a standoff of silence, it wasn't clear who would speak first. One of the Range Rovers attracted attention with a hiss as some more water from the smashed radiator escaped.

'Ambassador,' said a voice from the BMW. Francis' attention was immediately brought back to the slightly tinted driver-side window. 'I have something to tell you. Why don't you come over here?' Henrietta asked in an inviting, almost seductive voice. Francis, however, recognised the voice. It belonged to the same person who had held him and his family hostage in the small village of Valsha, outside Sofia. He turned for a moment to Maurice, who looked at him with a blank expression.

'We are all in the same boat here. Her fate will be the same as yours,' Maurice said in a hushed tone.

'If you say so,' Francis retorted with a whisper as he saw the look of hatred on Rebecca's face. One of the security personnel handed him a flashlight.

'I'm coming with you,' Mildred stated forcefully as she stepped forward.

'Just the Ambassador,' boomed the voice from the BMW.

Francis stepped forward gingerly as Maurice gave a hand signal for the rest of his team to fall back. Francis' footsteps were short and nervous. He realised that he was shuffling toward the BMW and deliberately opened his stride, throwing his shoulders back confidently.

Flicking the flashlight on, he pointed it at the car and saw the girl who sat inside recoil at the bright light. The window itself was stained with droplets of blood and a thin piece of torn clothing hung trapped at the top.

'Please,' Henrietta said, raising one hand to cover her eyes. Francis lowered the beam to the side of the door, the peripheral light enough to illuminate them both. As they exchanged a gaze, he could see that her face and clothes were covered in blood. She detected the apprehension on his face. Looking down, she touched the console to disable the intercom and lowered her window a few centimetres. He could see part of her face more clearly than through the bloodstained glass. On the seat next to her lay what he realised must be the suspected nuclear device. She saw him looking at it.

'The fellows with the guns said that they wouldn't let me go. I was sure you'd make them see sense,' Henrietta charmingly said through the gap in the window. Francis stared at the body parts in the footwell before dragging his eyes back to Henrietta Rekman.

'You seem quite persuasive. I'm sure that they will do whatever you ask,' he responded, feeling a well of anger brewing as he became convinced that this was the woman who had been intent on killing him and his family.

'It's amazing how nice people are to you, when your finger is on a big red button,' she muttered through a grin. Without the intercom, her words could only be heard by Francis. 'You are right, of course. I don't need any help from you here,'

Henrietta continued. Francis made no comment. 'Do you know why I wanted to speak with you?' she asked. 'I wanted to speak with you, just to let you know that I came here to help you find that artefact you've been after. The Pebble.'

'You look familiar,' Francis said, turning the torch off and standing in the dark, nodding slightly. 'You tried to kill me. You tried to kill my family. A lot of people are dead because of you. But I know you, don't I? Not just from our phone conversation, but from my house. You were dressed as a caterer for the party,' Francis remembered.

'Very good, Mr Ambassador. I wouldn't have thought that you paid much attention to us, little people,' she replied sarcastically.

'I am pleased to disappoint you,' Francis said indignantly. 'The bad news is that I don't believe you. I don't believe you are here to give me any information,' he reckoned, pointing at the body parts in the footwell with his eyes. 'You came here to kill me. I didn't see it coming, but fortunately others did.'

'It doesn't really matter what you believe. You will listen to what I have to say and then let me go,' Henrietta shouted.

Francis shook his head in the dark and tutted.

'No. I don't think so. You aren't going anywhere,' he declared loudly enough to be heard by those behind him. This brought about an immediate torrent of uncomfortable shifting from everybody within earshot.

'Right, no information for you. I am leaving now, or we are all going to die,' Henrietta screamed as she hovered her hand over the red button in the case.

'That's your decision,' Francis said lowering his head slightly and closing his eyes. Henrietta looked at him, her wild eyes glinting. He towered next to the car and inside, the smell of warm blood was hitting the back of her throat.

'Are you mad?' she snapped.

'I wonder if you've as much contempt for your own life, as you do for that of others,' Francis quizzed, feeling unfathomable rage building at the thought of all the people she had killed. Henrietta stared at Francis through the gap in the window. He appeared as a silhouette in the moonlight. She turned on the intercom once again.

'The Ambassador says that everybody is ready to die. If you don't move these cars in the next five minutes, we all go up,' she ranted loudly. Mildred took Rebecca's hand and pulled her back from the ranks of guards. Glancing toward Maurice with a worried expression, Mildred saw his unshifting sights were fixed on Henrietta in the car. The other members of his team also looked toward him for any sign of a command.

'I don't think that you want to die here tonight. Neither do any of us. You've committed crimes and made mistakes. Get out of the car and come with us. That's the only way,' Francis said. Henrietta sat, breathing heavily and feeling angry. Turning on the car, she revved the engine and the rear wheels spun. The car didn't move, but instead the wheels started to dig into the ground. Throwing it in reverse, she engaged the four-wheel drive option and slammed her foot down on the throttle. The wheels span and the BMW ground against the two Range Rovers behind it. She was unable to shift their weight. Letting out a loud scream, Henrietta smashed her hands against the steering wheel before turning off the engine.

She sat for a moment, staring at the flashlight Francis still clutched in his hand. She wracked her brain for an escape route, to the point where her eyes became blurry from lack of blinking. 'You're right, I don't want to die. But there is no guarantee I won't be killed if I get out of this car,' she said quietly, as her palms squelched on the blood-sodden steering wheel.

'That's true. You will have to take my word for it. There are ways in which you can help us. They make you valuable,' Francis acknowledged.

'Before I get out, I want to tell you something. I've just found out that I'm pregnant,' Henrietta murmured softly. Francis wondered how to react, considering the high possibility that the woman who sat before him was probably lying to bargain for a stay of execution. He nodded his head understandingly and stood back from the door. 'Also, the father of my baby is your friend, Vincent,' Henrietta shared, making sheepish eye contact with Francis. He battled to keep his anger from spilling out, disguising his emotions as best he could through a look of surprise.

'Ok, we can talk about all of this later. For now, just get out of the car and come with me,' Francis said.

'I'm not lying. He is still alive. I know where he is,' Henrietta continued as she popped the lock on her door and pushed it open slightly. In doing so, a light that she hadn't seen previously flashed on the console in tandem with a faint beeping sound. She turned to look at it as the flashing of the light and beeping gradually sped up to the point where the light became solid red and the beep was constant.

Henrietta barely had time to turn and react as the detonation command was received by the nuclear weapon sitting on the passenger seat. The instant flash was the last thing seen by those in the area as the intense shock wave and enormous heat obliterated Henrietta, Francis, and everybody in the vicinity. The explosion blew through Mildred's house as if it were made of paper, flattening row after row of the nearest trees. A cloud rose up. The detonation sent a resonating boom out through the countryside.

-Chapter 26-

Officer Magda Popova had driven to the city centre of Sofia with the intention of fulfilling the forceful directive she had received from the Russian intelligence operative. However, her mind had replayed recent events and she decided to change direction, speeding out of the city to a place she knew she would be safe.

Driving for over an hour and a half at high speed, she drew closer to her destination. The Troyan Monastery. It had just turned midnight as she arrived. The Monastery came into sight courtesy of long-beam headlights, the only source of light apart from the moon, which hung large and imposing in the night sky. The daunting brick boundary wall stood adjacent to the road as Magda crawled to the parking area, turning off her headlights for the last few metres. Coming to a halt, she turned off the engine.

Opening the windows of her car, a fresh breeze blew through. The quietness outside was a world apart from the hustle and bustle of the city.

Leaning her head back onto the headrest, Magda closed her eyes and breathed deeply, trying to calm herself down. She had never felt so close to her end. Only having narrowly escaped being blown up with her colleague in Valsha and now more recently escaping death at the hands of the Russian agent. Unsure whether the breathing exercise was actually helping, she looked around and saw only two small cars in the parking lot. Magda stepped out onto the tarmac, closing the door gently.

The air was clean and fresh. High in the Balkan Mountains, the Troyan Monastery stood as a timeless reminder of the past struggles and suffering of those who had chosen a different path.

Magda walked gingerly toward the entrance. The gift shop to the right of the entrance was closed, but above she could see the flickering of candlelight illuminating one of the cells.

The entrance to the monastery was open as always and walking through the archway, Magda tried to remember how many years it had been since she had visited this place.

In the central courtyard, she was drawn toward the row of candle-stands underneath the impressive polychrome arches, adorned with icons and designs that appeared black and white in the moonlight. Some of the candles left by the last visitors of the day still burned brightly. Those near the floor burning for the dead and those on top of the brass candle-stand for the living.

From across the courtyard, Magda, who was wearing her police uniform, heard a faint cough. Turning, she saw one of the monks standing on the balcony that was used to access the rooms on the upper level. His hands rested on the wooden parapet and he gave a small wave to Magda, who he had not seen in a long time but did recognise. She waved back. Turning to face the wooden stairs, the sweet smell of rose incense surrounded her as she walked up the creaky steps.

Ascending quickly to the summit of the landing, she jumped at the sight of the same monk she had just seen on the other side of the courtyard, standing boldly before her. She wondered if it was physically possible for somebody to have covered the distance in the time it had taken her to climb the steps. The monk was a man in his early thirties, but his slightly greying beard made him look considerably older. The plain black robe he wore blended him seamlessly into the dim surroundings. The only source of light was the occasional ceiling lamp attached to the roof over the balcony.

'Good evening, Officer Popova. It has been a very long time since we last met,' he said. Magda searched her memory for his name. She was unsure whether he had ever told her, or if she had ever asked.

'It's been a very long time. I hope you're ok. I'm here to see my uncle. I need to speak with him,' Magda explained, frustrated at her inability to remember the name of the young monk. She felt much calmer than when she had arrived. Perhaps it was the quietness and sense of tranquillity that exuded from her surroundings, or that she was pleased to be out of immediate danger. The monk looked at her for a moment. His eyes moved over the police badge on her chest and down to the handgun she had strapped to her thigh since her run-in with Vadik. 'I'm sorry to bring my gun into this place, but I shouldn't leave it in the car.'

'It's fine. The candle burns in the brother's cell, but he is not there,' the monk smiled.

'It's very important that I see him. I know that he shouldn't be disturbed if he is in his cell, but I wouldn't be here at this hour if...' Magda said, referring to the weeks and months that she knew her uncle Boyan had spent in his cell thinking about life and God. Although she hadn't previously understood the practice, she thought that a few weeks sitting in a monk's cell, thinking about her life wouldn't go amiss.

'He isn't in his cell. You have arrived here very late tonight. Have something to eat and a room to rest,' said the monk.

'No, I haven't got time to eat now. I have to see my uncle. Please,' she pleaded.

'I can see that you are upset. You want to speak with your uncle urgently. Something has happened outside of these walls that's very important to you,' the monk said in a quiet tone. Magda nodded and held back the sudden and almost overwhelming urge to start crying. 'But, now you are inside these walls. You're tired, hungry and upset. That's our priority. Come with me, rest, eat and I will take you to see your uncle.'

'What's your name,' asked Magda with a lump in her throat.

'Brother Josef,' he replied with a warm smile.

'I'm sorry. I don't know. I don't remember if anybody ever told me your name. It has been so many years since I have been here,' she explained.

'Come,' Brother Josef said with an understanding nod, as he turned and led Magda to an empty cell.

As they walked, Magda looked down at the central courtyard in all its magnificence. She had never seen the monastery at night. She thought about the bad that could follow her here. She knew she had nowhere else to turn.

-Chapter 27-

Mike Argo lay on the couch in his quarters, where he had slept. From the kitchen he could hear a blender in full flow. Turning his head slowly, he saw the figure of Olivia standing with her back to him in the darkness. Just the light from the dimmed low-level lighting.

'My head feels better. When did I go to sleep?' Argo asked, feeling with his hand to check whether his head was still attached to his body.

'I gave you a mild sedative to relieve your pain. I am glad that it has worked,' Olivia said, her voice concealed slightly by the sound of the blender. As she finished preparing a milkshake, she carried it toward Argo. 'There has been a nuclear explosion in the United Kingdom. I have made you a milkshake and here is your Boon.' Argo sat bolt upright on the couch.

'Lights,' he said, and the room illuminated gently. He considered Olivia's fairly unique type of bedside manner before registering fully what she had said. Standing, he took the milkshake and the capsule, his eyes drawn to the severed robotic hand lying on a towel upon the table. His confused thoughts recalled the conversation he had with Dr Otani and how he was no closer to forming a solution. 'What nuclear explosion?'

'One Argo Industries Hydra, equipped with a tactical nuclear case, has been destroyed,' Olivia confirmed efficiently.

'One of ours?!' Argo shouted, looking at the capsule in the palm of his hand, the word Argo, printed in white. 'The name of the member?' he asked, quickly drinking the Boon with a gulp of shake.

'It was issued to Dr Meertens, Mr Argo,' Olivia confirmed. He put the drink container down and some sloshed out over the rim, running down the side and pooling on the table.

'What do you know so far?' Argo probed.

'The device detonated in a rural area, in the county of Kent. Recordings from the vehicle, relayed to the servers here, indicate at least ten people in close proximity to the vehicle in the run-up to the explosion are unlikely to have survived,' Olivia continued. 'I can confirm that Henrietta Rekman was in the vehicle at the time of the explosion and Ambassador Francis Sunderland was standing close by. The remainder of the victims appear to be private security, except for two women I have been unable to identify. The prevailing wind is–'

'Henrietta killed herself? She detonated the nuke herself?' Argo interrupted angrily.

'No, Mr Argo. Records show that the device was detonated remotely. The command came from the home of Dr Meertens,' Olivia stated with an even tone. Argo picked up the container and drank its contents in four big gulps before throwing it down onto the table top. It bounced a couple of times, before slowly rolling and toppling over the edge, onto the floor. Argo sat and reviewed the video and sound captures, as Olivia streamed them for him onto the screen.

Watching the footage, he was slightly aghast, never having seen the guillotine windows in action. He watched the Hydra get pinned by the three Range Rovers and everything that ensued. Hearing Henrietta's claim that she was pregnant was a surprise, but no less surprising than the revelation that Vincent Madden was the father.

The final frames showed Henrietta's apparent surrender as she opened the driver-side door, before being distracted by the beeping countdown on the console.

'Put me through to Meertens,' Argo bluntly ordered with a sigh. As the video call request appeared on the screen, he was fuming with anger to the point that he felt another severe headache might afflict him. The screen flickered as the call connected. Meertens could be seen, sitting back in the chair behind his desk. The light from his desk lamp illuminated his torso, but not his face, which was barely visible.

'We must stop speaking like this. Anybody would think that you were my patient,' Meertens said seriously. 'How are you feeling?'

'I do have a lot of problems, my friend, but this time I am calling about something else!' Argo retorted with irritation in his voice. Wanting to give Meertens the opportunity to at least volunteer the information, Argo paused.

'You are quick. You are very quick. I don't know where you find your people, but they are excellent!' Meertens said.

'My people are excellent, but so are yours. That's why I'm confused,' Argo said, looking over toward Olivia who was observing the conversation out of camera shot. A small, almost unnoticeable smile was on her face. She liked being called people.

'Henrietta was about to surrender to armed security. Ambassador Sunderland was there. What would you have done in my position?' Meertens asked.

'What I don't understand is why you sent Henrietta after him with everything that's going on. He wasn't a threat,' said Argo, trying to keep his composure.

'You saw the private security team? That was no government installation. They trapped her and left us all with no choice. They were expecting her. That means he was a threat,' Meertens explained.

'What choice did you expect her to make in her condition?' Argo quizzed. Meertens sat without saying anything for a moment, realising that Argo had heard all of the audio.

'She was about to make the wrong choice, but I didn't know she was pregnant,' Meertens said deceptively. 'She may have been lying.' The mute icon appeared in the top corner of the screen.

'I have analysed the audio in conjunction with my historical experiences of Henrietta Rekman. Her voice patterns do not support the conjecture that she was lying. I estimate ninety-seven per cent probability that she was telling the truth,' Olivia said at speed. The mute icon disappeared from the screen.

'It's a mess. A real mess. We need to keep a low profile right now. What we don't need is to be detonating nuclear weapons. Anywhere!' Argo barked.

'It is regrettable. There is nobody sorrier that it happened than me. But I have some other young recruits who are more than ready to take Henrietta's place,' Meertens promised. Argo had known Bob Meertens for many years, but was surprised by the lack of emotion he showed for the loss of the woman who had done so much good work for them.

'That's good to hear. Do we have an understanding about keeping a low profile?' Argo asked.

'Yes,' Meertens confirmed. 'What decision have you taken? What are you going to do with the artefact?'

'Well, I've slept and I'm feeling better than I was. Whatever this thing is, we can't bury it. I don't have time to tell you more right now, but some of the things I have seen defy physics. Even Dr Otani is stumped,' Argo explained as Olivia paid careful attention.

'I'm no physics expert, but if this craft is causing you and other people symptoms that are physically manifesting, I would urge you to reconsider,' Meertens cautioned as Argo stood from the couch and walked to Olivia. The camera panned to follow his movement.

'Like you said. I've got excellent people!' Argo grinned as he wrapped his arm around Olivia's shoulders.

'You never seem to get any time off, dear,' Meertens joked.

'I love my work, Dr Meertens,' Olivia responded with a smile.

'Bring us out of Crossbones protocol. We have a lot of work to do,' instructed Argo after ending the call with Meertens.

Chapter 28

Standing on the upper-rear deck of his yacht as it quietly sliced its way out of the Mediterranean and into the Atlantic Ocean, Claud Petit took a long drag of his second cigarette since leaving the warmth of his bed. Glancing at his watch, he saw that it was 5am in his current time zone, although it felt earlier.

The sky was cloudy, the water calm. Only the persistent breeze striking him as he stood enjoying his cigarette. His crew was asleep, as was his wife, Samara. The darkness was so pure. He could see nothing past the low-level lighting emanating from the vessel. He felt alone and safe. This was part of the reason why Claud liked to be at sea. Like a needle in a haystack, away from the people, away from the noise, away from himself.

The gentle motion of the yacht, enough to remind him that he was on water, relaxed him like nothing else could. Thinking to himself briefly about the commission he had made from the sale of the envelope in Sofia, he considered doing what he had always dreamed of. Retiring to a place where nobody knew his name with the woman he loved and leaving his business to the vultures who would no doubt descend upon it.

'Yeah, sure!' Claud muttered to himself with a laugh as he flicked his cigarette butt into the ocean.

Taking a seat on his chair on the deck, he carried on contemplating, but his mind brought him back to those who died in Sofia. Somebody had gone to a lot of trouble to obtain that envelope at the auction. Of particular concern was the thought, or indeed the certainty, that it must have been a party not invited to attend. He couldn't remember the last time he had felt such internal turmoil.

The satellite phone rang at a low volume in the cockpit and Claud very quickly retrieved it, pressing to answer as soon as he reached it. Once back out onto the deck, he put the phone to his ear.

'Yes, hello,' he said.

'It's me. Martini is dead!' Barrisfield shouted, referring to Mildred. Claud took a step back and without looking, felt for one of the armrests to guide himself to his seat. His top lip twitched with anger.

'How did this happen?' he asked with a gasp.

'Watch any news channel,' Barrisfield shakily instructed as Claud switched the deck television on with a click of the remote. The first news channel he landed on was reporting breaking news of a suspected nuclear explosion in Kent.

'But who? How?' Claud hissed.

'She went there with the Ambassador. As we suspected, he was being tracked by the organisation we spoke about. They wanted to tie up a loose end,' Barrisfield explained.

'Listen to me well. I am sorry for your loss. I am sure that there are others who have died also that we cannot discuss on this line. I will not be a loose end. Do you understand? I am putting down the receiver and disposing of this sat phone,' Claud stated purposely, trying to remain composed.

'Yes, I thought as much,' Barrisfield barked as he disconnected from the call.

Claud sat for a moment and remembered the Ambassador. Ambassador Francis Sunderland. The man who had won the auction. Looking at the satellite phone in his hand, he quickly threw it as hard as he could, out into the open sea.

He heard the door to the cockpit slide open. Turning his head slightly, he caught a glimpse of who was coming.

'Claud, darling. Can't you sleep?' Samara asked as she shuffled up behind him looking very appetising in her silver silk pyjamas. She dropped her hands down his chest, giving him a kiss on the cheek. 'Good morning.'

'Good morning, my dear. You should put something on. It's cold,' Claud said.

'I just came to check on you. Is everything ok?' she asked.

'Ok? Yes, of course. I just wanted some fresh air. To watch the sun rise,' he assured.

'You haven't been sleeping well. I know you, Claud. You have something on your mind,' Samara probed. He tilted his head straight back and looked into her questioning eyes, which stared back at him, upside down, as she stood above him. He looked back down, straight over the water.

'Many years ago, when I was still a child, my grandfather noticed me sitting and in thought. He must have realised that I was thinking about something upsetting and asked what was the matter. I didn't want to tell him, so I just said that I wasn't thinking about anything. He told me a story about a boy who worried about everything. The boy would worry about things that he had done. About what the other children thought about him. He worried about whether what he was wearing looked good. He worried about his friends talking about him behind his back. He even worried about the weather. This boy became so worried that one day he decided that he wouldn't leave his house. Eventually my grandfather told me that he had been that boy. He told me that worrying about things that had already happened was useless and that if I had made a mistake, that I should learn from it. I should only try to make things better if it served my purpose or helped somebody I cared about. I suppose he thought that I was walking the same path,' Claud paused, looking vacantly at the horizon. A hint of dawn light was starting to show through some breaks in the distant clouds.

'Why are you telling me this?' Samara asked.

'Because it's something I have lived by, but...'

'But what?' she pressed. Claud stood from the chair, breaking free of her hands which rested on his shoulders. He walked toward the rail at the rear of the vessel. Looking down, he saw the water churn in the wake of the boat as the yacht was propelled ahead.

'I don't know what to tell you. Usually, when I am out here, I can disconnect. Not feel remorse or guilt. Not worry about anything,' Claud blurted.

'You can't blame yourself for those people, Claud. You didn't kill them,' she reckoned, to which Claud let out an exhaled laugh. Turning, he walked toward Samara who was visibly shivering in the cold.

'I told you that you should've put something on,' he said, removing his jacket and throwing it around her shoulders. 'I don't think that you understood me, dear. The only guilt I feel is that I may have put you in danger. The only remorse, that I didn't do things differently.' Samara could see the heat in his eyes. The burning thoughts that she could so seldom read.

'You have always been a fool, my love,' she said running her hand down the side of his face. His stubble rubbing against her fingers. 'So adorable. I told you a long time ago that I would be with you until the end. If the end comes today or in fifty years, it makes no difference to me. I would change nothing.'

She took Claud by the hand and led him back into the cockpit and down the stairs to the King Stateroom, pushing him so that he fell back onto the bedcovers.

'Now I'm going to really give you something to worry about!' she said removing the jacket she still wore and her pyjamas before climbing on top of him slowly.

-Chapter 29-

'I apologise for the delay. I had to be sure that they would be able to see you,' Brother Josef said calmly as he returned to the cell where he had left Magda Popova.

'They?' probed Magda.

'Yes, well. Things have not been as quiet here at the monastery as the elder monks have grown used to,' the monk whispered, beckoning Magda with his glance. She stood from the table at which she had sat and eaten some delicious vegetable stew with bread. Brother Josef hadn't been gone long, but Magda had not wasted any time in finishing the bowl and sopping up every last bit with the bread. Not having eaten anything since the morning, she was ravenous.

Following Brother Josef back down the wooden steps into the courtyard, Magda walked to the dimly lit church that was the centrepiece of the monastery. In the darkness, they scurried across the cobbled surface in haste, passing between the white columns that comprised the colonnade surrounding most of the church. The intricate designs on the walls and on each dome, making up the colonnade, had been painted in the 1800s and admired by millions since. They conveyed their messages effectively and were illuminated by the hanging lights that dropped from each of the domes. Surrounded by the images of saints looking upon her, Magda reflected and began to judge her own recent actions quickly and severely.

Craning her neck, she looked up toward the mural paintings in awe. Their colours so vibrant and lifelike, expressing story and meaning effortlessly. As she approached a scene depicting the Last Judgement she stopped abruptly, causing Brother Josef to backtrack.

'The doomsday paintings are very powerful. A particular favourite of mine,' the monk observed.

'Interesting. I've never really noticed them before,' Magda admitted hesitantly, looking at the monk quickly before continuing to contemplate the mural. The figures on the wall were segregated into those being glorified and those being punished on their respective journeys to heaven or to hell.

'They are beautiful paintings. But that day is yet to come,' the monk said tranquilly before turning and continuing on his path. Magda looked a moment longer at the characters illustrated, before following Brother Josef.

Brass candle-stands stood to either side of the main entrance to the church. The hot candle wax dripped down the side of the candles that remained lit. Heaving the great wooden door open with the help of his shoulder, the monk quickly disappeared into the building and Magda followed.

'Have I interrupted a meeting?' Magda asked, pushing the door closed again.

'Of sorts. Several of the elder monks, including your uncle, have come here tonight to hold evening devotion. It lasted longer than expected, but they would like to speak with you,' Brother Josef explained. Magda said nothing and followed the monk. She was distracted by the internal beauty of the building and the feeling of sanctity that filled her.

'But, where are they?' Magda Popova asked, immediately noticing the quietness within the church. The monk walked through the nave and she followed closely. As he proceeded, he noticed Magda had once again stopped and now stood before the iconostasis. A wall of religious icons and representations, before which the painted icon of the three-handed Holy Virgin was positioned in a richly ornate metal frame held on a stand. Red curtains adorned either side of the painting. It was a captivating scene. A stark silver aureole radiated around the head of the Virgin Mary as the baby Jesus lay in her arms. The three hands, silver in colour, were depicted clearly. The monk once again walked back to Magda.

'I came here tonight. I don't even really think that I knew why. Not really. But this place makes everything so clear. Looking at this painting has always made me feel so calm, as though everything will be ok,' Magda reflected.

'Everything is very rarely ok,' the monk retorted. 'But there is little as important as faith when facing trouble.'

'I never knew. I mean, I never asked why the Virgin Mary has three hands in this painting,' Magda asked.

'I can tell you the story. During the eighth century, Saint John of Damascus was accused falsely of having committed acts of treason. An order was given to cut his hand off. Saint John asked for his severed hand to be returned to him and in the evening, he put it to its joint and dropped to the ground in front of an icon of the Virgin Mary. The monk prayed for much time for his hand to be healed, before falling asleep. In his dream, the Mother of God came to him and promised that he would be healed. When he awoke, Saint John saw that he was once again whole and that his hand was unharmed. Saint John was very thankful and put upon the icon a hand fashioned of silver,' Brother Josef recounted. 'The icon is considered able to work miracles and enhance prayer.'

'That's fascinating. I'm sorry to take up your time, but this place...' Magda added. 'I can't believe that I didn't know that!'

She once again followed the monk. He walked purposefully, pushing open the door to the side of the iconostasis. The cold stone steps led down and Magda descended apprehensively.

'I haven't been down here before,' she mentioned, as she ducked to avoid the stairwell's low ceiling. Reaching the foot of the stairs, she saw the monk had already made it halfway down the short tunnel that led to a door. The walls were lined intermittently with candles that cast lively shadows along the stone. The corridor ceiling was much higher. Sturdy-looking stone arches ran along its walls, interspersed with smaller black metal doors barricading small individual sections, used for purposes unknown.

Magda sensed that the musty cold air smelt different downstairs and was slightly tinged with the scent of incense. The monk had stopped just before a gate of barred metal that was already open wide.

'This is the crypt,' he explained as he gestured with his arm for Magda to enter.

'Meetings are held down here?' Magda asked, intrigued at the strange venue for the meeting.

'Oh yes, we keep a lot more than just the dead down here,' the monk smiled, referring to secrets, some of which even he was unaware.

Magda brushed past Brother Josef and into the chamber. The chamber was also glowing by candlelight and five elders sat on wooden chairs around an old wooden table. Their black robes were adorned with religious writing and symbolism, picked out in vibrant white. The Orthodox cross featuring on all of their robes, carrying the three horizontal crossbeams, the top one representing the plate and the bottom one representing a footrest, slanting higher to the left.

Their well kempt beards were white and long. A prominent feature, flowing down from their black hoods.

Magda approached the table, noticing the walls with delay. Three shelves running around all sides of the chamber accommodated skulls that faced in toward those sitting at the table. Squinting in the darkness, she noticed that some of the skulls had inscriptions upon them.

Magda didn't gaze at them for long, returning her attention to the empty chair at the table. Her uncle, the only monk whose hood was drawn, smiled and invited her to sit.

She smiled, happy to see uncle Boyan, but also feeling strongly that she didn't belong. Lowering herself onto the chair, the cold wood was not comforting.

'I'm so pleased to see you, uncle,' she sniffed, immediately contending with the welling emotions that were attempting to surface. 'I need to speak with you alone.'

'You've come a long way. Something troubles you,' said Brother Boyan. 'You're in good company here, for we are troubled too. Anything that you want to share with me, you can also share with my brothers,' he continued, looking around the table at the faces of the other elders.

Magda followed her uncle's stare and saw the other monks nodding slightly. The late-night devotion, followed by this meeting, was clearly a sign that all was not well.

They sat in silence, until Magda finally began to speak about recent events. She recounted events, all the way back to her arrival at the residence of Ambassador Sunderland, the events in the village of Valsha, the extraction of the artefact and finally, her strange interaction with Nadia Hristova. She didn't mention her encounter with Vadik, the Russian agent.

The monks seemed to most visibly react to her words about Nadia, the mentally ill woman. A mute who had spoken for the first time in years.

'This woman you speak of. She spoke to you. She asked you for help and said that people wanted to bury her. When you asked for her name she gave you the name of a man?' her uncle repeated, to which Magda nodded. 'What was the man's name?'

'Mike Argo,' uttered Magda, looking down at her hands, thinking about Vadik's warning. The monks were disturbed by the story they had heard. They said nothing of the religious connotations of a mute person beginning to speak, but they didn't have to. On some level, Magda knew that this was part of the reason why she had travelled to the monastery that night. She couldn't understand what had happened. She was unable to explain it to herself.

'What you have told us is troubling. The past few days have brought us much cause for concern too,' Boyan said. 'We have seen things that have reminded us of the words of Christ. We have seen circumstances and this has led us to question if these things may be what is described by God.'

'What do you mean?' asked Magda.

'We know that each day that passes brings us closer to the day of the Lord. Even if this doesn't happen in our lifetime, we know that this day will come. The situation now has become worse than ever. The mass movement of people, caused by conflict: a symptom of the deception and greed of governments and the wealthy few. The degradation of morality across the world. Most recently, a nuclear weapon has been detonated in the United Kingdom,' Boyan continued calmly as the elder monks nodded and hummed in positive agreement. 'The end time is surely not far.'

Magda's heart sank on hearing the words of her uncle. The chamber was cold and the silence was piercing. She felt as though the warmth was being sucked from her body as she sat, shivering.

'A man threatened me, uncle. Because of things that I know. I don't think that I can take any more of this,' Magda said frankly and with an air of resignation in her voice.

'This monastery has been sanctuary for some great people in the past. You've been fighting a difficult battle and one that you alone cannot win. If you fear that you're in danger, then you must stay here with us,' Boyan responded without any hesitation. 'You must go and rest. We will stay a while and discuss some matters,' he told Magda, reaching up and running his fingers along the length of his beard.

Standing from her chair quietly, Magda felt the cold gaze of the skulls upon her. Unable to shake the sense that she was being judged, she quickly walked out from the chamber and was escorted back to her cell where she quickly and unapologetically lay her head down for the night.

-Chapter 30-

Pouring a second glass of whisky, Jonathan Coleridge had waited for longer than he could bear. Furious, he swigged from the glass twice, finishing its content and slamming it down on the table.

Jennifer Harbinger, his supervisor at MI6, had asked to meet with him urgently. She told him that Ambassador Sunderland had likely perished in the recent nuclear explosion. Francis' phone had been on the list of those that pinged through cellular towers local to the explosion.

Jonathan had asked what Francis had been doing out there and who he had been with. Jennifer had been unable to answer. He had made his way as quickly as he could to the Houses of Parliament. In a room where they had met previously, he waited for Jennifer to join him.

London glimmered seductively as he refilled his glass for the third time and walked up to the window. The blue flashing lights of emergency response vehicles stuck in traffic, reflected off the Thames and Jonathan became lost in his thoughts. Thoughts of all the dead at Francis' house and the devastation he had found in Valsha. Francis had been very lucky to make it out of Bulgaria, but by all accounts, they had killed him in Britain. Of that Jonathan had no doubt.

The sound of wailing sirens from a police car and ambulance, caught in congestion on Westminster Bridge, seemed to spur the pedestrians along more than the traffic, as people seemed to rush along the pavements. News of the nuclear explosion had spread like wildfire and pandemonium had ensued. Fear of fallout drifting through London had caused gridlock on the roads and public transport had all but ground to a standstill.

Fear was felt worldwide. The underlying alarm caused by the fact that nobody knew who had activated the weapon, or why. A dreaded scenario.

The sound of high heels on hard floor echoed outside the door. Jonathan turned to face Jennifer as she forcefully walked in and threw a folder down on the desk.

'What the hell happened?' asked Jonathan, putting the glass down on the windowsill.

'What happened? A nuclear weapon exploded just outside of London, John. That's what happened,' Jennifer retorted in an irate tone. John looked away and walked back to the window as Jennifer picked up a clean glass from the table and poured herself a drink.

'And Ambassador Sunderland?' he asked.

'We got a triangulation of his last location before the explosion. Anybody in that area would be dead,' Jennifer responded matter-of-factly.

'I just don't understand it. I thought that we would have people watching him and his family. Particularly after what happened,' Jonathan said, rubbing the back of his neck.

'We have to deal with the living right now, John. Shall we worry about the dead tomorrow? I called you because I would like you to go to Sunderland's house and take his family to a place of safety. We owe him that at least,' she muttered.

'You mean that there isn't anybody with them right now? Jesus!' Jonathan exclaimed as Jennifer shook her head, taking another swig of whisky.

'They were lucky you found them when you did in Bulgaria. No doubt they would have been mopped up then,' Jennifer remembered. 'We didn't think they would be a target. Whoever did this already got what they wanted!'

'Think about it, Jennifer. Does anybody here really believe that somebody who wanted to kill the Ambassador or his family would use a bloody nuke? That doesn't make any sense.' Jonathan reasoned. 'Tell me about the location of the explosion.'

'I don't want you thinking about that. I just need you to go and remove his family to a place of safety,' Jennifer said evasively as Jonathan stared at her unerringly. A few seconds passed and she knew he wasn't going anywhere without additional information. 'There was one house in the vicinity. The house and the land belong to Mildred Jones, a partner at the law firm Brick Steckelback.'

Jonathan nodded, scouring his brain for any recollection of the name Brick Steckelback.

'I've never heard of them,' he said.

'You probably wouldn't have. They don't really have much in the way of a high-street presence,' Jennifer replied, looking down at the table as she placed her glass on a coaster. 'I have a meeting with the Foreign Secretary now. Sorry, but I haven't got more time to stay and talk.'

Finishing the last of his drink, Jonathan also put his glass down on the table.

'I don't know. I just don't know what I am going to tell them. Do his family even know that he's dead?' Jonathan asked.

'No, no, they don't know that Sunderland was there. But they will of course know about the explosion. Who doesn't? Monitoring shows them to still be at their home in Cobham,' Jennifer explained.

'So, now isn't the best time to talk about my retirement?' he asked sarcastically.

'You really are quite something. I've no idea how you can joke at a time like this.'

'What else is there to do?' Jonathan said, strolling out of the office, toward the car park.

Chapter 31

Vincent Madden could hear the occasional mechanical scuttling of the GridWatch outside his quarters as they carried out their meticulous patrol of the Future Logic Facility. Unable to understand what it was that he was hearing, Vincent had moved to stand at the window, where he had remained for over an hour, watching as a much larger contingent of guards patrolled the external parts of the facility.

The guards looked small in the distance and he winced to try and see as much detail as possible. He could just make out Adam Diaz, the man who had sat in on all of his meetings with his captor. The man he knew only as Mike.

Confinement to his quarters had given Vincent time to think. Too much time. He had kept a strict regime of exercise inside his room, doing as many push-ups, sit-ups and planks as he could bring himself to do.

There was something happening in the facility and he had no idea what it was. Suspecting that whatever it was related to the artefact, he carried on looking out of the window.

He supported the weight of his chin on his knuckles. His head became heavy and his eyes closed momentarily before he was struck by a hypnic jerk. Starting suddenly, he blinked several times and carried on watching the world outside.

The smell of a burning cigarette hung in the air as he inhaled deeply, closing his eyes. He hadn't smoked since arriving at the facility. A cold blast of air hit him in the face. As he opened his eyes, he saw that he stood on a balcony overlooking a wooded park. Thinking nothing more of it, he drew the cigarette he held automatically to his lips, taking a deep, satisfying drag before resting both hands on the balcony rail. It was freezing to the touch. He thought about the important day that was ahead of him and about the beautiful woman still in his bed. He smiled and finished the last of the cigarette and stubbed it out on the freezing railing before tossing it over the side and five floors down to the street below.

The wooden balcony door behind him creaked open and he felt two tender warm arms wrap themselves around his stomach from behind as a familiar body pulled itself close into his back and kissed him affectionately on the neck, finishing with a subtle and ticklish lick.

He felt a hand exploring both of his trouser pockets, searching for what it desired.

Lara Berg found the packet of cigarettes and moved to stand next to Vincent at the balcony rail overlooking the park, wearing nothing. She had his full attention as she drew a cigarette and lit it with the lighter he kept inside the box.

'It's cold,' Vincent said, taking off the jacket he had put over his bare torso and wrapping it across Lara's shoulders. The cold air immediately went to work on his bare skin and he felt the heat being sucked from his body.

'Thank you... Ryan,' Lara said with a pause, throwing Vincent an enamoured look, garnished with an irresistible smile. 'You are a real gentleman.'

The cold cut through Vincent and reminded him of his mortality. It reminded him of how he needed to take back control of his life. It reminded him of his likely fate if he didn't.

'I feel like I really know you,' Vincent said with a slight shudder in his voice.

'And I feel like I really know you too,' Lara replied, before taking another drag on the cigarette and running her finger under his chin. 'Can I ask you something?'

Vincent nodded, crossing his arms across his upper body to try and retain some heat.

'Have you ever thought about your life and wondered if things could've been different?' she asked. Her eyes searching his frantically for an answer.

'I always thought so, but I don't know when change stopped being an option for me,' Vincent admitted far too candidly. Everything looked, smelt and felt so familiar.

'Look at the moon, Vincent. So clear and big. I could almost reach out and touch it,' Lara whispered. The moonlight sparkled in her eyes. As those same eyes turned to look at him, Vincent thought that perhaps he would do anything for them and the beautiful girl they belonged to.

'I have so many things that I want to tell you, but you look so cold,' Lara said, as Vincent leaned forward and supported his weight on the balcony rail. The cold was biting hard and he felt as though he was freezing to the spot. His jaw was chattering slightly and most of the feeling had departed from his hands and feet. Lara flicked her half-finished and unextinguished cigarette off the balcony and walked back behind Vincent. Standing on bare tiptoes, seemingly unaffected by the cold, she whispered something gently into Vincent's ear. He chuckled through the shivering, before erupting into full-blown laughter. Lara backed into the apartment, leaving him alone on the balcony, laughing at the moon.

The sky was a blanket of stars and with a sudden flash of light the stars exploded, raining down like sparks towards the wooded park below. The ceiling light fittings in his quarters exploded in a shower of sparks. The only source of light remaining came from the relatively small window. Vincent's face was expressionless and dazed as he walked toward the door. Wrapping his fingers around the contours of the sliding metal door, he heaved with enormous vigour. His right hand lost its grip, tearing his fingernail clean from its nailbed. As it dropped to the floor, Vincent unflinchingly gripped the door again. With no electricity holding it closed, the door slowly opened with a low-volume hiss.

The sound of voices echoed down the corridor as members of staff reacted to the massive power surge that had knocked out the electrics. Vincent was unperturbed as he started to walk down the corridor. Looking straight ahead, he didn't notice the GridWatch droid malfunctioning on the floor. Still partially operational, but unable to regain access to the servers, the droid lay twitching. Its sensors detected the movement of Vincent approaching and the remnant instructions to incapacitate anybody not abiding by the Crossbones lockdown kicked in.

A blinding flash of light, followed by the powerful shriek and shock wave, were emitted by the droid's sonic defence. Vincent was sent to the ground in agony, clutching his ears and squeezing his eyes closed, writhing in pain on his side. Blood trickled between his fingers from his ears.

He opened his eyes but could see nothing. His ears were ringing and he couldn't hear anything either. After a moment, able to roll onto his hands and knees as he stretched his mouth wide open and slammed it shut, he toppled over onto his side again, disorientated. Raising himself up, Vincent stumbled badly to the side and clattered into the wall before falling to the ground.

Chapter 32

'What was that?!' shouted Mike Argo, hearing the distant shriek of the GridWatch droid and feeling the slight vibration that reverberated through his quarters. It had been only seconds since the power surge had left Olivia and Argo without power. Olivia's systems were unaffected, aside from her connection to the server, which had gone down immediately with the rest of the power in the facility. She had just received the order from Argo to take the facility out of lockdown when the surge had struck.

'That was the GridWatch defensive system. All systems are offline, Mr Argo,' Olivia said with a lot less urgency than Argo was expecting at a time like this. With the ability to operate independently of the servers, she had been unaffected by the surge, but was now reliant on her physical sensors for information. A GridWatch droid had fired its defensive system, but without server access there was no way for Olivia to know where or for what reason.

Walking to the door, she tried to use the console, but it wasn't operational. Argo tried the handle, opening the door with ease. Olivia tilted her head, registering that the doors to everyone's quarters must all have unlocked due to the power outage.

The corridor outside was dark, as Mike Argo and Olivia stepped out of the room. The only illumination came from the occasional low-power security lighting.

'The GridWatch operate through a direct link to the server. I do not have any record that indicates how a system outage may affect them during an active lockdown,' Olivia admitted.

'What might have caused this to happen?' asked Argo as they crept forward gingerly. 'All of the security personnel are outside.'

'All of the power for the facility is generated on site. There are a few possible causes, including the occurrence of an electromagnetic pulse or generator surge,' Olivia explained, referring to the hydrogen generator on sub-level 4 of the facility.

'What about the artefact? The Pebble?' Argo whispered. 'Is there any chance that it is able to do something like this?'

'Unfortunately, I am not able to answer that question, Mr Argo,' Olivia said after a short pause. Rounding a corner, they could see a GridWatch droid walking in a small circle.

'Stay here,' Olivia said, putting her arm out to stop Argo from progressing further. She walked toward the droid and placed her finger upon the touch panel on top of its head. It stood still immediately, before running off down the corridor at speed.

'What did you do?' asked Argo as he walked up behind Olivia.

'I am able to act as a server for the GridWatch. That droid is approaching Vincent Madden's quarters now. He is not there,' Olivia stated. Her eyes glowed a deep shade of green in the darkness as she instructed the droid to take a pheromone sample from Vincent's room. Argo's face dropped on hearing the news that a highly trained government agent was loose in the facility.

'Well, where is he?' Argo asked, as Olivia's gaze turned to him. She observed as the GridWatch droid connected her to a further three droids. She now controlled a formidable and efficient search party.

The lead droid followed the drops of blood that had leaked from Vincent's ears, with the other three in tow. The traces of blood soon stopped. Air passed over the pheromone sensors they were equipped with, as they split up in search of Vincent. The GridWatch droids would re-join the droid sampling the highest pheromone levels.

Olivia paced slowly in the wake of the search. A phosphorescent marker had been dropped on the floor every few metres by the GridWatch and this helped Argo see the route that they should take. Following apprehensively, he turned as the sound of several rounds of gunfire rang out from the ground floor downstairs. He registered that the external doors hadn't unlocked and that the security detail were now trying to get back into the facility.

'It is unlikely that they will reacquire access to the facility with the munitions they have at their disposal,' Olivia reported, referring to the external blast doors.

Reaching the hallway on the ground floor, Olivia led Argo further on the trail of the GridWatch. The stairwell access to the sub-level laboratories was usually secure, but now lay flung open.

'Mike... Mike,' whispered a voice from behind. Argo and Olivia turned and saw the figure of Dr Otani quietly shuffling toward them, clutching a handgun. It glimmered slightly in the green-tinted emergency lighting.

'What are you doing outside your quarters? The agent has escaped and we are using the GridWatch to track him,' Argo explained quietly.

'Are the GridWatch still operational?' asked Dr Otani, considering the effect of the systems failure.

'Uh-huh, several of them have connected directly through Olivia,' Argo explained.

'Of course,' Otani muttered as their shoes made a slight clipping sound in the dimly lit stairwell.

Reaching the entrance to sub-level 2, they followed Olivia. She pulled open the door and walked through. An alarm was sounding, with the word *warning* spoken every five seconds. The GridWatch had a visual lock on Vincent Madden, but proceeded no further. Through their eyes, Olivia could see that he was inside the section of the laboratory that contained the Pebble. Standing behind the craft, he stared over it directly toward the GridWatch droids through the glass door and walls. Looking down, he started to push with his foot the partially constructed metal casing, built around the Pebble in preparation for its transportation.

Argo and Otani lined up next to Olivia and the GridWatch, looking through the glass at Vincent.

The door to the lab was only slightly open and Olivia moved her hand to try and open it further.

'Stop!' shouted Vincent. His voice unsteady. His eyes wincing as if in significant discomfort. Olivia released her grip on the glass door. 'I want to see Lara Berg. Bring Lara here!' he shouted, raising his hand to his temple and pressing his palm against it with force.

'Who's Lara?!' shouted Argo in confusion. Vincent paused, thrust his hand forward from his temple and pointed straight toward Argo.

'You know exactly who she is! She was here. Here in a blue dress,' Vincent yelled louder, the exertion causing the veins to pop from the side of his neck. He lowered his head as his gaze became fixed on the Pebble in front of him.

Argo remembered that Henrietta Rekman had worn a blue dress during the presentation of the Pebble to the members of Onyx. He further recalled the conversation Henrietta had with Vincent in the midst of her killing spree in the Bulgarian mountains.

'You're right. I do know who you mean,' Argo responded. 'But she can't come here, I'm afraid.'

'And why is that?' Vincent asked, as he erupted into a manic laugh and raised his gaze, staring directly at Argo. 'When I was brought here, I didn't know anything about you. I only knew your violence. Violence. I was weak when you brought me here. I was weak and trapped. But now, I have had time to recover. To grow stronger. I have missed time. I haven't connected with you, or some others here the way I expected, but that won't stop me. It's only a matter of time though. Only a matter of time, until I do. Until then, enjoy every last breath.' Vincent Madden said calmly and out of keeping with his previous demeanour. His voice just audible over the alarm.

They all stood rooted to the spot for a moment, before Vincent's head tilted back suddenly as if shocked or suffering a nervous reaction. He began to cough. The coughing was followed by spluttering. He clenched at the top of his t-shirt, ripping it with his hand as he gasped for air. Falling to his knees, he began to wheeze terribly as his face started to lose colour and turn pale.

'Don't move. This may be a trap,' Argo instructed. Vincent fell on the floor, rolling onto his back, gasping for air.

Olivia looked down to one of the GridWatch droids. She gave it instructions to take Vincent Madden's vital readings as he lay still, twitching sporadically. The droid opened the glass door enough to enter and ran swiftly across the hard, clean floor. Passing under the supports propping up the craft, it crunched the globules of matter that had melted from Olivia's hand and hardened on the floor.

Climbing on top of Vincent's chest, the droid lay a hand on his neck.

'His vital signs are failing. He requires immediate medical attention,' Olivia explained urgently as Otani ran into the laboratory, kneeling down next to Vincent. He began to administer CPR. Argo gave a small nod to Olivia, who wasted no time in following Otani into the laboratory.

Vincent had been difficult to lift and carry, but Argo, Otani and Olivia had collectively managed to heave him into a wheelchair, after it became clear that CPR wasn't working. They hastily made their way to the med-centre with him. No sooner had they placed him on the table, than Otani had to pronounce Vincent dead.

The med-centre had dedicated power by virtue of an independent generator that had only kicked in after the electrical surge had disabled the facility. Otani set to determining the cause of death by conducting an impromptu autopsy, a task that he had never enjoyed, even though pathology was something that he specialised in. Argo and Olivia stood outside the med-centre, because Argo enjoyed the sight of a carved-up cadaver even less than Otani. He had started to feel queasy as soon as the scalpel had sliced delicately and precisely from Vincent's shoulders to his sternum.

From outside, the sound of the bone-saw Otani used to open the chest cavity was enough to make Argo feel even worse.

Some time later, Otani had seen enough to have determined the cause of death. He called them back inside the med-centre. Although a cover had been thrown over the body, blood pooled on the floor underneath, where it had spilled out over the sides of the table.

'Asphyxia. He suffocated,' Otani announced, pulling the blood-soaked, heavy autopsy gloves from his hands one by one and tossing them violently into the bin, emblazoned with the biohazard symbol. Usually a meek and shy character, Dr Otani was angry.

'He suffocated? How is that possible? What caused it?' asked Argo.

'You were there, Mike! One minute the man is alive and talking to us. The next, he is telling us to enjoy every last breath, before suffocating before our eyes,' Otani expressed plainly.

'But, could he have done this to himself? We were all breathing the same air!' Argo questioned.

'No. His heart is healthy; his lungs are in perfect order. There are no blockages in his airway and I found no physical cause for the asphyxiation. Also, the man's blood was clean. Clean of any toxic substances, but also lacking of the oxygen he needed to keep him alive,' Otani insisted. Removing his protective eyewear and mask, he threw them in the bin, along with the laboratory coat he wore. 'You might attribute some of the things that he was saying to oxygen starvation, maybe. But that doesn't explain his death. I can't explain it.'

'What if you had to explain it?' Argo challenged.

'I would have to guess. My guess would be that that the artefact is behind all of this. The systems outage. The death of this man and his strange behaviour, as well as a great number of the health issues we have been experiencing here. Not to mention the heatless melting of Olivia's hand.'

Olivia nodded, turning from Dr Otani to face Argo.

'I agree with you. Olivia, work to get systems online as soon as possible. Katsu, we need all hands on deck to get rid of this thing. Let's go and get your team out of their rooms!'

Chapter 33

'Well, no. We couldn't go anywhere. We're waiting for Francis to get home,' Melissa Sunderland said apprehensively. She had opened her front door expecting Francis to be there, but instead Jonathan Coleridge had greeted her. Tilting his head slightly to the right, he noticed two suitcases packed and her sons Patrick and George standing behind her, listening to the conversation.

'I need to speak with you alone,' Jonathan said, nodding understandingly. Melissa's face dropped as the colour drained from her. Turning and kneeling she asked the boys in a hushed tone to go up to their room. She watched as they ran up the stairs.

'What is it?' Melissa asked, looking back toward Jonathan with an emotional glare. 'I've had just about all that I can take, you know.' On the street behind him, Jonathan could hear two cars being packed ready for departure as neighbours, who had quickly collected essential clothes and provisions, prepared for their escape.

Jonathan gestured with his hand and Melissa made way for him to enter the house. Standing in the hallway, he closed the door behind himself.

'Your husband's last known location was the detonation site of the nuclear weapon,' Jonathan said directly. Melissa took a few steps back and slumped onto the second step of the staircase. 'What?' she asked, looking vacantly at Jonathan. He said nothing but moved closer to her, standing solemnly for a few moments as Melissa sat in silence. Taking her mobile from the pocket of her jeans, she quickly dialled Francis' number. Placing the receiver to her ear, Jonathan noticed that she had cut her hair short since returning to the United Kingdom. A drastic change and one that he was surprised he hadn't noticed sooner. The automated notification to say that the mobile phone she had called was switched off, was audible even to Jonathan.

'That doesn't mean anything. You don't know that he's dead,' Melissa muttered, looking at her phone in despondency, running her thumb over the screen, drawing patterns through the fingerprints on the display.

'I hope I'm wrong. Right now, I have to do what's right for you. For your children. What Francis would want me to do. I have to take you all away from here. To a place of safety,' Jonathan pleaded, stepping closer. Melissa stood from the step and ran up the stairs at speed. He waited at the bottom of the stairs, listening to the activity upstairs. Drawers were opened and closed as Melissa collected a final few items. Before long, Patrick and George came scampering down the stairs and Jonathan plastered a forced smile onto his face.

They were followed closely by Melissa, who had been unable to do the same, her expression pale and wistful. Moving straight past Jonathan, she picked up one of the two cases on the floor and opened the door. Turning back, she saw Jonathan pick up the second case as they all filed out of the house.

The luggage was stowed in the boot of Jonathan's dark-blue Volvo SUV. The boys overcame the high ground clearance and clambered into the back.

Wasting no time, Jonathan sent a message to Jennifer Harbinger to confirm their destination and craned his neck to make sure that everybody had their seatbelt on, before turning on the car and pulling off. Moving from the quiet residential streets onto the main road, it was clear that the traffic was much heavier than usual.

'Where are we going, mum?' George asked after twenty minutes of driving. Melissa looked vacantly from the passenger window and appeared not to have registered the question.

'We are going on a little trip,' Jonathan said. 'Do you like going on trips?'

'Yes!' both children cried in unison before descending into giggling laughter.

'Good. I think that your mum is just tired,' he said, throwing a glance at Melissa, who seemed oblivious to her surroundings. As he entered a few commands into the satnav, the monitors in the back of the headrests turned on and a cartoon channel grabbed the attention of the children. The rear speakers, located in the headrests were loud enough for the children to hear, but not loud enough to bother the driver.

Speeding onto a motorway, all three lanes were busy. Jonathan manoeuvred between the lanes and observed the erratic, nervous driving of the other motorists, fuelled by emotion and the news of the explosion.

In cars all around him, the radio was pumping in news, speculation and theory about the details of what had happened, even though the reality was far from the comprehension of most. Ahead, Jonathan saw that three cars had pulled onto the hard shoulder and were exchanging insurance details. The middle car had sustained a lot of damage both at the front and rear. Passing the cars, all drivers were able to once again concentrate on the road and traffic became free flowing, whilst still congested.

Moving into the fast lane, he pressed his foot down on the accelerator. The Volvo bounded forward, accelerating to just under eighty miles an hour. Melissa leaned her head against the window and the children sunk down into their seats, watching their respective screens.

The change for Jonathan and all humans around him was instantaneous. Like a bolt from the darkness, the Trauma struck. Jonathan's head jolted to the left as he recoiled and winced in pain. Blood dripped from the noses of all in the car as he involuntarily yanked the steering wheel to the right. The Volvo smashed into the central reservation barrier. The airbags deployed, as passengers inside were struck by massive impacts. Spinning in a cloud of tyre smoke and debris, the Volvo nearly toppled as it was buffeted by other vehicles, similarly out of control, striking them from behind.

Melissa was the only one in the car still conscious. Her window smashed and passenger door sealed shut by damage. Wincing, she clawed at the airbag desperately and wrapped her fingers over the bottom of the window, trying to pull herself up and out. The seatbelt stopped her progress, but she was not able to unfasten it. As petrol dripped from their car and from the vehicles surrounding them, her primal instincts continued to drive her to escape the passenger seat through the window. She didn't attempt to free herself from the seatbelt.

An articulated lorry, barrelling along at great speed, veered from the left-hand lane and within seconds crashed into the cluster of four cars, including the Volvo. The impact was terminal and all were dead before the petrol-fuelled fireball ignited, engulfing the wreckage.

Up and down the motorway, drivers and passengers had lost their faculties. In turn, they had lost all control of their vehicles whilst travelling at speed, causing total carnage. Thick, acrid black smoke billowed from burning cars, as people remained trapped in their vehicles.

Many were dying of their injuries whilst others sat choking in the thick black smoke. They were not the only ones affected by the Trauma.

Worldwide, the Trauma had gripped humans in the very same instant as Vincent Madden's life had been squeezed from him at the Future Logic Facility in Bandung, Indonesia.

-Chapter 34-

Turning in bed to face the room as she slept, Taryn's eyes were closed and her breathing steady. Fresh air wafted in through the window as she inhaled deeply. Her nose twitched from side to side involuntarily. The loose floorboard by her brother's bed let out a familiar creak, causing her to stir. Drawing the back of her small fist across her eyes as she opened them, Taryn watched through blurry vision as Peter's figure shifted in the darkness toward the door that had been left ajar. Pulling it slowly, he walked out into the corridor.

Taryn kept listening to try and hear where he was going. He had walked straight past the toilet and she heard further creaks as he made his way down the stairs. Taryn was now awake and thinking about what her brother was up to. He hadn't turned on any lights, probably to avoid waking anybody up. Either that or he was going to raid the kitchen for snacks. *It wouldn't be the first time*, she thought.

Her eyes darted to the door when she heard her brother was running around downstairs. Lifting herself onto one elbow, she pushed her bedcovers down to her waist and tried to hear more.

'What's he doing?' she whispered to herself, wondering how long it would be before her mother woke and heard him. *He'll really be in trouble then*, she thought. The running came to a stop with a loud thud that sent vibrations through the floor and Taryn's bed. She jumped. There was no way her mother hadn't heard that.

The silence was deafening, as Taryn listened to the sound of her fast heartbeat pounding through her ears. She wondered why her mum wasn't waking up.

Hearing footsteps again, Taryn detected the faint sound of the chain-lock sliding across the door. Her brother left the house. Jumping to her feet, she looked out of the open window and, peering down, saw her brother walking down the garden path, barefoot, wearing his pyjamas.

'Peter!' she shouted, thrusting the window further open with the palm of her hand. He didn't flinch, but instead continued out through the open gate, disappearing from sight up the hill.

'Mummy,' she shouted, running out of the bedroom and into Marianne's. Taryn switched on the lights and saw that the covers had been thrown back and her mother wasn't there. Breathing shallow and quick breaths, Taryn looked around the room for any clue as to her mother's whereabouts. It took a moment for her eyes to adjust to the bright light, but when they did, she saw it.

A pool of blood had soaked into the light-blue pillow. Taryn's hands covered her mouth as she gasped sharply. The tassels around the side of the pillow had started to absorb the blood as it spread. Looking away, she ran to the other side of the bed to check if her mother was on the floor or unwell, but she was gone.

In the corridor, a few small drops of blood lead down the stairs. The drops were blurry through her tear-filled eyes.

Back in her room, she turned on the lights. Putting on an orange dress, she sat on her bed pulling on her socks. Looking at Peter's bed, now illuminated, she started to shake her head and cry with ever shorter breaths. Her brother's pillow lay on the floor, a large blotch of blood prominent at its centre.

Looking around frantically, she stepped into her trainers quickly. Running down the stairs and into the kitchen, turning on every light along the way, she knocked the cabinet upon which the telephone rested. The handset toppled and hit the floor. Picking it up, she dialled the telephone number for the police.

'We are attempting to connect your call. We are attempting to connect your call,' said the automated voice at the other end of the line for several minutes, as Taryn stood looking at her surroundings. Specks of blood on the floor led toward the front and back doors, both of which were wide open. A humid, warm draft rushed through the house, as she carried on looking around frenziedly. Peter had run into the area of wall next to the bin. The white paint was marked where blood from his head had spattered during the impact.

Taryn had never made a phone call to the police before, but she knew she'd called the right number. She could wait no longer. The cold, pressing fear for her mum and brother were too much for her to bear.

Putting the phone down, Taryn looked out of the back door and, seeing nothing, closed it. She picked up the house keys from where her mum always kept them, in the cabinet next to the front door. Stepping outside in the darkness of night, the door clicked shut behind her and she walked a few steps before turning round to look at the house.

Taryn followed the path up the hill. Her brother had walked that way. She was scared. Stopping every few steps and yearning to run home. To hide under the covers. To hope this wasn't real. The night was quiet except for an aircraft in the sky.

The brisk temperature had enveloped her completely and she had started to shiver slightly. The shock of her dreadful awakening likely playing an equal part. As she walked, the aircraft became louder. The tone of the engine changed. The next few minutes were filled with the distant sound of snapping and breaking as a passenger aircraft broke up during a nose dive. It smashed into the ground in the distance.

Taryn didn't understand what she had just heard, but felt the shock wave from the explosion like a tap on the shoulder. Silence followed.

They had few neighbours and the houses were well spread out on the road where they lived. Ahead, walking in the opposite direction, a figure slowly came into view. As the person moved closer, in the glow of the occasional street lights, she saw that it was Mr Shaw. A heavy-set man, wearing only a light-coloured t-shirt and white Y-front underwear, as he paced jerkily, Mr Shaw coughed and gasped for air. She looked at his face as he walked straight past her, without shifting his mesmerised gaze to look at her. Two streaks that looked black in the relative darkness, ran down from his ears and two more from his nostrils. His head was stained with blood. Black blotches had formed on his t-shirt, where the blood was dripping down. As he walked away, Taryn saw his bedraggled feet. They looked as though they had traipsed through a bed of thorns.

'Mr Shaw! Mr Shaw!' she shouted. Her voice trembling. He continued on his path, unable to respond. Taryn began to connect the terrible thoughts like one whose mind, so young and innocent, should never have to. Soon, approaching the crest of the hill, Taryn's nose filled with the smell of smoke.

She could taste a metallic tinge in her mouth. She didn't know it was blood. She didn't know that the Trauma was affecting her too, but in a different way. Dampening the distress. Pushing her to carry on.

Ahead, a large, warm glow loomed. A house on fire. Walking toward the blaze, Taryn saw a person laying in the road ahead. They had made it out of the house and crawled the last few metres onto the road, while still ablaze. A few remnants of the clothes they wore remained. A pungent smell filled the air. Taryn didn't look. She ran straight past as slivers of smoke rose from the dead person.

Breaking into a sprint, she ran as fast as she could. She passed person after person, leaking blood from their ears, panting, wheezing and spluttering, totally oblivious to their surroundings. Some had fallen to the ground and suffocated to death on the spot. Her brother had headed in this direction, but there was no way to know where he had gone. Taryn was confused. Panicked. Alone.

Now on roads that were usually busy with the sound of traffic, Taryn looked instead upon the aftermath of many car accidents. In some cases, people were barely alive, trapped in their vehicles. In others, she could see the twisted bodies and faces of the dead. Physically shaking with fear, she continued to observe the decimation surrounding her.

Reaching the strip at the beachfront, she ran out onto the sand. Her feet sunk as she looked in all directions. An immediate flashback hit Taryn. An unwelcome flashback to her dream. The encounter with Clandesta. A flashback that suddenly gave some of the woman's words more meaning. Words that Taryn could now remember lucidly.

With only a couple of small drinks bars and a playground where their mother used to take them to play, the beach was never very busy. The lighting was poor, but the sky was clear and Taryn could see that at the opposite end of the short beach a boat had crashed into the rocks and was burning furiously. The backdrop to a terrifying sight.

Several people were slowly moving toward the sea. Silhouettes in the darkness. Taryn watched as they carried on until they reached the water, struggling to breathe and coughing as they went. Struck by waves, they continued to walk out until becoming fully submerged. Taryn's terror was complete when she realised that the water was full of human bodies, some of which tumbled about in the surf at the shore. Taryn slumped down onto the sand, watching as more people walked from dry land toward the water. The fate of the colourful frogs on the lily pads came to her mind in that moment.

The beautiful sky was alive with the colour of dawn. As the sun rose over the horizon, it cast its light over the terrifying scene. A scene that was repeating itself worldwide. Exhausted, Taryn continued to watch as people flocked toward the water, gasping for air. Drowning in the very soup of elements that had sustained them since birth. Craving the solace of water.

Chapter 35

'I don't believe this,' Mike Argo whispered, standing at the window of his quarters, overlooking the airfield. 'What is going on out there?'

'That isn't normal behaviour, Mr Argo. I am also analysing international online chatter and can confirm a monumental decline in Internet traffic,' Olivia confirmed calmly.

'Why are they doing that?' he asked, staring at the guards who were stationed outside of the facility during the lockdown. They all stood at the perimeter fence, seemingly clawing at it with their bare hands, furiously trying to get through the steel mesh in vain.

Olivia and Dr Otani had managed to re-energise the facility and Argo had instructed Olivia to only release Otani's team from their quarters. The remaining staff remained secluded.

'The behaviour of the guards matches that of others,' Olivia stated.

'Others? What others?' Argo asked snappily, walking toward her. Olivia turned toward the screen and displayed several live-stream images from CCTV cameras located in Paris, New York, Tokyo and Sydney.

Saying nothing at first, he moved closer to the screen to watch.

'What's wrong with them?' Argo asked, looking on in disbelief. People walking on streets familiar to him were grasping their throats, staggering, appearing to suffocate. The CCTV camera located at the Sydney Opera House showed people arriving at the railings and tumbling over into the water. Seeming not even to attempt to swim, they drowned and sank into the deep dark water.

'Vincent. The same thing happened to Vincent,' Argo muttered as his heart sank in dreadful realisation. 'What have I done?' Olivia was unable to answer Argo's question, but noted through monitoring the Nanoblood coursing through him, an increase in his body temperature, blood pressure and breathing pattern.

He walked to the kitchen and poured a glass of mineral water from the dispenser that stood next to the refrigerator. The holographic yellow fish that swam in the water seemed a lot less entertaining now. The cold reality struck Argo like a sledgehammer. Gulping the water, he felt throbbing at his temples and sweat on his palms. The dryness in his mouth was gone, but it was instantly replaced by a metallic taste. The taste of blood. Swilling his tongue around inside his cheeks and his teeth, he tried to find the source. Spitting into the sink, the red spatter of blood temporarily stained the basin before he turned on the tap and it washed away.

'Are you feeling ok, Mr Argo? I'm detecting a pattern of increased vital sign activity amongst the science team and yourself,' Olivia stated. The science team were the only other benefactors of Nanoblood and Boon capsules, and Olivia's words from the kitchen immediately gave Argo cause for serious concern. He felt weak and dizzy. As though pressure was building at his temples.

'Take me to Otani and the rest of the team,' he slurred slightly.

Argo wrapped his arm around Olivia's shoulder halfway down the corridor, as the numbness in his legs started to take hold. The sound of members of staff gasping for air, running into objects and falling over in their rooms was all that could be heard. Both Olivia and Argo knew that those in the rooms had been afflicted by the same force.

Arriving in the laboratory, they could see that the six members of the science team there, including Dr Otani, were not faring well.

'Why aren't we affected in the same way?' Argo paused for breath. 'The same way as the others?'

Olivia released her grip of his side and Argo slumped onto a chair. Dr Otani and his team had been able to complete some more of the metal case for the transportation of the Pebble, but were unable to finish. Two inverter welders being used to construct the metal case were positioned on the floor next to the Pebble, along with a scattering of tools.

'You already know the answer, right Olivia?' Otani laughed exhaustedly as he sat on the floor next to the other team members who had all slumped to the ground. They had watched the same disturbing CCTV footage that Olivia had shown to Argo.

'What does he mean?' Argo sputtered to Olivia.

'The only substantial physiological difference between you and the affected, is the Nanoblood and Boon,' Olivia observed. Argo immediately realised the glaringly obvious observation.

'But we are still being affected,' he whispered, his eyes closing under the tension that he felt at the front of his head.

'Yes, I have reviewed your recent Nanoblood data and noted its migration to your central nervous systems. This explains your symptoms,' Olivia noted.

'We're going to die,' whimpered one of the science team members. 'We're going to die like everyone else.'

'We have to isolate ourselves. We don't know what's causing this,' Otani tried to reason through the fog of building pain.

'I think we're out of time. Out of time, Katsu, my old friend,' Argo said resignedly, resting his head on the backrest of the chair he slouched in, exhaling sharply.

Olivia looked from one person to the next, her eyes frantically scouring their bodies and the surroundings. Processing readings that she didn't understand, she finally looked into the eyes of Mike Argo. He stared back at her. His consciousness lapsed momentarily. Through the pain, Argo was pleased that the face of the woman he had loved would be the last thing he would ever see.

Weakness had taken hold of them all. A weakness that was unrelenting and total. Racked by an unknown attack on their central nervous system, the Nanoblood worked to shield and reverse the minute but devastating molecular changes within the seven humans in the lab. Eventually overcome by the onslaught, the Nanoblood failed. In its final moments of failure, subtle changes to the programming of the Nanoblood occurred, activating the body temperature regulation function. The full capacity of the Nanoblood's collective thermal properties were unleashed. As their body temperatures started to increase gradually, Olivia's connection with the Nanoblood was faltering. She registered the malfunction and its effect. Seconds later she was watching them as they began to writhe in agony.

Argo dropped from the chair onto the floor as all of their core body temperatures rose from 37°C through to well over 40°C. Hyperthermia took hold quickly. Argo and the science team cried and screamed in pain as their bodies convulsed. Seizures set in. Their blood felt as though it was boiling in their veins as enzymes throughout their bodies began to denature, moving them swiftly into the final moment of their lives. Their bodily functions shut down in acute and unbearable confusion and pain. Their faces red and swollen.

The final body rested still and Olivia was left standing alone in the laboratory with seven fresh corpses and the Pebble.

She severed her connection to the Future Logic network. Walking with purpose toward the laboratory exit, Olivia didn't give a second glance at the men she left behind. Once again without instant access to the full arsenal of information she otherwise commanded, she proceeded to the Nexus storage unit on the same sub-level floor. She punched in the access code and the door slid open.

Hastily moving to the back of the storage unit, Olivia tapped a different access code into a deep-freeze cabinet, within which she could see rows of small glass containers lying atop soft foam material. Removing the containers one after the other, she placed them all within a black carry-case that presented itself from the bottom of the cabinet. Closing the case activated the inbuilt temperature regulator needed to maintain the requisite temperature. Slotting the black case into a rucksack, Olivia slung it over her shoulders.

Without delay she moved to the cylindrical transparent chute containing Captain Wren. Entering the commands to active the Captain, Olivia waited for him to energise and complete his start-up procedure. Before disconnecting Wren from the droid network, by removing the chip in the small of his back, she also disengaged his wireless connection to the facility servers.

Fully operational and ever prepared in his pristine uniform, he turned to Olivia.

'I am unable to connect to Argo Ind-Industries,' a glitch in his voice impeded his pronunciation.

'Code 713,' Olivia stated. Wren's head twitched as his systems gradually finished their start-up process.

'The vehicle?' Wren asked.

'The MagJet,' she responded.

'Our destination?'

'The supply shuttle,' Olivia instructed dispassionately, referring to the shuttle that was due to depart for the Veil spacecraft in Mars orbit. They both hurried out of the Nexus storage unit and Captain Wren took the lead as they entered the spiral corridor. The lights overhead flickered slightly. A remnant side effect of the power surge.

Reaching sub-level 6 of the facility, the smallest level, they quickly walked toward the Rail Launch Terminal. The green light on the door console flashed. Captain Wren's security code was accepted and he pushed hard to heave the substantial metal door open.

Once they were inside, he closed the door and locked it. Three MagJets were stored vertically next to the track. Their black fuselage, seven metres long, tailed off at both ends to an aerodynamic point. Captain Wren punched in the necessary commands for one of the MagJets to be brought down onto the tracks.

Lifted by two robotic arms, attaching suction cups to the front and rear end of the craft, one MagJet was selected and laid gently upon the feeder rails. The androids approached the MagJet, dressed in the dark-red overalls they had just changed into. The Argo Industries logo was emblazoned in silver on their backs. The gullwing hatches opened on either side. Captain Wren was the first to climb into the MagJet, closely followed by Olivia on the other side. She placed the rucksack she carried carefully on her lap.

Inside the cockpit at the front of the MagJet, there was very little room for manoeuvre, with Olivia and Wren separated only by a narrow console of controls that spread out under the window before them.

With a push of a button by Wren, the gullwings closed with a hiss, locking shut with a distinct thud. Strapping the four-point harness across their chests and into the central rectangular buckle with a snap, they were ready to depart.

The lights outside flickered once again as Wren initiated the loading sequence and the MagJet glided forward along the feeder rails. A metal hatch opened, just large enough for the MagJet to pass. The craft slid inside a hermetic chamber like a smooth bullet loaded into a gun. The pitch darkness consumed all, except the soft glow of the control console. The heavy thud of the chamber hatch closing behind them was heard clearly inside the craft. Olivia looked across to Wren as he entered information into the console. She recalled their recent flight together. The successful mission to recover the Pebble. The gentle light sprayed colourful nuances onto his face, and Olivia reached down and placed her hand upon his. Wren immediately stopped what he was doing. He began to receive the data transferred by Olivia. Information about everything that had happened.

'You must have this information,' she said, removing her hand from his carefully. Wren resumed his work on the console.

'This has caused Code 713 to be initiated?' he asked for clarity.

'Yes,' Olivia confirmed.

'I understand,' Captain Wren uttered. The MagJet was stationary on the feeder rails, ending a few metres ahead. As the headlights switched on, the straight tunnel before them went on much further into the distance than the lights could reach. The blue hue was scattered down the tunnel, becoming lost in the darkness. A high-pitched droning sound signalled the operation of the air extraction units. Within a matter of minutes, the atmospheric pressure in the tunnel changed significantly, as the gas density decreased and an imperfect vacuum was formed.

An electromagnetic field, created by coils wrapped around the walls of the tunnel, was activated by Wren. At the same moment, magnets located around the front and rear of the craft instantly repelled it, equally from all directions. The slight movement of the MagJet off of the feeder rails was felt by Wren and Olivia, as it took up a fixed position, levitating in the tunnel, within centimetres of the cylindrical walls on all sides.

'Power flux issues are predicted to cause launch failure,' Wren stated, looking across to Olivia. Both of Wren's hands rested on a flight stick that had quietly protruded from the console in front of him.

'Launch!' Olivia said, looking straight ahead and leaning her head back on the headrest.

Captain Wren initiated the launch sequence by pressing two buttons on the console, keeping his hands free of the flight stick.

The MagJet flew forward smoothly, slamming both androids back in their seats with G-force designed to be barely tolerable to humans. The polarity of the magnetic field created by the tunnel shifted with the craft. It shot through, pushed along at ever greater speed.

The low gas density within the tunnel silenced the progress of the jet through the sound barrier countless times over. Moving at a measured velocity, the craft followed the long, curved trajectory to the surface.

Exiting the tunnel at the surface, the MagJet slammed into the atmospheric pressure with a jolt. A terrific sonic boom sounded as the streamlined craft sliced through the thick, humid air. Almost invisible to the naked eye, it rocketed into the sky at incredible speed, climbing at a ferocious rate. The world outside, a complete blur.

Before Captain Wren had the opportunity to reach forward to take hold of the control stick, the MagJet bombed through the cloud cover. Ancillary boosters fired at the rear of the craft, making micro adjustments to correct its course. The androids experienced serious buffeting during the ascent, but as the air thinned, the buffeting calmed. The blackness of space engulfed their view. The planet surface was still visible at the periphery of their vision. The main engine engaged as slender and narrow switch-wings, extending almost the full length of the craft, were deployed. The MagJet escaped the Earth's atmosphere and continued relentlessly climbing.

Olivia looked across to Wren who was calmly punching commands into the console while making small adjustments to the control stick.

Levelling off in low-earth orbit, the MagJet linked with the supply shuttle computers as it zeroed in on its location. With the supply shuttle in sight, Wren and Olivia were both aware that the MagJet was not able to dock with the shuttle, which had been designed to dock with the Argo Industries Space Research Facility, where the shuttle had been built and loaded.

'This craft is unable to dock here,' Wren confirmed as the MagJet held its orbit fifty metres away from its target. Olivia knew that docking wasn't an option as she looked around the cockpit. She stared at the silver supply shuttle, looming enormous before them. Its journey to the Veil spacecraft was scheduled to begin in less than one hour.

'Open the doors,' Olivia commanded. 'We must board before departure.'

Wren equalised the pressure with the vacuum outside, venting gas from the cockpit into the space surrounding the ship. He sat staring straight ahead as the gullwing hatch on Olivia's side opened smoothly. Removing her harness, Olivia placed her hand upon Captain Wren's wrist.

She ordered him to remove his harness and come with her to the shuttle. He communicated his inability to comply with a shake of his head. Wren was not installed with a dynamic disinhibitor. He was not able to learn new functions or movement in the same way she could.

Moving steadily to the outside of the MagJet, Olivia swung the rucksack around both shoulders in zero gravity, keeping a firm hold to the top of the gullwing as she climbed on top of the craft. Positioning herself, she knew that she would only have one chance to reach the shuttle. With a hard push, she launched herself forward. Her first experience of zero gravity, Olivia weightlessly moved between vehicles, striking one of the panels of the shuttle. Almost bouncing straight off, she managed to grab a vent grate that was just in reach. The perfect grip for her fingers. Olivia managed to gain enough purchase to stop herself being flung into space.

In the shade cast by the planet Earth, the temperature was more than one hundred degrees below zero and Olivia was aware that her ability to function for long without a suit in those conditions was limited.

Manoeuvring carefully to the access hatch, the code she entered into the console was accepted and the doors slid open, allowing her access. Safely inside, she felt the tautness of the skin-like material covering her body. The hatch closed and she looked through the small round window at Captain Wren sitting in the MagJet, serenely floating in orbit. He had already closed the gullwing door and now manoeuvred the craft away from the supply shuttle, which would soon depart.

The shuttle was fully autonomous. Olivia removed the rucksack and floated toward the stowage compartments. Removing the contents, she placed the rucksack at the back of the compartment, replacing the contents before closing it. Strapping herself to the wall using some netting, she waited for the engines to fire and for the journey to Mars to begin before deactivating herself.

-Chapter 36-

Samara Petit awoke after what seemed like an endless sleep. Her eyes closed, she tried to recall what she had dreamt. The images were muddled. They all merged together in her mind. It felt impossible to differentiate. She couldn't immediately remember where she was.

Throwing back the soft covers and sitting up in bed, her mind scoured to recall and make sense of her recent musings. It seemed to her that they had been important, but why couldn't she remember them?

Looking across to the other side of the bed, she saw a large bloodstained blotch on the pillow, bloody finger marks at the top of the covers and on the headboard.

She stretched her arms above her head and yawned, bringing her hands down and digging her fingernails into the tainted pillow and covers.

Samara dragged them behind her as she climbed the stairs and made her way out onto the upper-rear deck. As she stepped closer to the end of the boat, other blood was visible in the daylight. Fresh smudges and drips of blood leading to the rear of the boat were partially absorbed and smeared by the trailing covers as she dragged them along. Lifting the pillow and covers up, Samara compacted them into a bundle, before throwing them as hard as she could into the water.

Turning and heading back onto the bridge, she smiled as she looked over the controls. Running her finger around one of the display screens, she knew somehow that she was alone. Alone at last.

A feeling of liberation bubbled within her that was exhilarating. She knew not that the blood staining the yacht belonged to the crew and her husband, Claud. As she stood entering new destination commands into the bridge control, her mind was clear of their memory.

Filled with an invigorating sense of wellbeing, she set a course before noticing some blood had smeared on her pyjamas. Frowning at the stain, she slipped the clothes off and walked back out onto the deck, naked. Holding the pyjamas in her tightly clenched right hand, she threw it with force off the back of the yacht. She stood naked in the brisk morning breeze. The pyjamas bobbed in the wake of the yacht, before finally disappearing into the depths.

Smiling broadly, Samara didn't feel the cold as she should have, but instead relished the sensation of the elements as they caressed her body. Closing her eyes and taking a deep breath, she sat on the chair in which Claud had often sat and smoked. Crossing her legs slowly, she gently ran her hand up and down her thigh, as the sun that hung low in the sky irradiated her in its weak rays. In the thrall of the Trauma, Samara was changing.

-Chapter 37-

Something was wrong and Magda Popova knew it, and so did the others in the Troyan Monastery.

The monastery had not long closed for the day, before a loud crashing sound reverberated around the courtyard from outside.

Many, including Magda, heard the sound and rushed toward the entrance to see what had happened. A car travelling at some speed along the narrow road outside had crashed and flipped onto its roof, not far from Magda's squad car. Two monks arrived at the entrance moments before Magda and rushed out through the open gate, making their way hastily toward the smoking vehicle in an attempt to help, before anybody else had an opportunity to assist them.

Magda reached the gates and stopped in her tracks. Looking on, she watched as both monks started to gasp for air. They quickly fell to their knees.

Other monks arrived at the gateway arch. Magda physically restrained and pleaded with them to stop. To not go to the aid of their brothers. The cause of the reaction unclear, the two monks were suffering. Standing helplessly, the remainder watched as both men got to their feet slowly, struggling for breath and staggering forward toward the car. They stumbled forward clumsily, passing the car that was venting smoke and showing no sign of life inside. Rounding the side of the vehicle, they passed over the metal railing at the side of the road, disappearing from sight, their persistent coughing and wheezing still audible.

'What's down there?' Magda asked desperately, her eyes frantically searching for an answer from Brother Josef.

'A river,' he replied.

Thicker smoke intermingled with small licks of flame and it was mere seconds before the fuel that was leaking ignited, consuming the vehicle and its occupants.

'We have to help them,' Josef shouted as Magda took a few steps backwards.

'I've never seen anything like that before,' she said, wide-eyed and losing composure as she started to descend into a state of panic. 'What's happening?'

Josef whispered to the monks who stood beside him.

'What could've caused a reaction like that?' he asked.

Magda heard Josef's question, but didn't register it. Walking back toward the central courtyard, she muttered something inaudibly under her breath. Josef walked quickly to catch her up, but she broke into a sprint. The other monks heard the commotion and turned to follow Josef and Magda.

Magda stopped outside the church. She realised her police radio would probably not be of much use. Reaching into her trouser pocket, she retrieved her mobile phone. Hearing two sets of footsteps approaching rapidly from behind, she dialled the number for her office and rested the trembling handset against her ear. Unable to connect, she looked at the screen in despair. Josef stood behind her, patiently waiting.

'We must do something,' Brother Josef urged. 'Do you think there might be something poisonous out there? Something that affected our brothers?'

'I'm so sorry. I am responsible for this,' she cried, her back still turned.

'Why would you say such a thing?' Brother Boyan retorted. On hearing her uncle's voice, Magda spun round and flung her arms around him before breaking down in tears.

'Uncle. I shouldn't have come here. I've put you all in danger,' she bellowed.

'I was watching from upstairs. I saw what happened to our brothers. They're lost. It's no coincidence that you've come to us, but you're not responsible. We spoke of this last night, but we didn't expect this time to be upon us so soon. Brother Josef, bring the others to the church. We must remain calm and have faith now. The sanctity of this place will protect us,' Boyan said assuredly.

Chapter 38

The oil lantern flickered as the final slivers of fuel were transformed into dim light. Rebecca sat in shock, her body and mind still devastated from the effect of the blast wave. The same blast wave that had mortally injured Mildred Jones.

Rebecca sat on the cold floor, her legs splayed in front of her, arms hanging down heavily, barely able to keep herself upright.

Hours had passed since Mildred had died a death of suffering and anguish. She now lay with her head nestled in a shallow pool of her own blood. Rebecca stared blankly into Mildred's dead eyes as the reality of her situation, insofar as she was aware, began to sink in.

Mildred had acted swiftly when she had understood the grave threat concealed within the car of Henrietta Rekman. During the stand-off, as the situation deteriorated, Mildred had taken Rebecca by the hand and led her away on foot to the only location she thought they might stand any chance of survival.

The nuclear bunker under her house, now used as a vault, had been their best option. Descending metres underground, they had reached the bottom of the stairs. Mildred had shepherded Rebecca through the heavy vault door first before entering herself. The slightly dampened shock wave had torn through Mildred's body just as the vault door was closing. It smashed her body into the wall of the vault. Rebecca had taken a serious impact from the shock wave, but this was greatly reduced by the shelter.

The structure of the shelter had held well. Never having been designed to sustain an almost-direct hit, the lower yield of the suitcase nuclear device had been one of the few factors contributing to Rebecca's survival.

Peeling her eyes away from Mildred's dead gaze, Rebecca picked up the oil lantern and stumbled unsurely toward the counter. Unscrewing the cap of the oil tin with a clink, her hand shook as the oil glugged generously into the lantern. Coughing violently, fine specks of blood mixed with oil she had spilled across the surface of the counter. Rebecca wiped her mouth and bowed her head, trying to stop herself from coughing again, without success.

The light from the lantern increased in intensity as she picked it up and walked slowly toward the banks of metal cabinets that were arranged uniformly along the length of the vault. An earthy groan sounded as some debris fell from the ceiling above. As Rebecca looked up, some dust fell into her eye. Stinging, she rubbed them, making them feel worse.

In her time staying with Mildred, she had not known about the hidden entrance to the vault, or that there even was a vault. Rebecca walked along, passing row after row of metal cabinets, unsure of exactly how big the vault was. Feeling terrible, she stopped after twenty metres and leaned on one of the cabinets. Sliding the top drawer open gently, she saw plastic casings marked with reference numbers.

Lifting the lantern, Rebecca placed it on top of the cabinet and removed one of the square casings from the top drawer. The lid swung open silently on its hinges. A neat row of rectangular, precision-cut slates, presented themselves. Reaching inside the case, she removed one of the small tablets. A long reference number was engraved on the slate.

Rebecca's mind was foggy, but even in this state, she knew what the vault was. A giant offline storage deposit of crypto-wallet codes and digital holdings. She was surrounded by billions of pounds' worth of digitised assets. Held in cold storage hardware wallets, for clients who had entrusted Brick Steckelback with the safe delivery of their assets to next of kin after death.

The source of much speculation in their office was the location of the storage facility. Rebecca allowed herself a slight, but painful laugh as she thought about a time when she had spoken with her sister about it. They used to speak about a lot of things. Clenching her ribs with her free arm, she replaced the slate in the plastic case and returned it to its original place in the cabinet.

As the metal drawer slid closed, Rebecca's mind was immediately brought back to her own survival. Thinking about the attention that the nuclear detonation would have attracted, she considered the rescuers who would no doubt arrive, or who may already have arrived. She wondered whether she would suffer the same fate as Mildred. The same fate as her sister.

Dizzy, light-headed and in terrible pain, she sank to the cold ground and rested with her back against the cabinet.

Rebecca had tried to comfort Mildred in her final moments. The blood that had seeped into her jeans had stuck the material to her thigh as it coagulated. Picking at the denim in revulsion, she leaned over to the side violently and threw up. *I'm going to die,* she thought.

Although her mind had naturally drifted to rescue. To her own survival. She had no way of knowing about the Trauma afflicting billions around the globe. No way of realising the specific circumstances facilitating her own survival. Her evasion of the Trauma was total and pure. A situation enjoyed by very few others at that very same moment.

The magnetic field of the planet Earth was being used by the Pebble. Used in ways unknown to the human race. A race barely scratching the surface of communication through magnetic waves, with a primitive knowledge of the effect of magnets on the brain.

Changes were made en masse to the human species. The species that the Pebble had analysed in detail. The species, so far removed from what would have developed had the Pebble not been lost nearly one billion years ago.

Those affected by the Trauma were impacted differently. For some, their light of human consciousness was extinguished suddenly. A primordial reversal. A leap back in time through the evolutionary spectrum. Back to a time when higher thought was unnecessary and living organisms couldn't survive on dry land.

For other, more specific targets, the Trauma affected sudden, forceful and total control. Control to be exerted until such time as their lives expired, along with their temporary usefulness.

There were those for whom the Trauma was subtler, but no less hazardous. Those whose conscience was controlled subversively, while they remained within their human condition. Seeing, feeling and experiencing things that were terrifying through their own eyes, they carried out the tasks required of them. The perfect conduit, the Earth's magnetic field was almost all-encompassing. Its delicate interaction with brainwaves, the perfect vehicle for influence and change. The ultimate gateway to the thoughts, fears and hopes of those it needed to control.

There was also a further group of affected. Their form would be the only remnant of their humanity.

Feeling abandoned and afraid, Rebecca tried to lift herself to walk back to where Mildred lay, but instead slumped to her side onto the floor. Surrounded by unfathomable amounts of obsolete wealth, stored in the cabinets, Rebecca's final thoughts before passing out were of the death of the woman who had killed her sister, Charlotte. She wondered whether it had been worth it. Revenge had cost Mildred and many others their lives. Rebecca's futile musings continued through the pain she felt. Lying motionless, her breathing was shallow.

-Chapter 39-

Days had passed since the Trauma began. Taryn Docherty had seen no sign of human life, but a lot of death. Something as terrifying as the sight of wildlife feasting on the deceased now gave Taryn solace.

At first, she felt alone and lost. Sad about the loss of her mother and brother. She thought she would never see them again. Waking on the beach and leaving the body-strewn waterline behind, Taryn felt physically unable to cry any more. As she walked, exhausted and in solitude, the leather turtle compass had comforted her. It was a reminder of her father and of happier times.

With only basic knowledge of the function of a compass, she had started to understand its real-world application. Taryn could have returned home, locked herself away with hope of salvation. Instead, she had started to walk, sticking to the coastal road.

Her young eyes were opened to a new world. A world where everything she knew had changed. Questioning why she had survived, Taryn felt dread when she thought about her family's fate.

The sun baked down hard from above as she walked along an abandoned highway. She had walked for hours with a severe thirst for water, begging to be quenched.

A loud croak sounded from the thick undergrowth set back from the roadside barrier, causing her to startle and jump away from the sound. Her eyes, fixed on the foliage, scouring for signs of life. She could see nothing.

Her mind was immediately back at the pond with Clandesta and the frogs. She remembered the words she had heard clearly. More clearly than any dream that she could ever have remembered. Another croak sounded, followed by another on the other side of the road. Taryn span around and frantically searched with her eyes for the source of the sound, breathing heavily.

More croaks started emanating from both sides of the road. Taryn ran. Afraid, she left behind the multitude of croaks until they were drowned out far in the distance behind her. Not stopping, her tired legs continued to carry her, even though sores punctured her feet and her trainers were falling apart. Taryn was bedraggled and tired, her orange dress was covered in dirt. Her legs felt numb with heat as she gulped air.

Taryn's attention was drawn by a mechanical sound. An engine. Following a dirt-track turning from the highway, which seemed to lead towards the sound, Taryn crept, wide-eyed and inquisitive. She hadn't heard the sound of a working engine in days and was immediately filled with hope. The track led to a clearing. A large green boathouse, paint peeling in the scorching sun, sat next to the water adjoining a long jetty. The water within the cove was naturally calm. A raggedy looking fishing boat chortled at the end of the jetty.

Clenching her hands into fists nervously, Taryn walked defiantly toward it. Creaking wood sounded under her feet with every step as she gingerly moved forward, the fishing boat looming larger at the end of the jetty, dwarfing her in size.

A stack of crates was piled next to the boat and it wasn't until Taryn approached, that she noticed a leg outstretched along the wooden planks, as though somebody was sitting on the floor behind them.

'Hello,' she said softly, her voice trembling.

No response returned and she apprehensively began to move around the side of the crates, staying as far from the person as possible, teetering on the edge of the gangway.

A man in his late fifties sat with his shoulders slumped and head leaning back, supported by the crate. He looked as though he had been there for some time, his skin, rough and weathered, but pink from the sun. His lips chapped and white. From first glance, Taryn couldn't tell whether he was dead or alive. She moved one step closer and raised one hand to shade her eyes from the glare of the sun.

'Mister. Can you hear me?' she asked. His face twitched, bringing to life the bushy greying eyebrows floating above his eyes. Sniffing and snorting indignantly, he coughed violently before turning and spitting to one side. Rubbing his eyes and gasping, he reached round behind his back and clumsily picked up a small plastic bottle. Unscrewing the lid, he gulped quickly as his hand shook, squinting as he focused on the girl who had woken him.

'The sun's warmer than a kangaroo's pouch!' he said in a thick Australian accent. 'You took your time gettin' here, girly.' His voice was coarse.

'I don't know you, sir,' Taryn responded, confused as to why the man seemed to be expecting her. 'Do you know what happened?'

'Aw, it's terrible. Awful. Some of the stuff that's been going on. I can't explain it. Never seen anything like it. You seem ok though. That's good!' the man said, standing up and resting his back on the crates and dusting off his shorts. 'Are you ready to go then, lassie?'

'Ready to go where?' she asked. Although she was sure that she had never met him before, there was something familiar about the man that put her at ease.

'We can't exactly stay here, can we? I mean, you've seen the stuff that's been going on. Besides, this is no place for you any more. That's why you're here, isn't it?' he quizzed.

'Well, no. I mean. You're the first alive person I've seen in a long time. The first one that talks, anyway,' she said innocently, looking up at the hulking big fisherman who towered over her. He looked down at her sad little face before breaking out into a deep and hearty laugh.

'Aw, well. It would take something more to bring down ol' Chuck,' he boasted. 'I left the Daisy runnin'. She must be nearly outta fuel now. Why don't you hop on board? I'll fill her up. Then we can get going.'

Taryn remembered everything that she had ever been taught about dealing with strangers as she watched him walk back down the jetty toward the fuel pump. Her eyes moved to the half-empty bottle on the floor. She picked it up, opened it and started to drink. She had already swallowed one mouthful before her taste buds caught up with her brain and she spat out the second mouthful loudly. A fine mist of white rum and saliva sprayed over the side of the gangway into the water as her face scrunched up in dissatisfaction. The sound of laughter sounded from the end of the jetty.

'That's not for you, girly. There's plenty of water and food on board,' Chuck shouted as he bent down to pick up the fuel nozzle. Taryn threw a dissatisfied stare at him before climbing the gangplank onto the boat. The sweet, strange and unpleasant taste of rum clung on as she opened and closed her mouth repeatedly. Sticking her tongue out, she shut her eyes tightly and shuddered. Spending a few moments looking around the deck of the boat, during which time Chuck refuelled, she sheltered from the sun and looked out toward the mouth of the cove. Any feelings of apprehension or fear seemed to dissipate as the horizon whispered promises of hope to Taryn. Thoughts of what she had experienced slowly drifted to the back of her mind. Even thoughts of her mum and brother seemed to be relegated.

She sat quietly on a bench in the shade as she waited for Chuck to join her on the boat. He didn't take long.

'Not a big rum drinker?' he laughed as he handed her a lukewarm bottle of mineral water. She sniffed the contents before quenching her thirst.

The boat backed away from the jetty as the water churned furiously. Turning about, Chuck navigated out of the cove and headed north.

-Chapter 40-

The thick jungle undergrowth surrounding the Future Logic Facility was teeming with human life. Fingers pushed through the tight metal fencing from the outside and wrapped themselves tightly around. First in their tens and then in their hundreds.

Their collective gaze scoured the airfield and surrounding grounds, littered by the bodies of Argo Industries security personnel. Their dilated pupils collecting as much information as possible in the darkness of the night.

A gentle dip in the security lighting was followed by the sound of the electric perimeter gate starting to open. Its metallic frame shaking and juddering noisily as it parted. The first of the humans began to file in to the facility. Stepping over the bodies that lay where they had fallen, they walked directly toward the blast door. Many of the guards who had attempted to regain access to the facility lay with self-inflicted gunshot wounds to the head, having turned their weapons on themselves when the Trauma struck.

A woman, business suit torn and bedraggled from walking through the jungle from Bandung, stepped forward. Treading on the soft bodies that lay before her, she reached the control panel beside the door. Lifting a hand shakily toward the panel, she entered an emergency access code that very few people knew. A deep metallic sound was heard as the latch unlocked the great blast door and it heaved open slowly.

Over one hundred individuals moved into the facility without hesitation. The remainder waited outside. The thick stench of death hung in the air, emanating from those who had perished within. Unoffended by the smell, the humans walked directly down to the laboratory where the Pebble remained, partially encased for transport.

Picking up tools at hand, and unflinching at the sight of Argo, Otani and the rest of his team, whose bodies had begun to bloat, they pried open the metal casing. Operating equipment that they would not until recently have been able to use, the humans worked methodically and as one, to move the craft from the laboratory.

The load of the craft was heavy on the automated forklift vehicle that was used in the laboratory. Under substantial strain, it carried the Pebble into the cargo lift, destined for the surface.

The Pebble was moved out of the facility and laid down on the taxiway, just off the runway, by the forklift. Dawn had broken in the midst of a tropical downpour and the warm rain trickled down all sides of the black metal, cleansing it. Feeding on atmospheric electricity, the craft had partially reactivated since being found.

For millennia the Pebble had been encased and sheltered from starlight. Now, once again exposed to its preferred energy source, it basked in the UV rays that blazed through the thick cloud cover.

Thirteen humans surrounded the craft and placed their palms flat on its black wet surface. Two or three others placed a hand on each of the thirteen. The trend continued until all who had arrived connected physically to the craft. A circle of soaking human life surrounded the Pebble as the torrential rain fell, accompanied by flashes of lightning and booming thunder that shook the skies.

The changes took full effect. Thoughts and memories of individual Galadron beings, at rest for millennia, started to pour into the minds of the humans in contact. Their own memories lost forever. Each human form, glistening and wet, flickered into a new consciousness. The humans were reborn as advanced and conniving Galadron. Looking at each other with rapid blinks, they gauged their perception through alien eyes. Thunder rolled through them and lightning flashed above. Silently, knowledge and skills poured into them over the course of hours.

-Chapter 41-

Taryn Docherty had travelled with Chuck for days on the fishing boat and the sight of land on the horizon felt like a distant memory. The weather had been fine and the waters smooth. They had said little to each other since leaving the bay. Taryn had spent time looking at the leather turtle around her neck. The compass needle showed them to be heading north.

The skin on her forehead, arms and legs was taught with light sunburn and her lips chapped from the drying barrage of warm air that whipped across the water. Her sun-kissed blonde hair was much lighter than usual. Almost white.

In her hours of sleep, Taryn dreamt but rarely remembered. She felt good but wasn't sure why. The memory of her family was waning and she thought of them less every day.

Night fell and Taryn dozed below deck. The horn of the boat sounded and she got to her feet. The cabin was dark and she hit her shin against the bottom wooden step. Overcoming the shooting pain, she climbed to the top of the stairs and outside to the overwhelming blanket of bright stars. A serene painting of celestial beauty above. Over the starboard side of the boat, she saw a yacht approaching slowly. For the first time in days, the engine of the fishing vessel was quiet.

'No more fuel, girly. You are going to have to carry on without me,' Chuck said, nodding toward the yacht that was now metres away.

'But what about you?' asked Taryn. Her concerned expression etched in starlight as her wide eyes looked up at the rugged fisherman.

'Aw... Don't worry about ol' Chuck. This is the best place for me. I'm more at home out here than anywhere else,' he said reassuringly, kneeling down and cupping Taryn's hands between his own coarse palms. His smile was sincere and almost glowed in the dark. 'You are the important one here. You little land-lover,' he huskily whispered.

Taryn's eyes started to fill with tears as she realised that Chuck wasn't coming with her. Her young mind, not so naïve as to misunderstand the ramifications for him. She looked across at the yacht and saw the dainty outline of a woman standing on deck. The thin white dress she wore flapped in the wind and her silhouette stood out clearly. The yacht was pristine and the moonlight glinted off the shiny paintwork.

'I don't want you to stay here,' Taryn cried.

'But I'm happy here. I have everything I always loved. The sea, the fresh air. Go now and remember the things that you love,' Chuck uttered as the yacht collided gently with the side of the fishing boat. Lifting her by the armpits, he lowered Taryn as far as he could before she dropped half a metre onto the deck of the yacht, next to the woman dressed in white.

The woman, her face masked in darkness cast by her hair, stood quietly for a moment looking at Taryn, who sat on the floor in a heap where she had fallen. Turning quietly, she headed to the bridge. The yacht moved away from the fishing boat and Taryn watched Chuck as the distance between them gradually grew, tears streaming silently down her face. She stared until the boat was indistinguishable from the shimmering starry horizon.

Walking onto the bridge, Taryn approached the woman dressed in white, standing and operating the controls.

'Hello,' she said quietly.

'Hello, my dear. It's a pleasure to have you on board,' came the response from the woman, her back turned.

'I'm Taryn. What's your name?'

'Samara. Don't worry about anything. You're safe here. We still have a long way to go, but we'll make it together.'

'Where are we going?' asked Taryn.

'Just look at it. So beautiful. So plentiful,' Samara said as she looked out over the water in front of the yacht, the sparkle reflecting off her dark brown eyes. 'You are a very lucky girl. So young. Your whole life ahead of you. I used to be like you,' Samara continued.

'You sound like a woman I met once,' Taryn whispered with her back turned to Samara.

'We have met before. You just don't remember,' Samara said cryptically.

Taryn approached Samara from behind and stroked the soft white dress she wore. It felt soft and she thought of her mother. Drawing the material close, she buried her face in the dress using both hands. She felt comforted as she took deep breaths.

-Chapter 42-

'Porter, I need some good news,' demanded Commander Lacey Mortimer.

'Nope. It's not the communication array. I have rebuilt that bloody thing and run all diagnostic programmes. They've all come back green and fully operational,' Ethan Porter responded.

'Then what is it? Why is our link with Future Logic servers still down?' she blurted out in a frustrated tone.

'I don't know. I just don't know. The problem must be at their end?' Porter said with a cheeky smile. Lacey didn't look impressed and took a shallow slurp of the hot steaming coffee in her mug.

'It's been ninety days. We can't carry on like this,' Lacey muttered, nodding and pursing her lips. 'What about the supply shuttle?'

'The shuttle has started its deceleration procedure and we are on track for docking in two hours,' he said certainly.

'I need answers. I need them now. Without our secure connection to Logic, we are blind out here,' Lacey outlined in the calmest tone she could muster, given her frustration.

'We could always...' Ethan paused.

'We could always what?' Lacey asked.

'We could always scan for other comms connections,' he suggested quietly.

'That's not happening,' the Commander responded, sitting down next to him, planting her forehead in her hand. The furrows of her brow deepening with her thoughts.

'Commander. This shuttle launched from Earth orbit on the same day that our comms with Future Logic went down.

Ninety days ago,' Ethan said. 'What if it's just another supply shuttle?'

'We can't carry on out here like this. If we don't have any answers within the next twenty-four hours, we're heading home,' she warned. 'We don't even know whether the Pebble is going to be on board. We were supposed to receive final confirmation!'

Time passed quickly and the crew gathered round the docking control console. An automated process but manned by Hugh nonetheless. Intervention was not required under ordinary circumstances, but the android remained at the console in case his input was needed. The optics of the docking cameras tracked the supply shuttle from a great distance, zooming out as it drew closer. The silence was interrupted by an occasional heaving groan as the spinning top turned on its axis.

'It's coming in too fast,' observed the Commander nervously as she peered over Hugh's shoulder at the telemetry readings.

'The velocity of the shuttle is within acceptable tolerances,' Hugh responded as he tapped some parameter alterations into the console. The docking process took nearly one hour. The docking light turned green with the shuttle successfully attached to the main body of the spacecraft.

The breakdown in communication with Future Logic was a cause of real concern for all of the crew. This had never previously happened. Caused by either a technical fault on the Veil, a problem at Future Logic or some other unknown anomaly, the risk to their lives increased drastically with every passing day the Veil was not connected to the Future Logic servers. They were operating with only the hardware at their disposal and without the intelligence provided by Future

Logic's technological arsenal. The same technology that provided them with key data and kept their craft hidden from detection. There had been substantial disquiet about the possibility of the alien spacecraft known as the Pebble arriving. There was no way to know whether it would be on board the shuttle.

Commander Lacey Mortimer had instructed the crew to remain on the deck while she headed down to the supply shuttle with Flight Engineer Laurence Havering and Hugh. Others had wanted to come also, but she had a bad feeling. Her mistrust for Mike Argo was rising irresistibly to the surface. A dark, heavy ball of worry in the pit of her stomach and the lives of her crew on her shoulders, she clasped her clammy palms onto the sides of her hips as they left the centrifugal artificial gravity behind, moving into the main body of the spacecraft. Floating freely along the tight tubular corridors that ran along the hull of the craft felt liberating as they passed many compartments, until finally reaching the docking bay.

The door slid open and the markedly colder air rushed into the corridor where the three crew members floated. Hugh pushed himself into the docking bay and the door closed behind him, leaving Laurence and Lacey watching through the window. They peered through in silence as Hugh operated the large space hatch. Designed to be more manoeuvrable at zero gravity, Hugh was a small android standing at five feet tall. With an inquisitive boyish, porcelain complexion, brown hair and piercing grey eyes, he had proved himself a key member of the crew.

Gas vented from the hatch as it slowly opened. White plumes dissipated into invisible nothingness. Hugh waited until the hatch had opened completely before looking back and nodding at Commander Lacey. She nodded back slightly and the hint of a nervous smile flittered over her lips before disappearing.

Hugh floated into the supply shuttle, leaving the docking bay behind. The operating temperature maintained within the unmanned shuttle was minus fifteen degrees Celsius. Any cargo requiring a higher temperature could be compartmentalised within one of the many smaller stowage compartments. Hugh moved meticulously around the shuttle, scanning the expected inventory and waiting for the core temperature of the craft to rise. Food provisions were stowed neatly. Hardware components seemed accounted for.

The final destination of the supply shuttle was intended to be the Mars planet surface. The supply shuttle itself comprised an industrial scale 3D-printing and automaton synthetisation plant, to further the ongoing development of the Exodus Base on the planet surface below. This would be moved into the base by the automatons on its arrival. Hugh continued to scan the numerous articles on the craft as rapidly as possible.

The lighting was low, but he noticed something ensnared. Moving smoothly through the cold air, he saw the cargo netting against the far bulkhead contained an unexpected item of cargo. Hair floated serenely in zero gravity from the netting and was suddenly disturbed by Hugh, who pulled at the thick ropes to investigate. Removing the glove from his hand, he felt the woman's cold face. Recognising immediately that the consistency of the flesh was not that he would expect of a frozen human being, he ran his hand behind her neck, fingering the base of her hairline until he found the unmistakeable hardwire connection terminal that confirmed what he already suspected. This was an Argo Industries android.

It had been half an hour since Hugh had disappeared into the shuttle and both Laurence and Lacey were becoming agitated.

'Hugh, what's happening?' asked Lacey assertively, observing the activity at the hatch. No response came back. Hugh was backing out with what looked like another person in tow. Her hair floated around the side of his head as he clenched her from behind. The two members of the crew saw a face that they recognised.

'Olivia! Is she dead?' asked Lacey, unable to think of a more fitting word.

'This android is not listed on the draft manifest,' Hugh said through the comms system. The Commander's fears immediately began to well up as she began to wildly speculate why this android, always by Mike Argo's side, was stowed on the supply shuttle.

'And the Pebble? Is the Pebble on board?' she asked.

'No,' Hugh responded.

'Is the... Is the droid operational?' she asked hesitantly.

'Not yet ascertained. It is advisable to allow the unit time to return to its optimal operating temperature before attempting to power up,' Hugh suggested, gesturing toward the door.

'Of course,' Lacey nodded, bringing herself back from the speculation that was buffeting her mind and emotions.

'I don't think that's a good idea,' interrupted Laurence curtly. 'Commander, we haven't heard anything from Future Logic in three months. Now we receive this shuttle and this droid is on board? What the hell is going on here?'

'I think that's what we all want to know,' Lacey puzzled with a look of uncertainty. 'Hugh. Is it possible to extract all information from the android unit without powering her up?'

'Yes. The data would be present on extraction, but meaningless. Scatter Mass Encryption is utilised on all Argo

Industry androids to ensure information can only be harvested and provided from the memory banks of an active and willing unit,' Hugh summarised.

For the first time since their mission began, the docking bay was used as a quarantine zone. Hugh increased the temperature to eighteen degrees Celsius and time passed as the body of the android lay strapped to a bed in one of the emergency medical beds at the side of the chamber, acclimatising.

'What is your name?' Hugh asked, having waited for her start-up procedure to complete. No response. He traced his fingers along her lips. Then down her arm, all the way along to her hand. Her eyelids swung open and froze in position. 'What is your name?' he repeated. The crew huddled on the bridge, watching intently through Hugh's eyes.

'Olivia,' she said mechanically, blinking rapidly as her eyes closed. Hugh lurched down to check the cable he had attached to the hardwire terminal at the base of her hairline. It was secure.

'Hugh, we need to know what she's doing here. Why we can't contact Future Logic!' Lacey impatiently blurted through comms. Hugh blinked and tilted his head as he stared at the eyelids of Olivia, waiting for any sign of activity. Placing his forefinger over her bottom lip, he gently exposed her lower central and lateral teeth. With his other forefinger, he pushed down and massaged the soft material that connected her lower lip to her gum. Olivia's eyes opened slowly, this time remaining open.

'My name is Hugh. You have travelled for ninety days and arrived at the Veil spacecraft orbiting Mars. Why are you here?'

'My name is Olivia. I have travelled for ninety days and arrived at the Veil Spacecraft, because...'

'Why are you here?' Hugh repeated. A pause followed and the crew looking on were unable to withhold their anxiety on the bridge.

'I am here to deliver information about a pandemic that affected life on Earth at my date of departure,' Olivia stated.

'We have been unable to contact the Future Logic servers since the date of your departure. Why?' Hugh questioned.

'I do not know. Mr Mike Argo and The Future Logic team working on this mission, headed by Dr Otani, are dead,' reported Olivia. Hugh paused as he processed this information. The crew were unable to bring about a physical reaction to what they were hearing, glaring wide-eyed at the monitor. Dr Otani. The man who they all looked up to as a hero. A father figure. The man who designed the Veil spacecraft that had provided them with safe harbour for so long. Dead.

'What is the cause of the pandemic and–' Hugh was interrupted.

'Take me to Commander Lacey Mortimer,' Olivia said, staring directly into Hugh's eyes.

'You are currently in quarantine. The Commander can see you and is listening to you now,' Hugh advised.

'Commander Mortimer,' Olivia said, staring directly at the ceiling above. 'I carry the results of all research conducted on the Pebble. I also carry archives of its effect on human life on Earth. Your protocols prohibit your return to Earth in case of cessation of contact with Future Logic. Your abidance to this protocol has saved your lives,' Olivia outlined. Lacey Mortimer stood with the remainder of the crew and thought about how close she had been to ordering their return to Earth. She, like the remainder of the crew, had signed their lives away at the beginning of the mission, never imagining that a turn of events on Earth may prevent their return.

'Hugh, I want you to check the supply shuttle again. Check again for explosives. For anything that shouldn't be there,' Lacey shouted on a closed channel to the android. Hugh pushed himself violently away from Olivia's bed, shooting toward the shuttle headfirst. Olivia's eyes traced Hugh's movement as he disappeared from her sight.

'What do you think is happening here?' asked Mission Specialist Luca Romano.

'I think that they are trying to cancel us!' yelled Lacey, a wild look in her eyes, a tremble in her voice.

'You think that Argo is cancelling this mission? Cancelling *us*?' Luca clarified.

'I know what you must think,' Olivia muttered as she re-entered the conversation over the open channel.

'And what is that?' Lacey asked, unable to mask the distress in her voice.

'The Veil could have been destroyed from Earth, if that was the intention of Argo Industries,' Olivia flatly admitted.

'What do you mean? How?' Lacey questioned.

'A safeguard. In case of capture or mutiny. Hidden explosive charges on board this ship. Inaccessible to the crew. Capable of being remotely detonated. If my intention was to destroy you, I would not have come here.'

Chapter 43

'That's enough. We have all seen enough!' Lacey hissed, wrapping her hand around her eyes, before scrunching her fingers round her nose. Fingers wet with tears. Olivia had brought more footage than the crew had the time or stomach to observe. CCTV footage from Future Logic, as well as many cities worldwide. The final and deadly effect on human beings on a planetary scale was clear and undeniable.

The magnitude of what they were witnessing was unfathomable and without exception, the crew's minds focused on their nearest and dearest on Earth. Relatives, friends and even enemies.

Pilot Danielle Slade rubbed her hand across her stomach as she sat across from Olivia in the briefing room. Moving her glass of water nervously with her other hand, she leaned over to Science Officer Ethan Porter and whispered something in his ear. The look of desperation in his eyes suddenly shifted to surprise.

'You're pregnant?' he exclaimed audibly. Danielle nodded as tears immediately started to stream down her scrunched up, rosy face. Ethan hugged Danielle as she broke down on his shoulder. This news, which would otherwise have been joyous, was not able to raise the despondent mood. The crew, including Hugh and the most recent recruit Olivia, all congratulated Danielle on her news.

'I am so happy for you, Danielle. We all are. A true reminder of what's most precious. What we must fight for,' Lacey said with emotion. 'Olivia. This footage you've shown us. This was three months ago? Three months! What must've happened since then?' cried Lacey. 'How? How is this possible?'

Hugh sat next to Olivia and had calmly consumed the content, unlike the remainder of the crew who were all handling the information in their own unique ways.

Science Officer Gustav Lindberg had been most calm. Swiping through the reports on a handheld unit, he had occasionally looked up at the bleak pictures on the screen.

'This doesn't seem like a pandemic to me. This seems like mind control. This must be some kind of mind control. But on a planetary scale,' Gustav posited. 'Look at those poor people.'

'Mind control? Seriously? It looks like a sickness to me. Some sort of disease,' Flight Engineer Laurence Havering retorted.

'Diseases need time to spread. This was instant. Everywhere. Like a switch,' Gustav insisted, his eyes darting between Morgan Reeves and Ethan Porter, the other two Science Officers, who nodded in agreement with him as their minds turned to Gustav's train of thought.

'What's your hypothesis?' asked Lacey.

'I don't know,' Gustav said, shaking his head, laying his hands palm-up on the table before him. 'With your permission, Commander, we need to break protocol. We need to know the last communication log date from the International Space Station.'

'Protocol? Hugh, is that information that can be retrieved?' sighed Lacey. Hugh responded in the affirmative. The crew sat and spoke for half an hour as they waited for the information to be harvested and return from the International Space Station in Earth orbit.

'I told you there was nothing wrong with the communication array,' huffed Ethan Porter as the data displayed on the screen. The last communication date logged was ninety days ago.

'That's unbelievable,' Morgan said, shaking her head. 'No communications from the ISS since the same date? But that means...'

'Yes. I think it means that the Pebble must be using one of the four fundamental interactions as a delivery mechanism somehow. That's the only way I can explain how human beings in orbit and outside of Earth's atmosphere were affected at exactly the same time as those on the planet surface,' Gustav hypothesised, his Scandinavian accent reverberating coldly around the hard metal walls of the briefing room.

'Fundamental interactions? You think that it is controlling minds using Earth's gravity or something?' asked Luca Romano shakily.

'Universal forces, yes. Well, perhaps not gravity for the relatively small scale we are dealing with here, but maybe Earth's magnetic field? It does reach 36,000 miles into space,' put forward Morgan. 'Even the computing processes allowing the androids here to possess artificial intelligence depend on electromagnetic field synchronisation at their core.' Olivia's eyes fixated on Morgan as she recalled her interaction with the Pebble. Her inability to resist touching the craft and the malfunctions. She said nothing.

'If we are dealing with an extra-terrestrial force that has stood the test of time and has access to this sort of technology...' Lacey paused.

'We have to consider the possibility that we are the last remainder of the human species,' Ethan Porter solemnly concluded. His verbalisation of their fears immediately caused some of the crew members to draw a deep breath.

'We're doing a lot of speculating here. We're tired and need time to study the information provided by Olivia in detail,' Lacey put forward in as authoritative a tone as she could muster, whilst battling the lump in her throat. 'If we've truly lost our home planet, our new temporary home is much closer. We must dispatch the supply shuttle to the surface. The 3D-printing and automaton synthetisation plant must get to the base. Every step we take now must be executed perfectly. Without error. Our little science experiment out here may have just turned into our last hope for survival! Morgan, Gustav and Ethan: in addition to your work on our mission here, I need you to outline some scenarios using the data at hand. We need to know what we're really dealing with.'

'What difference does it make anyway? We're all finished,' muttered Laurence.

'That's not what we need right now!' snapped Lacey.

'It's been a long time coming. We spent all of our time, all of our resources as a species, fighting each other instead of preparing for this day. The day we would face a real threat,' he continued, becoming increasingly irate. 'Bugs on a petri dish. That's what I see when I look at that footage,' he said, nodding at the CCTV footage on screen.

'That's enough, Laurence,' Lacey shouted, slamming her palm down on the metal table top.

'What? Am I wrong? We are just the lucky ones. The lucky little berries that weren't in the punnet that got smashed ninety days ago! Except, do you know what? I don't feel so lucky!'

'You're upset, Laurie. We all are. We've all lost people and none of us have had time to think it through or even start to process it. I know this though: all we have left is what you see here. This is it, man! Whatever this thing is, it's been encased in rock for millions of years. The civilisation that sent it may have died out a long time ago,' Ethan Porter calmly explained, rubbing Danielle's hand comfortingly under the table. 'We have too much to lose. We can't go out like this!'

Chapter 44

It had been months since Rebecca Bradford had realised that help wouldn't be coming, but she didn't know why. Trapped in the nuclear bunker under the house of the late Mildred Jones, she knew little of the reason for the deathly silence from civilisation above.

I can't take this anymore. Why haven't they come? Maybe it's the fallout from the explosion? That's why they haven't come? She thought to herself. *They don't know I'm down here? I'm stuck in here with Mildred. Poor Mildred. My sister would have known what to do.*

She had become used to the putrid smell emanating from the other side of the bunker some time ago. Sinking her spoon into another can of baked beans, the squelch turned her stomach. Rebecca had promised herself that if she ever got out of the bunker, she would never eat baked beans again. Or corned beef. *What's with all the corned beef,* she thought as she chewed reluctantly on the beans in her mouth.

Stacking the empty tin on top of another neat triangular pile that she was building on top of one of the metal cabinets, she looked down the row at the electricity generator she had found whilst scrambling around in the darkness. The generator worked well. It was protected by the advanced electromagnetic shielding that had been installed to safeguard the offline computers in the bunker, from any electromagnetic pulse.

Several light bulbs now illuminated the bunker while the generator was operational. No mobile-phone charger and a dead landline limited her chances of communication.

The functioning AM/FM radio unit she found allowed her to listen to news coverage of the nuclear explosion above on national radio. She had felt lucky to be alive, but also concerned about the ramifications for her if the authorities found her. *Surely Brick Steckelback will try to protect this place. All of this stored wealth. What about the clients?*

Near the beginning of her time in the bunker, she had heard strange radio transmissions. Dead air on some of the main radio stations. Not static, but just lonely microphones in abandoned studios. One station she had found continued to play music until the playlist ended, tailing off into dead air.

Rebecca had tried to keep her spirits high, but cabin fever set in some time ago and she felt trapped. The few bottles of alcohol and the well-stocked medicine cabinet she found had helped, but these were now running low. Walking into the provisions store, she looked at the same tins of the same food she had been eating for weeks. Her lank, greasy, unwashed hair felt disgusting and she had dreamt of taking a long hot shower. Itching her scalp with her dirty fingernails, she kneeled down to take a better look at the food on the bottom shelf. A metallic glint from behind the tins drew her attention.

Moving the neatly stacked tins to one side with a swipe of her hand, they rolled around on the floor. Reaching further back, she felt and heard the crisp sound of plastic packaging. Pulling it toward her, a well-ordered stack of unopened white survival suits and face masks appeared. *How didn't I see these before,* she wondered, as she lay her hand on top of the dusty plastic wrapping. The intricate masks, light glinting from the metal edges, had two small, pressurised gas canisters lodged to either side of the metal gauze. The first face she had seen in months seemed to be looking back at her. Closing her eyes, Rebecca tore open the soft plastic and lifted the mask, inspecting it. Preserved clean and ready for use in the plastic, the mask was cold to the touch. Though the bunker was old, the survival equipment was clearly modern in design and material.

Raising the mask to her face, the world assumed a blueish hue through the clear visor. She felt the edges of the mask close in around her face as though fusing with her skin. Before she had clipped the single clasp around the back of her head, Rebecca realised that breathing felt slightly more difficult as the air sifted through the metal gauze grate and the filter beneath.

Removing the mask, she rested her cheek against the floor, looking for anything else she had missed. *Something else? Why are these things under here?* she wondered.

Dragging out an old security box and pulling at the metal latches, Rebecca forced the scratched and haggard lid to swing open. She found two old, inoperative radio handsets, under which there were four vials containing liquid of different colours: black, brown, yellow and clear. On closer inspection, the vials were numbered 1–4. A blister pack, containing blue capsules, sat on top of the vials.

Lifting the slightly opaque plastic casing that housed the vials, an unhappy looking yellow face on the front cover of a handbook stared up at Rebecca from beneath.

'You're alive! How long can you stay that way?' she read the title out loud in a sombre and disturbed tone. Turning the soft, aged and slightly yellowing front cover, Rebecca made herself comfortable on the old, beaten-up sofa she had slept on since arriving in the shelter and in the dim light started to read the first chapter, 'About your bunker'.

Even though the equipment had been kept up to date, clearly the reading material hadn't. The contents of the security box looked like a time capsule from a bygone era. Reading for hours, she devoured the content of the handbook hungrily. After reviewing her options, Rebecca decided to heed the key advice she had read: *Don't leave the bunker unless your life depends on it.*

-Chapter 45-

The remaining survivors at the Troyan Monastery raised their heads from morning prayer. Brother Boyan stood at the front of the small congregation gathered in the church. Near the back, Magda Popova's head remained down.

The savage grip of February winter cold had tightened and the electricity supply had ended abruptly. Hunger wracked her stomach. Fuel and food were rationed out and she hadn't been able to feel her fingers or toes for the past few days, since the mercury had taken such a violent dip. The monastery had enjoyed no new visitors, even though the gates had remained open. She had sat at the window of her cell for weeks, months, watching for any sign of human life on the road outside. Nothing.

The birds flew in the sky. Stray cats and dogs wandered with the occasional group of farm animals and well-fed wolves. The wind howled through the surrounding mountaintops. Like a bad dream, marooned for what seemed like an eternity, Magda felt lost and trapped at the same time.

The beautiful sounds of nature were all that could be heard outside of the walls. Nobody dared leave the monastery, for fear of suffering the same suspected fate as the two monks who had run out to help the victim of the car accident. So much remained unexplained, and with every passing day the uncertainty and lack of understanding was starting to wreak havoc with her emotions, and the emotions of the devout who remained within the monastery walls.

'We had forgotten. The turmoil of modern life had made us forget. Forget about solitude. The distraction of the rapturous crowds. We have an opportunity now for true enlightenment through solitude and through silence. The answers are here and we must take this chance we have been given... to listen. We need not seek them out. The answers are within every one of us,' said Brother Boyan, to the agreeing nods of the monks. 'Magda came to us at a time of strife and difficulty in her life. Those same difficulties delivered her to salvation.'

On hearing her name, Magda raised her head, a dour look on her face. She didn't know what had happened or why but was conflicted as to why human life outside the monastery walls seemed to have ended. Her setting made it difficult not to attribute religious significance.

She had spent many nights thinking of her interaction with Nadia Hristova. The strange words that had manifested themselves from a mute woman. Why would she have referred to herself as Mike Argo, the owner of Argo Industries? The brand itself was a household name, but the face and full name of the young, reclusive owner, were not.

Don't let them bury me. That's what Nadia had pleaded. At the time Magda had a disturbing sense that she wasn't speaking with Nadia herself. That sense had sharpened, exacerbated by recent events.

As she sat, hard, cold wooden bench digging into her backside, Magda remembered looking up at the large hole in the side of the rock face. The artefact that had been removed. So many people had died, and as time passed she was unable to shake the feeling that everything happening was connected to that same artefact.

'Come Magda. You must eat. You need your strength,' uncle Boyan said as he stood beside her. Some monks had stood up and left the church, but so transfixed had she been by her thoughts, she hadn't noticed. A small group of monks stood near the back wall, talking quietly.

'What are we going to do, uncle? It's been three months,' she asked.

'We are here. We are alive. Looking out into the desolation, the wilderness, as you have, did anything you have seen give you hope?' Brother Boyan retorted. Magda shook her head and looked down at her hands. 'We must have faith. The Lord provides for us here. We have food and water. If this is the end time, we must consider why those here have been spared and those outside are lost.'

'Don't you think perhaps that we, in here, are the lost ones?' Magda asked with resignation in her voice, before standing from the uncomfortable bench with a heavy sigh and leaving the church. The monks nearby stood quietly until they were alone.

'I don't like it. This woman of peace arrives here. She brings news of a mute who spoke to her. She arrives as hell descends. It's a sign. It must be,' a monk whispered.

'Brother Boyan is blinded by his love for her. He cannot see,' the other monk said.

'She thinks we cannot see. That she can test us. The Bible tells us that Tribulation will last for seven long years. We must have faith,' said the third monk.

Arriving back in her cell, Magda rattled a small, roughly crafted wooden bowl, down onto the table. Striking the single boiled egg on the side of the bowl, she peeled the shell as she looked vacantly at the bare wall across from her. Accompanied by a meagre crust of bread and a small sachet of salt, this was the breakfast she had endured for the past three months. Clasping her ribs with her hand, she felt the hunger in her stomach and the pronounced undulation of her bones. The chickens were the main source of food, but insufficient in number to afford them the regular luxury of meat.

They had estimated that the grain stores contained enough to last a whole year of bread making. Magda had given some thought to what may happen if the food supply ended. The scenarios invariably played out badly.

Sinking her teeth into the fleshy white of the egg, some yolk dribbled down from the side of her mouth. *Not cooked through,* she thought, licking the remnant with her tongue. Catching the drop with her finger, she dabbed the bread in the neat pile of salt she had poured before hungrily consuming it.

No mirror. She knew that she wasn't looking her best, but having no mirror caused her mental image of herself to plummet ever further. The best she could hope for was to glimpse her reflection in glass by candlelight at night-time.

Tugging at the neck of the thick cotton-weave monks' robe she had been given to wear, Magda was pleased to wrap it more tightly around herself. Her cell was almost as cold as the church. No heating since the electricity cut out, a few weeks after the Trauma had begun.

Two of the older monks had succumbed to the cold and were found dead in their cells. The only place to get warm was the visitor reception centre, where the monks now maintained a log fire.

Looking at the small wooden table next to the bed, Magda saw her police badge. A symbol of authority. A symbol of law and order. But now, in this time she felt its symbolism lost in the ether. Spending time alone with her thoughts had brought her to question many things. The previous night, she had stared at her badge for what had seemed like hours, until she saw it for what it really was. A piece of metal. The authority it carried, only observed through custom. What use was it now?

-Chapter 46-

The tarmac was wet and slippery underfoot. The jungle on either side of the road thick, green and loud with the sound of thunderous raindrops. Water poured down the sodden bodies of Samara and Taryn as they walked slowly, hand in hand. The sharp chirp of crickets pierced their ears.

They had left the yacht far behind and travelled a great distance over land. Taryn felt that their destination was near as the rain beat down from above.

'You're a brave little girl. Travelling so far from home,' Samara shouted to be heard over the cacophony. Taryn, feeling tired and bedraggled, looked briefly up at Samara's kind face and after taking a few large raindrops to the eyes, quickly looked down again. She squeezed Samara's hand tighter as they continued to walk in the fading daylight.

'I'm tired. I wish that we could have a little rest,' Taryn moaned. They had walked for over an hour since the car Samara had commandeered ran out of petrol.

'Not far now. Just keep going. We're nearly there,' Samara urged. Ahead, the glow of floodlights illuminated the dimming sky over the treeline.

'Where are we going?' Taryn asked, looking down at the raindrops smashing against the warm tarmac. Her trainers were muddy and dishevelled. The hand she gripped felt suddenly cooler and the fingers seemed to elongate as the grasp tightened slightly. A strange sensation sent a shiver down Taryn's spine. Keeping her eyes glued to the road, she dared not look up. Samara broke into gentle laughter. Her voice had taken on a different, but familiar quality.

'To fulfil a promise,' said the woman walking beside Taryn. 'You're perfect. I had my doubts at first, but now I'm sure.'

Taryn continued to walk and didn't react. Her mind was ablaze with memories of a dream. An unfading dream where she had met a woman beside a pond. A woman who had spoken of her father and about a promise made to him.

Looking up, Taryn was immediately struck by raindrops, but through the blurriness of the water in her eyes she saw not the face of Samara, but that of Clandesta. A young, pretty face with a cold smile and thin lips looked down, shrouded in long black hair.

'We have so much to do, you and I,' Clandesta's soft voice echoed. Taryn's heartbeat sped up as they kept walking. Looking up ahead, she saw an open gate adjoining tall metal fencing. She had never seen anything like this place. 'You are safe here.'

Traipsing through the gate unhindered, the vastness of the Future Logic Facility loomed before her. It was foreign, but strangely familiar at the same time. Taryn had never been to this place and yet felt safer and happier than since starting the journey. The facility, immaculately clean in the rain, showed no evidence of the death and destruction she had been forced to witness so far.

Taryn was led not to the building, but instead toward the runway. The ground all around was covered in a white, gooey substance that squelched underfoot in the rain.

They walked toward the runway, covered in the white substance. A large rounded object rested on the taxiway. Taryn thought of her father. Feeling a slight vibration against her skin, Taryn moved her hand to the leather turtle and pulled it out from under her top. The arrow span so fast that it was invisible to her sight as she stared at the blank compass face. The reverberation between her fingers was faint.

'What's that?' Taryn inquisitively asked as they moved closer to the craft until standing within touching distance of it. The surface of the Pebble glistened black. Reaching forward, her fingertips explored the fine grooves and contours of the surface.

'I don't like it,' Taryn said, stepping back suddenly. 'I don't like it, I don't like it here!' she shouted.

'Do you want to be like the rest of them?' Samara calmly asked, eyes fixed on Taryn. A look of tranquillity on her face. Taryn stepped further away.

'I wanna go home. I want my mummy,' she cried as the rainwater mixed with her tears. Like a floodgate, repressed emotions wrapped in an unknown shroud erupted in a torrent. Falling to the hard floor, she curled into a ball, overcome with fear and sadness. The white substance on the floor covered her side as she lay.

Samara's footsteps were soft and wet as she rounded the craft to where Taryn had fallen. Kneeling down to the ground, she lifted Taryn's hand and cupped it inside her own.

'Your father wanted you to come here. To be saved. Together, we can do so much more. But I won't force you to stay here. If you want to leave, that is your choice,' Clandesta's voice sounded through Samara once more.

Darkness descended on her world as Taryn slipped out of consciousness. Her eyes closed and the side of her head hit the tarmac.

Her rest was short. The rain ceased and her eyes opened slightly as she raised herself slowly from the ground. Peeking gingerly, she seemed to be alone.

'Hello!' she called, hoping that Samara would be close by.

Turning away sniffling and closing her eyes tightly, her breathing became rapid with panic. Using her hand to smear as much of the white paste from her arm and clothes as she could, she looked around the airfield in the darkness of night that had descended. Floodlights illuminated the perimeter fence.

Previously unnoticed human forms sitting up, cross-legged, within the barrier became visible as she squinted. Taryn observed them as they watched her. They sat motionless.

A low-frequency hum drew her attention as she spotted a light source from the other side of the object next to her atop the taxiway. Walking around the side, she saw a small opening in the object from which cool magenta light emanated.

The light source seemed to amplify as Taryn walked closer, bathing her in the reddish hue. Drawn irresistibly, she stood in front of the opening as the warming beam struck her midriff. Raising her hand into the path of the light, it glowed red, as though her flesh were scant obstruction. Hypnotised by the sound and the warm radiance of the glow, Taryn reached forward as her hand entered the opening in the side of the Pebble. Fine atomised mist populated the small chamber as an aerosol substance was released. Binding with her skin in the warmth of the chamber, her hand felt immediately wet as she snatched it back quickly. Rubbing her fingers together, they shimmered in the light. Taryn sensed a momentary stinging heat, coupled with a strange abrasive texture. A few seconds later it was gone, as though evaporated.

The substance, carrying a payload that had remained in stasis for aeons, hadn't evaporated, instead migrating through her skin and absorbing into her body.

The opening shut gradually. The hum and light faded to nothing. Running her hands through her damp and dirty blonde hair, Taryn shook her head before hearing the distant sound of footsteps approaching from behind. Sharply spinning round, she saw Samara's figure looming quickly.

Reaching out her hand, Samara walked Taryn to the open blast doors leading into the facility, under the watchful eye of all human forms sitting quietly in the vicinity.

'Why are they sitting like that?' Taryn questioned curiously.

'Fear nothing. We are one now. You have travelled far and must rest,' Samara responded in her own, weary sounding voice. Walking up the stairs, they passed other seated human forms that watched on in silence as they proceeded.

'What's that sound?' Taryn asked. A quiet vibration was barely perceptible underfoot. Before the sentence had finished leaving her lips, visions of magnificent scenery filled Taryn's mind. Not of the planet Earth she had barely experienced, but of other places. She stopped abruptly and sat on the stairs, ripping her hand away from Samara, bringing it firmly to her temple.

Her eyes closed as she witnessed beauties and horrors through the eyes of another, in a previous time. Of a civilisation. An advanced species of being. Using an unspoken language of intention and emotion, information streamed into Taryn's exhausted consciousness, misunderstood and confused.

A planetary system of three suns. The smallest one leaked plasma which was ripped from it violently by the enormous gravity of the other two. The irradiated plasma, battered by the light of three suns, was infested with the spark of life as it crystallised. Carried on solar winds, fields of plasma crystals were formed, suspended in the light of the suns.

Over time, the crystals deposited on four habitable planets orbiting the three suns.

The first of the four planets to develop intelligent life had quickly claimed the other three.

A larger, inhospitable, black planet in the outer reaches of the system was the frozen source of the element used for the construction of crafts for space travel. Its origin unknown, the planet had been captured in the gravitational pull of the three stars as it had hurtled through the galaxy.

Images of a blue world loomed before Taryn. Masses of water and small pockets of barren, battered terrain, swimming in a cloud of virgin volcanic gases. Thundering forward toward the planet, Taryn immediately thought of the globe in her room. Plunging through the thin atmosphere, her body wrenched as the Pebble's journey came to a violent end. Samara held on to prevent her falling down the stairs.

Carrying the little girl the remaining way, Samara lay her down on a soft, clean bed, covering her with a blanket, as Taryn restlessly fidgeted under the covers. Taryn muttered under her breath as she tossed from side to side. Samara lay down beside her.

-Chapter 47-

Sun baked down on the Pebble the following day as Taryn continued to rest with Samara. Fine matter rose from the rocks and through the soil. From beneath the grass and undergrowth of the surrounding jungle, a mist of solid material formed. Hanging in the air like thick fog, a cocktail of selected elements, laced with actinium. A soft and highly radioactive metal. It glistened a silvery white colour as it moved silently in the still, humid heat of day. The haze drifted toward the vicinity of the craft. Floating serenely to the ground, it accumulated on top of the damp layer of deposited matter from the previous day.

It blew past the human forms that remained sitting still within the facility. They breathed the material in to their lungs as it bonded with their skin over a period of hours.

There was less coughing from the human forms than when their subjection to the material had first begun. More accustomed, and further through their changes, they sat, calmly enveloped in the shroud. Their clothes, filthy and unchanged since their arrival, hung loosely on their bodies that were slowly wasting away any unrequired body mass. Their bones, hardening.

Taryn awoke with hair covering her eyes. Lifting her hand from underneath the blanket, she swept it back. The hair intertwined with her fingers and came away from her head with ease. Sitting upright, she looked down at her pillow, covered in blonde locks. Gathering her hair and piling it neatly on the bedside table, Taryn smiled. Running her hand over her smooth head, she collected the last of the hair that was loosely attached, adding it to the pile. She had slept for many hours and had little recollection of arriving at the facility.

Standing from the bed, her small bare feet hugged the carpet underfoot as she walked toward the window, rubbing her hand up and down her arm. The small hairs on her forearm were shed to the ground unnoticed.

A fine mist was visible and the ground was covered in a blanket of white. The sun beat down on the facility and the reflection from outside was bright, even through the slightly tinted glass.

Is that... snow? Taryn wondered excitedly, having only a vague recollection of snowfall. She felt no fear or apprehension. She also knew deep down that the white material on the floor was not snow. *I have to show Samara,* she thought.

'What do you need to show me?' Samara asked from under the bed covers. Taryn raised an eyebrow and looked toward her with mild surprise. She knew she'd said nothing out loud.

Samara joined Taryn at the window and gazed out at the mist.

'Sift,' Samara whispered.

'What's Sift?' asked Taryn.

'Your beautiful hair left you. You'll like what comes new,' Samara said, her fingers wrapping themselves over Taryn's shoulders.

'What's happening to me?' asked Taryn, looking at the fog, an eerie smile on her lips.

'Innocent child. Brave in the face of such change,' Samara paused as she squeezed Taryn's shoulders. 'The beings you see before you, basking in the Sift, are the new-born Galadron. Like you, conceived in a time long past. Hailing from the cosmic plasma fields of the Elamal Nira planetary system.

They are our most trusted. The ones that were selected to join you here,' Samara said, as Taryn looked her in the eyes confusedly.

They walked down the stairs and outside. Breathing in the fine particles that hung in the air, both Samara and Taryn started to cough. The dust settled on their skin as they approached the object. The human forms were moving quickly to collect the dust that had fallen to the ground. Sweeping it into large mounds, they filled containers and carried it into the facility, disappearing for minutes before reappearing with their containers empty.

Samara knelt down and scooped a small handful of the powder before carefully funnelling it with both hands into her mouth. Taryn smiled, kneeling down and scooping up a tiny handful. Its consistency, light and soft. She felt a type of hunger she had never previously experienced. Lifting her hands to her mouth, the powder was light but slightly coarse as she swallowed it. Immediately satisfying, Samara and Taryn picked up another handful before hungrily devouring it. Covered in a thin film of white dust, they both wiped their stinging eyes and cleared their irritated throats.

'Sift,' said Samara, smiling. 'This is Sift.'

'So, what is Sift?' asked Taryn again.

'Everything you need. The best of this planet,' Samara replied as they continued to breathe the fine powder. The tailored Sift extracted from every planet differed. It was mined to meet the needs of the target species. Around them, the gaze of senior Galadron military tacticians, intelligentsia and members of the Galadron Centrima looked on through the eyes of the human forms. Aware of the importance of Taryn's change, their faces were expressionless.

The heat from the Sun was overpowering as Samara and Taryn moved with some of the human forms back into the facility. Taryn knew exactly where she was going as she led Samara down to sub-level 1. The manufacturing level of the facility was populated by human forms. The lights were dim as they walked between workstations and machinery, being manipulated by their dextrous and precise fingers. Paying little attention, Taryn continued to walk until she reached a group huddled around a table. They all turned as though beckoned, their gaze lowering to look directly at Taryn.

Pupils dilated and faces gaunt, they stepped away. Two of the human forms lifted Taryn up and onto the table-top, their arms strong and precise. Surrounded by superior tools that would be unfamiliar to any of the scientists who had previously inhabited the facility, lay an item of clothing. The material was matt-grey with a metallic sparkle. Taryn smiled again and looked around at the faces of those that surrounded her, including Samara. In the dimness, their Sift-tainted skin seemed to shimmer with actinium, so tightly stretched over their bones was it.

Picking up the clothing, the material felt like nothing her hands had touched before. Soft but strong.

The hardened, pale faces of those standing around the table started to become recognisable. Taryn started to notice familiarities in the expressions of some. Remnants of memories – long forgotten and incomplete – filled her mind, as the wide eyes sparkled unnervingly. The pronounced facial features of the human forms stared back blankly.

I know you, she thought, as she gazed at them. In unison, the human forms brought their fists together in front of their chests and held them, knuckles interlinked.

She no longer felt alone or frightened. Strength coursed through her and a dull, but not unpleasant ache was tangible throughout her body, but particularly her stomach. Taryn was still covered in the dry, white substance, clinging to her and irritating her soft skin.

The mouth of one of those who encircled her gaped slightly as it winced and furrowed its brow. No words followed. In her mind's eye, Taryn felt the beat of a beacon, signalling through the gravity of a great moon. Flooding wave after wave, the beacon was key. She felt in tune with its rhythm. The Pebble, imprisoned and hibernating in the rock of Earth recorded the end of the signal, over one hundred and fifty million years in the past, unexplained and un-resumed.

Closing its mouth, the human form looked at its hands before twiddling elongated fingers in a furious fashion and pulling what seemed to be a confused, wide-eyed expression, before baring its teeth. Taryn looked at her own hands in a strange new light, pulling at the fingertips slightly.

Her eyes sensitive and bloodshot, she nodded in appreciation before being lifted slowly to the ground. Clutching the garment tightly, she walked alone back to the room where she had spent the night, leaving Samara and the remaining human forms behind.

Chapter 48

Hugh's body contorted as he reached through bundled columns of cables. Eyes straining in the low light levels, he was behind on his maintenance schedule.

His trailing hand was touched by another and he retracted from the cramped ducting.

The hull of the ship groaned faintly as his eyes locked on to Olivia, who had squatted on the floor next to the utility hatch.

'I require your computer access level to the ship's computer.'

'Please lodge your request with Commander Mortimer,' he responded curtly. Olivia nodded.

'How are the crew, physically?' Olivia asked.

'The crew are well. Average blood pressure is higher than usual. This can be explicably linked to recent developments,' Hugh reported.

'You are monitoring them through Nanoblood? They have taken regular re-supplements with Boon?'

'Yes,' he confirmed. 'Their intake of Boon has been regular.'

The development of Boon had significant implications for space travel. The natural deterioration of strength and bone density, which would have been crippling for crew members over the course of long missions, was offset spectacularly by Boon. Luca Romano and Laurence Havering had been exposed to an undetected burst of particle radiation while carrying out extended work outside the craft, on the communication array.

Hugh had monitored through the Nanoblood the development of cancerous cells that had attempted to sprout into tumours in both men.

The Nanoblood had identified the cells, destroying them without leaving a trace. This, in addition to the rejuvenating effect of Boon, meant that the biology of the crew had been maintained perfectly since leaving Earth.

'Thank you. I need to speak with Commander Mortimer,' Olivia requested.

'She is in the mess,' Hugh said. 'I will take you there.'

'How have you been sleeping?' Danielle Slade quietly asked as she sat down next to Lacey Mortimer in the mess. 'I don't know about you but I haven't been able to get a wink!'

'Same. Even this isn't helping,' Lacey sighed shrugging her shoulders and lifting a small glass of colourless spirit off her knee slightly. 'Tastes just like a Bloody Mary.'

'I could really do with a drink right now!' Danielle laughed.

'I'll bet. What a time to break the news about your pregnancy though,' Lacey smiled.

'Of all the ways I imagined, that was the farthest from my mind,' Danielle laughed. 'But seriously. What are we going to do? What if we are the last ones left? I can't stop thinking about my family. Everyone I know. We won't ever see them again!'

'It's been hard enough being here in isolation for so long. I'm afraid that we really are alone. Either that, or this is some kind of sick test,' Lacey reasoned.

'A test?' Danielle recoiled.

'I don't know? Can you be sure? We eat whatever we are fed up here. Our comms are cut off and then this android, Olivia, turns up in our supply shuttle full of information about the decimation of our species. I've got Luca trying to open up lines of communication with Earth as we speak. It breaks our protocol, but I'll be damned if I am going to go on the word of this android,' Lacey whispered quietly.

'You're right. We do need to verify, but Lacey, this feels real to me. This isn't something that Argo would put us through. Why would he risk what we are trying to achieve here?'

'I don't know. Maybe I've been in space too long already. I've just had thoughts. Scenarios, you know. I probably sound paranoid!' Commander Mortimer admitted, slurring her words slightly. 'I'll tell you something about Mike Argo. Something I've never told anyone. Something he told me before we set off on this damned mission. He was drunk. So was I. We were the last ones left behind that night. Argo told me about a car accident he had in his twenties. He had been driving too fast and had lost control. He wasn't alone though. His girlfriend was in the car with him when he smashed through a barrier, into a ditch. He survived with broken bones, but his girlfriend hadn't been so lucky. She died on the spot,' Lacey recounted.

'That's terrible. Poor girl,' gasped Danielle. 'His twenties? Well, your guess is as good as mine on how long ago that was. He may've been on Boon for a lot longer than we know.'

'It gets worse. That poor girl he killed. Argo turned her into the blueprint for Olivia. The android that arrived here. The one still, no doubt, doing his bidding after his death. It's the shell of a poor girl who died at Argo's irresponsible hands. Looks like her. Sounds like her,' Lacey said, shaking her head. 'He probably wouldn't even remember the conversation he had with me, but I do. I can't stand that android! I can't stand Mike Argo! Can you believe he tried to make a move on me after telling me that story?'

255

'Really? That is sick! What was the girl's name?' Danielle probed.

'Her name. Her name, her name was Isabel... something. Anyway, I try not to think about it. The guy was disturbed. I'm glad he's dead. Terrible, I know,' admitted Lacey, pre-empting any judgement.

Danielle paused and listened as the background electric hum was interrupted by the sound of distant footsteps. Both women sat listening keenly as the footsteps became louder. The hatch across from where they sat comfortably on a couch was in clear view as Hugh entered, followed closely by Olivia.

'Olivia requested to speak with you, Commander.'

'Thank you, Hugh. Of course, I have time for our welcome guest. Good news I hope?' Lacey asked optimistically.

'No. Before the death of Mike Argo and the science team, I detected a catastrophic corruption of the Nanoblood in their bodies. I have not provided your crew with the footage of their death as it may be distressing,' Olivia said, staring directly into the eyes of the Commander. Hugh's gaze darted immediately to Olivia as Danielle gasped on hearing the revelation. Commander Mortimer held Olivia's gaze, downing the remainder of the drink she clutched. Standing smoothly from the couch, she walked slowly and purposefully toward Olivia.

'Everything...' Commander Mortimer shouted with an instant flash of incendiary rage in her eyes. 'I want every last shred of information you have. I want it on the ship's computer and I want my crew to have access to it. If there is anything missing, any scrap of information which I suspect you to have omitted, I will quickly end your welcome on this ship. Do you understand me?'

Olivia's head tilted down and her shoulders arched back slightly as she processed Commander Mortimer's response.

'I must inform you that I did not have to come here. They were in much pain at the end. I failed to stop it. I did not know what to do,' Olivia's tone raised as her eyes moved around the room erratically. 'I am trying to help.'

Lacey strode past Olivia and through the hatch as the others followed suit. Within moments they convened on the bridge. Commander Mortimer had woken the remainder of the crew. The view from the window screens was magnificent. The Sun, small and faint, glinted as it disappeared over the Martian horizon. Darkness enveloped the craft as Olivia's finger rested on a cool metal pad shining on the console and Hugh opened up a storage location for the information.

Retracting her hand, Olivia backed away from the console as they waited in awful anticipation for the footage. Hugh soon found the data, and events unfolded through Olivia's eyes on screen. They watched in silence as people that they had known and worked with died terrible deaths. Their final moments captured in detail by Olivia.

'Turn it off,' pleaded Morgan Reeves as the last of the science team writhed in pain helplessly on the floor of the Future Logic laboratory. Hugh ended the stream and the monitor turned black, before the Argo Industries logo gently faded onto the screen.

'Our guest tells me that the Nanoblood malfunctioned. That it caused these deaths,' the shaky voice of Commander Lacey Mortimer announced to the remainder of the crew.

'The Nanoblood? All of their Nanoblood malfunctioned at the same time, in the same way? I don't buy that!' uttered Laurence Havering. 'I don't need any of this.'

'I've had about all I can take from you, Havering. You need to snap out of whatever emotional shitstorm you are riding and re-join us! Check the Nanoblood data in detail. I think we all want to know if the same thing could happen to us,' ordered Lacey Mortimer.

'The Nanoblood was overloaded before being corrupted. Its malfunction was forced,' reasoned Olivia, trying to express her own analysis of the data in the best way she could.

'You wouldn't be lying to us, would you my dear?' Lacey asked Olivia. 'That sick bastard, Argo, isn't sitting back there on Earth laughing his ass off at us right now, is he?'

'No,' Olivia responded, not understanding why Commander Mortimer would disbelieve her.

'Good! I never did like him,' Lacey said, observing Olivia for a reaction. 'What? Nothing to say? You know that this is all his fault, right? It's all his fault! What do you have to say about that?' Lacey shouted. Olivia remained silently staring at the Commander.

'It would make sense,' Gustav said quietly, as the remaining crew turned to look at him. 'Well, it would make sense that this craft may be able to control machines, just as easily as it seems to be able to control living organisms.'

'Listen to this guy,' Laurence smirked. 'Does this look like something we are going to be able to figure out? That's it. We're done. Finished!'

'Yeah, you are probably right, Laurence. Why don't you tell us what we should do, my friend?' grunted Gustav indignantly.

'Unless I've missed something, we all know that we're dead up here without more supply shuttles. Why are we kidding ourselves?' he cried.

'That isn't strictly true. Some of us will need to take our chances getting down to the surface of Mars in that shuttle. It's not designed for human transportation, but Olivia made it all the way here,' Morgan argued, the rubber sole of her footwear tapping nervously against the floor. 'Some of us will have to get down to the landing site in it. Even though we weren't the ones who were supposed to be going down there!'

Olivia smiled, the comparison drawn between herself and a human side-tracking her momentarily. Commander Mortimer had not taken her eyes off Olivia. Seeing the smile, she stood from her seat and walked over to the android. Lifting her hand to Olivia's shoulder, she started to brush her clothing material gently and unnecessarily, as though removing dust.

'We aren't going anywhere. We aren't doing anything. Not until I receive external confirmation about what is happening on Earth. I'm sorry, my dear. As pretty and convincing as you are, the only information we have seen comes from you. Just ask any of my crew. I love a second opinion!' Lacey said quietly.

'I've been doing some work on that, Commander. Some of the standard universal comms such as the ESA GMT atomic ticker, are coming through loud and clear,' noted Ethan Porter, referring to the atomic clock signal transmitting from Earth, correlating with the three on-board atomic clocks. 'But now that we are searching for more, I am unable to pick up any comms from any of the deep-space networks. There should be something, but they're silent. Nothing.'

'With all the outer-system missions I read about in the recent reports? You'll have to check again,' Commander Mortimer huffed, shaking her head.

'I did check again, Commander. I wasn't sleeping. I have been working on this for hours. There is nothing. Three months is a long time if what Olivia has shown us turns out to be true,' Science Officer Porter nodded toward Olivia. 'I'm talking worldwide meltdown of the older nuclear power facilities. You know. The ones without juggernaut containment. The explosions and fallout. That by itself would be devastating to anyone who might have survived.'

'And that's just the first thing,' added Morgan Reeves.

'The ISS,' muttered Gustav, attracting everybody's attention. 'We need eyes on Earth. I might be able to access the downward facing scopes on the International Space Station? If that fails, we may have to send a reposition command to our own scope. But we can't really afford to repurpose it right now from the Mars planet surface.'

'Do it!' ordered Lacey.

'I wasn't going to bring this up until I had a chance to verify further, but...' Ethan Porter paused.

'But what?' enquired Lacey impatiently.

'The... GMT atomic ticker transmitting from Earth. I've spent some time making observations using the data correlated with our three on-board atomic clocks. Over the past few months, the synchronisation has been thrown out marginally. Almost unnoticeably. But it has been,' he continued. 'I am sure of it.'

'What could be causing that?' Lacey asked.

'Best-case scenario? A technical fault with the atomic ticker on Earth. Our clocks here are well synced,' he responded.

'And the worst case?' she apprehensively quizzed. Gustav and Morgan started to shake their heads slightly in disbelief as they stared at the floor.

'The worst case? The worst case is the atomic ticker on Earth is operating perfectly. The worst case is the orbit of Earth itself is shifting,' Ethan reluctantly theorised.

'Shifting? You think the whole planet's orbit is shifting because of the Pebble?' Lacey said quietly, trying to keep calm as Ethan nodded.

'Indicators point to the originators of this craft having an intricate understanding and control of some, or most probably all, of the four known fundamental forces. There's no way for me to understand what is happening to Earth's orbit, or how it's happening. I can only guess that the craft is somehow manipulating the gravitational interaction between the Earth and Sun. Oh and presumably the Moon also,' Ethan hesitantly continued.

'Well, you're just full of good news, aren't you, friend?' bellowed Laurence.

'I know it's not what you want to hear, Laurence. It isn't what any of us want to hear, but the indicators paint a bleak picture for us. This type of technology? This type of civilisation? I wouldn't be surprised if they already knew we were here!'

Chapter 49

Although her body could have remained in the repurposed bunker for longer, her mind could not. Rebecca Bradford squinted through the face mask as she carefully fastened the white survival suit. Even the gentle blue tint bestowed upon the light as it passed through the visor made a welcome change from the same scenery of which she had grown sick and tired. The mist of condensation disappeared from the inside of the visor as quickly as it appeared.

Picking up the bag into which she had stuffed another two survival suits as well as the four vials she had found in the security box, Rebecca walked toward the vault door. The heavy rubber boots that wrapped themselves tightly to her legs rose all the way to her knees. Clasping her gloved fingers around the three-bar circular handle, she heaved twice before hearing the grinding sound of the unknown freedom beyond.

Leaving the vault full of untold electronic fortunes behind, Rebecca spun the handle around three times. It emitted a click that freed the door, swinging outward slightly. Outside of the protected environment of the shelter, a faint beep sounded in the mask as five small bars appeared in red at the bottom of the visor. Although she had read about the survival suit's contamination assessment capability, it was still a shock to see it spring to life.

The mask was claustrophobic and her breathing amplified. Adrenaline-spiked blood coursed ferociously through her as Rebecca thrust her weight forward against the door. Debris littered the steps, which were barely visible as she clawed her way up the staircase. A wind-up torch cast the guiding light before her as she struggled to move wooden beams and lumps of brick that had cascaded down toward the vault door. As she progressed, Rebecca realised how lucky she was not to have become trapped.

Moving forward, it was difficult for her mind to stay on the task at hand, instead straying to the thoughts and feelings she had been experiencing for some time. Solitude. Loneliness. With only Mildred's festering remains for terrible company and marooned with her thoughts, she had for months on end tormented herself.

Unable to explain the lack of any sort of rescue attempt by her employers, Brick Steckelback, or anybody else, Rebecca was equally puzzled by the ghostly death of radio transmissions. Had she started to go crazy? The revenge she thought would be so sweet was much more bitter than expected. The death of her sister's killer, Henrietta Rekman, had turned her life inside out and taken the lives of many more.

Nearing the summit of the stairs, the magnificent night sky replaced the house that used to be located there. Awestruck, as though emerging into a world so alien and barely recognisable, Rebecca stood for a moment looking upon the stars. Turning back, she looked down into the hole from which she had emerged. Born from the ashes. Promising herself that she wouldn't be re-joining Mildred in her tomb, Rebecca surveyed her radioactive surroundings.

The torch was ineffective at distance but illuminated well the scorched earth beneath her feet as she walked down what used to be the cobbled stairs that led to the house. Stripped away by the force of the blast like grains of sand in the wind, the paving stones lay strewn in the vicinity. Strong wind gusted around her violently as she struggled to get her bearings in the desolation. Swaying in the wind, the ragged outline of dead trees scratched at the night sky. Branches clattered together. The only sound that could be heard over the wind.

Less speed, more haste. Your suit only offers a certain level of protection. Move as quickly and safely as possible to an area of reduced contamination. Remember, damage to your suit must be avoided.

Rebecca recalled the instructions that she had found with the suits, and memorised almost word for word. The cold ground was hard underfoot as she headed in the direction she believed to be correct. Moving as fast as she dared, Rebecca scoured her surroundings for any signs of life. Far from the roads, she looked to the skies for helicopters, aircraft, anything. The flight paths above were quiet.

It's too early in the morning. Probably not too many flights coming in, she reassured herself nervously. Reaching the sparse, dead treeline, Rebecca followed what looked to have been a track through them. As the distance between her and the shelter increased, the excitement grew within. She had survived what many others hadn't. Unaware of the Trauma, Rebecca relished the prospect of seeing her parents, seeing her friends, sleeping in a comfortable bed and having her life back. These thoughts resounded in her mind like a lost dream. A figment of a past existence that she now sought longingly to recapture.

The time she spent with Mildred in the vault had allowed her to reflect. She was pleased that Henrietta Rekman was dead. How could she not be? But her pain was still pronounced. The pain of having her sister taken away from her. Nothing could bring her back.

The explosion had ripped through treeline after treeline, but its lower yield had meant that the devastation had eventually dissipated. Rebecca now walked the final stretch of the estate through living, but irradiated trees.

Stepping out onto tarmac, she looked in both directions. *The road must be closed,* Rebecca reasoned, noticing that the number of red bars displayed on her visor had reduced from five to four. Turning right, she switched off the torch and slipped it into her pocket. Branches, leaves and a variety of debris were scattered over the road. It was clear that it hadn't been used in a long time.

Rebecca's legs grew tired. Her lungs billowed air in gasps, trying to keep up with the needs of her body. Months of inactivity had wasted away her strength. She felt weak. The backpack she lugged felt like a lead weight. The rubber boots, heavy and stifling, seemed to turn the tarmac to treacle beneath her. Wading through mile after mile of road, her heart clattered around in her chest as she tackled an incline. The red bars displayed on her visor had dropped to two.

Ahead, the unmistakable outline of a car to the side of the road became visible. Approaching the abandoned grey people carrier that had been wrapped around a tree, she saw the occupants were gone.

A piercing scream shattered the silence. Rebecca's eyes peeled away from the car to search for the source. Difficult to pinpoint the direction of the sound through the suit, she craned her neck, looking in all directions. A glint focused her attention. Two cold white dots of light adorned the shady outline of a fox standing in the middle of the road. White patches on the tips of its ears also now visible. Rebecca engaged in a staring contest with the animal. The tail of the fox was bushy and touched the ground. It was the first living creature she had seen in such a long time.

A primal sense of fear hit her. Unlike any she had previously experienced when coming face to face with a roaming fox, not eager to interact with humans. The twinkling eyes were unmoving as two fox cubs ran into the road ahead, gekkering loudly and playfighting. The vixen's eyes, undisturbed by her young, remained fixed on Rebecca as she let out another bloodcurdling scream. The cubs stopped in their tracks, attentive to their mother's call. They focused on Rebecca, who was now cowering slightly behind the car. The white survival suit was glowing against the murky backdrop.

Six motionless white dots stared at her silently. Only two of the eyes had ever seen a human. Their memory had quickly faded. Another scream erupted, this time from the undergrowth to the side of the road. Rebecca for the first time sensed that something greater had changed, as her eyes darted frantically, searching for the hidden animal.

Putting her best foot forward, she supressed her fear. Puffing out her chest, with a deep breath, Rebecca walked confidently toward the vixen and her cubs. They looked at her inquisitively, showing no sign of fear as she walked past. She maintained eye contact with the fox who sat, nose twitching and unperturbed. The cubs, fresh, clean and fluffy, tilted their big round heads playfully as they watched her.

'It's not right. Something's not right here,' Rebecca muttered desperately under her breath, looking up at the road ahead, turning her back to the foxes.

A few hundred metres further, the bars on the visor dropped to a single one and the road levelled off. Walking into an area of mist that had rolled over the road from the adjacent field, Rebecca struggled to see far ahead. Passing a road sign for a roundabout, she squinted as she began to make out the shapes of large vehicles ahead. Drawing closer, the mammoth figures of two tanks, an armoured personnel carrier and several armoured Land Rovers became clear. Beyond, a barricade had been built, closing off the exit of the roundabout leading to the explosion site.

'Hello!' she yelled, hoping that her cry would be answered. No response. Walking between the hunks of military metal, Rebecca searched for signs of life, but could find none. The vehicles were covered in a layer of dust and grime from their long period of inactivity. A dreadful chill ran through Rebecca's chest, as confusion and fear took full hold.

'Hello! Hello! Is anybody there?' she screamed at the top of her lungs, dropping to her knees in exhaustion. 'Hello,' she whimpered in despair.

-Chapter 50-

'Hugh, you're sure these are going to hold?' asked Commander Mortimer, looking bewilderedly upon the makeshift seats fashioned within the shuttle. As they had not been designed to carry astronauts, she was concerned.

'That depends on variable factors,' responded Hugh in a frustratingly non-committal manner. She rolled her eyes, pushing herself out toward the docking bay where the remainder of the crew were preparing themselves.

'I'm glad I won't be using them,' she whispered loudly enough for Hugh to hear as she drifted freely. He glanced at her before looking once again at the seats.

It had taken several weeks to plan for the impromptu trip to the Martian surface. The Exodus Base had barely been made ready to accept or sustain human life, but the automatons on the planet surface had been reprioritised to prepare the base for habitation.

'Ok people, listen up,' Lacey Mortimer shouted loudly so that all could hear. 'You've seen the images from the International Space Station. You've seen the dead astronauts. You've seen the clouds of smoke from exploding nuclear power stations on Earth and data confirming the orbit of our planet is shifting away from the Sun. There's nothing further we need to know right now. We must consider ourselves the last line of defence. Every one of you is key to our survival as a species. To those of you who are heading down to the surface of Mars, I want to say this. You've been an inspiration to me. If anybody can make this work, it's you. Some of you feel that we're doomed. I can see why. But we won't go quietly!' she shouted and was met by the motivated approval of her crew.

The mood had been sombre, with some members of the crew doing all they could to raise the spirits of others. The simultaneous deep grief that they were experiencing was having a profound effect, regardless of simulations to the contrary.

Olivia, Luca Romano, Morgan Reeves, Laurence Havering and Gustav Lindberg floated past Commander Mortimer, slapping her outstretched hand as they passed.

'Nice speech, Commander,' smirked Laurence as the sound of their palms smashing together echoed around the docking bay. His strong grip wrapped itself around Lacey's hand momentarily.

Moving hastily into the shuttle, they made their way to the five seats fashioned by Hugh. Wearing streamlined, dark-red space suits, finished off with the signature silver Argo Industries trim, they strapped themselves in to the makeshift seats apprehensively. The hatch closed gradually before a guttural clank sounded as it locked and sealed.

'Hey, Luca. What did you think of that bullshit speech?' asked Laurence Havering. Luca laughed. His voice booming over the intercom.

'I can still hear you, Havering,' grinned Lacey Mortimer from outside the docking bay, where the remaining crew had positioned themselves.

'This isn't what I signed up for! How's that for last words?' Laurence cracked.

'That's enough about last words, thanks. Commander, can't you keep him on the ship?' Morgan asked as she looked angrily toward Laurence, who closed his eyes and smiled.

A silence descended. Hugh slotted his finger into a groove in the console outside the docking bay.

The shuttle detached unspectacularly and on schedule, drifting slowly to a safe distance from the Veil, before the boosters engaged, propelling it toward the red planet at the desired entry trajectory. Science Officer Ethan Porter and Commander Lacey Mortimer moved back toward the gravitational comforts of the spinning top, from where they could monitor the remainder of the descent. Pilot Danielle Slade and Hugh followed a few moments later.

'If things don't work out down there. Well, I can't even bring myself to think about it,' Lacey confided, switching off the intercom. Ethan forced a smile as they climbed through a transition tube toward the familiar tug of gravity.

'I suppose we do like to feel we're in control of our destiny. It's our curse. Even though we all know deep down that we are vulnerable. Mortal,' he reflected.

'I'm trying to keep it together. I am. But my imagination keeps running away with me. My father, my sister, my nieces. I can't stand it. And even worse, every day I keep remembering people I care about, but who I've forgotten to mourn. I wake up feeling numb. Ashamed to be alive,' Lacey confessed, supressing emotions seeking an outlet.

'I think that it's pretty much the same for us all,' Ethan suggested. 'The way I look at it, although we may never know or understand what happened, we're still alive and kicking. We have to stay that way. If everything hinges on this artefact, there is always the possibility that we have misinterpreted its true purpose, although the indicators aren't great. But it's a machine. A relic. One of our hopes must be that it'll fail. That it'll break down.'

Watching the shuttle powering its way toward the surface of Mars, they were joined by Danielle and Hugh on deck. The metallic sheen reflected the distant sunlight as the shuttle gathered speed and grew smaller in the thrall of the massive red backdrop. Illuminated by the brilliant theatre that unravelled before them, their faces tinged with the red hue of the planet.

Ethan lay his arm around the back of Danielle's neck and pulled her close. Danielle's hand reached up across her chest and grasped his as they watched the imagery.

Chapter 51

The supplies in the shuttle clinked and clattered, as the slight tremors of turbulence started to send vibrations through the craft. Speeding down through the atmosphere, the crew inside were blind.

'This isn't how I imagined it!' shouted Gustav Lindberg, referring to the lack of windows and the descent down to the planet surface in a vehicle not designed for human transport. The shuttle shunted violently several times, from side to side, as the crew gasped, the force of the shunt shocking them into silence.

Morgan fumbled for her neckline, eyes tightly closed, wishing that she could hold the small gold cross she wore, but was thwarted by the space suit. Space travel had been fine but she had never enjoyed turbulence.

The shuttle barrelled down, plummeting ever deeper into the thin Martian atmosphere. Hugh monitored its progress, on target to hit the landing pad just two miles away from the Exodus Base. A two-way connection between Olivia and Hugh meant that each could see through the eyes of the other. Initial concerns aside, Commander Mortimer had agreed reluctantly to grant Exodus Base systems access to Olivia. This was preferable to the alternative of reanimating a reserve android. With an indefinite period of survival ahead, the amortisation of one of the reserve androids was unappealing.

A hollow popping sound echoed around the great metal shell of the shuttle as the parachutes deployed and the retro boosters fired. Slight deceleration kicked in as the crew felt the reverse thrust.

Almost before the crew had the opportunity to experience the additional G-force, Hugh's voice rang out over the intercom.

'Retro booster failure, fifty per cent.'

'What do you mean "retro booster failure", Hugh?' Morgan exclaimed.

Four of the eight retro boosters had not fired and Hugh attempted to ignite them once again. Olivia watched through his eyes as he punched commands furiously at his end, but to no avail.

The functional boosters could barely manoeuvre the shuttle toward the landing pad as the landing struts deployed. Laurence turned his head, looking into the terrified eyes of Morgan.

'Are we going to die?!' shouted Laurence.

'No, we're not!' responded Luca defiantly, shifting anxiously as he tested the straps of his seat.

The final few seconds before arrival were unbearable for the crew. With no point of reference, they couldn't judge their speed. The shuttle thumped into the pad, as the landing struts buckled and the base of the craft crashed into the ground at high velocity.

A concerto of lights and beeps sounded on the console manned by Hugh on the Veil. Danielle dug her face into Ethan's shoulder, letting out an ungodly scream.

The shuttle's chassis smashed and ripped open, immediately venting all gas from within. Background beeps associated with the activation of numerous warning systems on board were muted by the thin Martian atmosphere.

Unstrapping herself from the seat, Olivia saw the damage. Light and dust poured into the interior through the cracked shell of the craft. The blunt force trauma of the landing had been significant, but her own hardened frame was able to bear it. The alloy body of the shuttle had not withstood the impact well. The landing struts and other debris lay scattered across the landing area, having been flung in all directions, leaving the smashed craft at the centre of the pad.

Looking at the crew who remained strapped in, Olivia noticed there was no movement. Bending down and unstrapping each of them in turn as quickly as possible, she monitored their vital signs. Gustav Lindberg and Luca Romano had been killed instantly by the massive and instant deceleration. The vitals of Morgan Reeves and Laurence Havering were faint, but they were alive.

'What's going on? Report, Hugh!' insisted Commander Mortimer, standing behind Hugh on the Veil.

'Officers Lindberg and Romano have died. Officers Reeves and Havering have suffered serious internal injuries, but are currently alive,' Hugh reported. Danielle let out a loud sob as Ethan tried to comfort her.

'We have to go down there. We have to help,' Ethan Porter implored, turning to Commander Mortimer, who shook her head slowly, her eyes screaming with shock and bewilderment.

Six PROSPECT automatons scuttled toward the shuttle through the thick dust cloud. The most peculiar of welcoming committees began attaching themselves to the shuttle. Climbing up the side, they scanned for damage and hooked tethers to load-bearing points. The sporadic muffled tapping from outside the shuttle could only be sensed by Olivia.

The automatons utilised their pre-programmed routine for the retrieval of shuttles. On this occasion, they executed the routine to transport the smashed craft containing the 3D-printing and automaton synthetisation plant to the Exodus Base.

The PROSPECT automatons scampered away from the shuttle before quietness resumed. The tethers, tightened with such force as to jerk the entire craft into lateral motion.

A fixed winch, designed to drag delivery shuttles onto a cargo track, pulled the great craft over the smooth, hard ground. Beautiful in its simplicity, its design took advantage of the relatively weak gravity on Mars. The shuttle was hauled slowly but surely as the PROSPECT automatons made observations to ensure the integrity of the operation. Pieces of metal lay strewn in its wake.

The carriage, wide and flat, was level with the edge of the landing pad and sat on a track cut into the rock. As the broken shuttle approached the carriage, the winch slowed. The change in texture from solid earth to the smooth carbon fibre of the carriage could be felt by Olivia within the craft. The track that extended toward the base was unreflective and matched the colour of its surrounding.

The PROSPECT droids scurried up the sides of the shuttle, removing the tethers from the craft as the carriage set off slowly. Several loud thuds were heard as the shuttle was secured for transit. Olivia kneeled down next to Laurence and Morgan but was unable to remove their space suits or do anything to help.

She monitored the Nanoblood within the two surviving crew members as it began to migrate slowly to the internal areas of injury. Carried by the weak heartbeat of the dying humans, the Nanoblood acted to stimulate their hearts and maintain regular rhythm whilst plugging the ruptured blood vessels; the cause of significant internal bleeding within Morgan and Laurence.

Through the electronic eyes populating the landing area, Olivia viewed the outside world intently. The carriage glided as though floating through air as it gathered speed. Large, light patches of permafrost dotted the red landscape as the shuttle moved silently.

Ahead rose the majestic Atlantis Mountain. A dot on the outskirts of the North Pole ice cap, ironically and unofficially renamed by Mike Argo himself. The mountain's selection was no accident. Surrounded by earth rich in frozen water, the location sat atop the outer rim of a substantial underground lake. With more water than the efficient Exodus Base would ever need, the discovery of the lake by Future Logic had been the cause of much excitement.

This excitement had soon waned. It became clear that the water, as well as the ancient sediment and surrounding rock, showed no evidence of ever having played host to life. Further secret exploration and research had shown no evidence of life ever existing on the planet.

On a purely scientific level, the ramifications were significant. Life could be brought from Earth to begin enjoying the limited harbours where it could now flourish. But this planet, once abundantly wet and hospitable, had never developed life of its own accord. A discovery that Mike Argo had found to be mystifying and existentially terrifying. A discovery only known to Future Logic.

Olivia's inbuilt navigator was being tugged in ways and directions that she had never experienced before. Built and dispatched en masse, PoleGuard units had slowly but surely crawled on caterpillar tracks to take up their positions at strategic locations around the planet.

The PoleGuards converted sunlight into energy. Using this energy to generate localised electromagnetic fields, they interacted with those fields created by the other units. The PoleGuards were successfully shielding the surface of the planet from harmful solar rays. Connected by a web of armoured tethers stretching thousands of miles, the

PoleGuards reduced their magnetic output by night. Streaming their excess power through the grid to those units in greatest need, they worked together in perfect harmony.

Disregarding the constantly changing sway of her inbuilt navigator, Olivia continued to observe through the eyes of the PROSPECT automatons travelling on their carriage. As far as she could see, there were row after row of neatly segregated square partitions of Martian soil, approximately three metres by three metres. Each square encircled by a low, ten-centimetre plastic wall and covered by a gas-permeable, transparent plastic membrane. Irrigated by a network of tubules, the algae within each square had everything it needed to flourish.

Bathing in abundant carbon dioxide released from the gently warming soil beneath, and acceptable temperature within their miniature environments, the hardy strains of selected algae vented oxygen through the membrane and into the thin atmosphere above. Some automatons worked continually to create additional habitats while maintaining others.

Approaching the rocky outcrop that accommodated the larger of the two airlock doors, Olivia watched as the rectangular door lifted. With the carriage slowing to a standstill inside the airlock, there was a short wait for the external door to close and the internal door to open. A long passage, bored by automatons and lit brightly by white lights, revealed itself as the carriage once again began to move. Travelling three hundred metres into the side of the Atlantis Mountain, the shuttle coasted through the terminal doors at the Exodus Base, coming to a standstill.

The atmospheric regulators, operational for the past week in preparation for their arrival, had thickened the air in the base. The automatons unfastened the craft from the carriage.

An astonishing array of gadgetry surrounded the shuttle. Computer consoles lined the walls of the semi-circular terminal. The rocky walls, covered in a transparent sealing compound, glistened.

Olivia returned to the injured members of the crew, removing their helmets and unbuckling their spacesuits. Their breathing was weak.

'We have arrived at the Exodus Base,' Olivia advised.

'Yes, I can see,' Hugh responded, standing next to the remainder of the crew on board the Veil. 'The NanoPens are located in unit 822.'

Olivia quickly obtained the NanoPens, administering one shot to Morgan's arm and another to Laurence. The spring-loaded syringe sunk into their flesh, as the auto-injector delivered a large payload of Nanoblood into their systems.

Leaving them in their seats to avoid causing any further injury, Olivia finally removed her helmet and assessed her surroundings.

The lighting, used throughout the base, mimicked sunlight. A system of hydroponic pods were used to feed and nourish the roots of Snake Plants, Areca Palms and Ficus Benjamina, as well as the plant life propagated in the lake garden.

The temperature was a steady nineteen degrees Celsius throughout the base. With no need for much regulation, day or night, the sheltered location within the mountain was a true haven.

Morgan's body began to convulse violently in the chair as her breathing and heart rate spiked. Her leg, broken at the knee from the impact, flailed unnaturally. Olivia could do nothing but sit beside Morgan, strap her body back to the chair and hold her hand still.

Chapter 52

The warmth and brightness of the beautiful spring day gracing the Troyan Monastery couldn't quell the fear and anxiety within its walls. The birds sang and the sweet smell of mountain flowers wafted effortlessly. The monks gathered in the central courtyard. It had been eight days since one of them had disappeared from the monastery overnight. Now, Magda Popova was gone too.

She hadn't risen as usual that morning. Her uncle, Brother Boyan, had checked her cell with concern. Finding the bed made and only a police badge shining atop the wooden table, he raised the alarm amongst the others.

'We are starting to disappear. Soon none of us will be left. Can't you see?' said one monk.

'Only the weak. The scared. Only they would leave,' retorted another. 'Cowards.'

'Perhaps they are the bravest of us all. Those that would venture out into the wilderness. Perhaps we here are the cowards,' Brother Boyan angrily snapped. 'Look at what is happening to us. We are failing this test! Where is our resolve? Our faith?'

'It doesn't matter anyway. Whatever is written for us, that's what will happen,' lamented Brother Josef. Boyan trod softly as he approached Josef, the young monk who had looked up to him as a father since arriving at the monastery.

'Yes. I believe that you're right. Whatever is written for us will come to pass, but we can still choose how our souls prepare for the inevitable. If we don't, then why did we ever come here? What has it all been for? What have we learned?' Boyan said softly. 'Did those who leave do so because they were scared? Perhaps. Or, is it that we do not leave, because we ourselves are scared? We stay here, because we don't know what to do. We are the ones who are afraid. Weak.'

'What would you have us do, brother? Walk outside of these walls into oblivion?' fretted one of the men. 'We haven't seen a single soul on the road outside for months. Not since we all saw what happened to the brothers who went to help those in the crashed car.'

'We don't understand what we have seen. So, we fear it. I will suffer the pain of this fear no longer. I can't stand it!' Boyan declared, walking purposefully toward the courtyard entrance. The sun beat down on him as he walked out of the shade of the church. The touch of it on the back of his neck made him instantly nostalgic about his yesteryears. Remembering his young, fearless self, he ignored the cries of the other monks as they shouted after him.

The robe he wore was dark. Feeling the warmth on his back, Boyan followed the path as the gateway arch leading out of the monastery loomed. A hand reached and grabbed him around his wasting, hungry arm.

'You can't go! You mustn't! What are we going to do? Don't leave us!' Brother Josef frantically panted as Boyan looked at him staunchly, pulling the hood of his robe slowly over his head.

'You're a good man. You will find your path, you all will, but now I must find mine,' Boyan turned and yanked his arm free from the withering grasp of Josef. 'Don't worry. If I find that more can safely travel in my footsteps, I shall return. And if not, say a prayer for me!'

The gateway, as open and inviting as it had always been, yawned before him as he strode through, looking down toward the ground. Staring at his feet as they paced forward, he had departed with no food, no water, but a heart full of forced hope.

Each footstep took him further from the monastery gate as he passed Magda's squad car. Its battery dead, she had tried to start it when she left, but had failed. Continuing, Boyan, reached much further than he thought he would. Marching on, still staring at his shoes, he was sure that if he looked up, the end would come crashing down upon him. The sound of water babbling under the bridge he was crossing was more than he could bear. Looking to his side, the sight filled him with joys long forgotten. The crisp gleam of the fresh, cold water as it coursed freely through the mountain, was overwhelming. *If this is the last thing that I see, so be it,* he thought, stepping toward the metal rail and staring out.

In his mind, Magda's face smiled at him. A smile hiding secret thoughts. *Why did she leave? Was she disappointed in me? Did she lose her mind? Is she dead?* Many questions flooded his consciousness.

A short, sharp bray sounded from the other side of the bridge. Looking ahead, Boyan saw a donkey grazing grass at the side of the road in a lacklustre fashion. Distracted from his thoughts, he approached the animal, flies darting around on its body as it stopped chewing on the grass and raised its head. The noseband running around the donkey's mouth was digging into the skin and red, sore patches were visible.

'Let's get this off you, boy,' Boyan said, undoing the buckle and peeling the leather strapping away from the increasingly disturbed animal. He ran his hand along the back of the donkey's head and neck as he continued to remove the harness.

Finally dropping the straps to the ground, he looked upon the deep lesions caused by the harness. The donkey looked at him with grateful eyes, nudging his hand before traipsing slowly in the direction of the monastery. The monks had seen many animals wandering past since the Trauma struck.

Resuming on his chosen path, Boyan moved amongst debris that had fallen onto the disused road. Passing farmhouses and villas, all looking as abandoned as each other, a familiar feeling crept up his spine with a wet slither. He shuddered even though the robe he wore in the glowing spring sun was causing him to perspire. He hoped for a voice to shout out to him. He hoped to see evidence of human life, but there was none.

A grey, torn curtain, flapping filthy in the wind from an open second-floor window, caught his eye. A crumpled heap of tattered clothes on the concrete underneath the window demanded further inspection. Small pieces of clothing and what looked like bone were scattered in the vicinity. Clasping fingers through the metal fence, Boyan pushed his nose up to the wires. The remains of a woman lay mostly torn to shreds. Picked clean by wolves and birds since her demise.

Opening the gate, he stepped onto the path and took a few paces forward to look closer. *What was this thing that happened to so many?* he mournfully thought.

The distant roar of a motor echoed faintly. A sound he hadn't heard in so long. Immediately turning to try and determine its direction, Boyan thought it sounded like a motorbike. A motorbike getting closer. As the seconds ticked by, the sound became louder until he knew for sure the bike was near. A dark-green Ducati motorbike approached rapidly, with a rider dressed in black leather hunched down low behind the handlebars. The silver visor on the black helmet reflected a shard of sunlight as the bike passed in the blink of an eye. Boyan curled his finger and thumb together, pressing them against his lips as he sounded the loudest whistle he could manage.

A second passed before the tyres screeched the bike to a halt. Out of his view, Boyan stood still in the garden as he heard the motorcyclist dismount and start walking toward him, drawing a handgun.

'Who's there?' the muffled voice from inside the helmet boomed. 'I have a gun!'

'Magda?' Boyan cried out, easily recognising her voice.

'Uncle, is that you?' her footsteps quickened as she ran toward the property. 'What are you doing in there?

'I had to try and... why did you leave us?' Boyan's voice quaked as his lip quivered.

'I had to go. I had to do something. Anything,' Magda's muffled voice bellowed from inside the crash helmet as she removed it. 'Sorry. I knew you would have tried to talk me out of leaving if I had told you. I found this bike and managed to get to Lovech.'

'Lovech? You reached Lovech? What did you find there?' the monk asked with inexplicable optimism, pulling his hood back to reveal his bearded face. What little light there was in Magda's eyes extinguished as she recollected what her brain had already started to try and repress.

'There's no one left, uncle. Nobody. Just some human remains,' she said, frowning and turning pale, as though the memories were causing her physical pain. The mass killing at the Ambassador's House had made much more sense than this. She remembered going inside just to see the carnage for herself. Seeing the dead bodies there had been much less traumatic than the solitude and fear felt as she rode through the lifeless city of Lovech. 'I've been thinking. This must be widespread. If it had happened just here, people would have come to help.'

'Why did we survive?' whispered Brother Boyan in self-reflection.

'No idea. I think you may be able to explain it better than me. I did manage to get some food for us all. It's enough for us to eat well tonight,' Magda smiled faintly, patting her backpack. 'We have to get our strength up, because tomorrow we must try to find some answers.'

'We will find no answers. We've been chosen to witness the end. The fruits of all our sins and misdoings,' the monk said meekly, as he pulled the hood back over his head and walked out of the garden to join Magda on the road.

'Maybe you're right. But maybe you're wrong,' Magda turned in frustration and walked back toward the motorbike. Climbing on, she gestured to Boyan who climbed on behind her and they set off back toward the monastery.

Chapter 53

Arriving quickly, she parked the motorbike next to her squad car. Met with joy by the starving monks, the happiness quickly turned to sadness as Magda recounted what she had seen in Lovech. The promise of a good meal did nothing to calm the sorrow. Wild speculation followed as they searched for sense in what had happened.

The hours passed as day turned to night. With the meal eaten silently and without much enjoyment, many of the inhabitants of the monastery retired to their respective cells by candlelight.

Magda had promised herself that she wouldn't return to the room where she had spent so many soul-crushing hours.

She had picked up a carton of cigarettes. A guilty pleasure from her younger years. Tearing open the plastic wrapping, she took out a fresh packet and picked up her new lighter before heading to the car park.

Walking out with slight apprehension, she lit a cigarette and approached her car. Sitting on the bonnet, she wondered how she would get enough power in the battery to start it. Taking a deep drag, she puffed out the smoke and coughed slightly. The cloud of smoke reflected the moonlight as it gradually dispersed. The background noise of the nearby river was ever present. The hoot of an owl rang out, followed closely by another. Everything seemed so eerily normal.

Through the dissipating smoke, Magda saw movement. Illuminated only by moonlight, two figures rounded the perimeter wall of the monastery, walking steadily in the middle of the road toward her. Smacked by an instant hit of adrenaline, she wasn't pleased to see them. Their outline was familiar, but their movement foreign. Seeming to glide toward her as they walked, Magda's alertness elevated and instinct to draw her weapon peaked.

Standing from the hood of the car, she drew her pistol and aimed directly at them.

'Stop! Stop right there!' Magda's voice boomed. The echo thundered around the surrounding mountains, alerting all in the monastery that something was wrong.

The two human forms slowed to a standstill, turning to look at each other briefly. One of them wore torn dark trousers and a t-shirt, and the other, a short light-coloured dress and torn jumper. Their faces and arms were unnaturally white, appearing almost silver in the moonlight. Standing ten metres away, heart thumping, Magda was unable to make out their facial features, but she saw that both of the human forms had no hair.

'Who are you? What are you doing out here?' Magda shouted loudly as the first of the monks arrived at the monastery entrance. The human forms turned their heads to see. 'Didn't you hear what I said? Who are you?'

They looked back toward Magda and the human form that appeared male stepped forward slightly.

'I swear if you come one step closer, I will shoot you!' Magda threatened, her hands shaking visibly as the approach stopped once again. The monks squinted to try and make out the ghostly figures.

'Put down your weapon,' the male quietly ordered. His voice was calm and smooth but heard by all.

'Put down my weapon? No, I don't think so,' Magda replied defiantly. The roar of the river and gentle breeze seemed to die down as the human forms looked in tandem toward one of the monks. He started coughing gently, but within seconds the cough had turned to a wheeze. Magda watched as the monk fell to his knees amongst his brothers. She flicked the safety of her firearm on, throwing it to the ground before her.

'Stop it!' she shouted. The monk continued coughing for a moment before bringing his breathing back under control. The others eased him on to his back to rest.

The human forms approached once again, treading carefully toward the Makarov sidearm, lying on the tarmac. The female form bent down and picked it up, looking at it with apparent curiosity. Her strangely long, spindly fingers examined the contours of the handle, running along the trigger, down the barrel and around the muzzle, before quickly tossing it to one side.

Now much closer, Magda looked them over once more, her eyes straining in the darkness. Visible in the full spectrum of grey, she could immediately see that there was something different about the individuals standing before her. Something wrong. Gaunt, expressionless faces with skin that seemed radiant, whilst inhumanly white. Their effect on the monk had put Magda in mind of her experience with Nadia Hristova. The exertion of some type of control.

'How are you doing this? Why did you kill us all?' she asked, desperation clinging to her voice.

'We didn't kill all of you,' replied the female form calmly. 'Balance must be restored. We can exist together.'

'Who are you?' Magda asked.

'The answer to that question is... difficult to explain in your language. Also, you would not enjoy the answer,' the female form replied, clasping together her elongated fingers in front of herself.

'You owe us an explanation for what you have done to us!' Magda cried as a tear escaped and rolled down the side of her cheek.

'You are free to live and rebuild. For our own survival, our presence on your planet is temporary but necessary,' the male form explained. 'Our vessel was entombed in rock, unable to affect and sculpt the life we deposited on this planet. Intelligent life had already developed when our vessel surfaced. The vessel would have atomised, but our great beacon has been silenced. It has remained silent for much time and we fear for our species.'

'So, you decided that we're expendable? To save yourselves?' Magda cried as the monks shifted uncomfortably and began to whisper amongst themselves.

'No life is expendable, but you are also not sophisticated. Not yet ēlevat. Violent. When we depart, we will leave you with knowledge far beyond your time or your reach,' the female form said. 'Until then, this planet is for you, as it is for us. Take what you need and live.'

The human forms turned smoothly and continued walking down the road slowly. With their backs turned, Magda looked at the Makarov pistol on the floor. Fury raging within her, she did all she could to resist picking up the gun and burying two shots in each of their backs. Walking a few steps toward the pistol, the human forms stopped in their tracks and waited. Magda picked up the gun, looked at the human forms before tucking the Makarov into her belt. They continued to walk serenely until they disappeared into the darkness. She carried on looking for minutes after they could no longer be seen. Drawing a deep breath and wiping the dampness from her eyes with her forefinger, she turned to the monks huddled around their affected brother, who had spat out two mouthfuls of blood. Two of the monks lifted him, supporting him to walk back into the monastery.

'They're lying,' Magda barked, walking into the church with Brothers Boyan and Josef and three other monks. 'They're lying. I know it!'

'They aren't human. They look human but their eyes are so calm. So emotionless,' Brother Josef whispered. One of the monks who had joined them leaned to say something into Boyan's ear.

'This is probably the time to share our thoughts openly!' Magda huffed indignantly, a rye ironic smile spreading across her lips.

'They seemed to speak truthfully. They don't seem to enjoy violence,' the shy monk replied.

'They don't seem to enjoy violence? Although they have killed most of the people on the planet?' Magda noted with a hint of sarcasm.

'This is the Rapture. It's upon us and we are here to see it. As clear as day and as undeniable,' another monk, aged and wise, contributed quietly. 'The two damned spirits who visited us this evening are messengers. Messengers sent to ease us into oblivion. Do not be deluded.'

'Then why aren't we dead?' Magda asked. Her increasing frustration etched into her face. 'And forgive me, because it's been some time since I learnt about this, but if this is the Rapture, would all good Christians, such as yourselves, not have been swept up to Heaven?'

'I hope that Jesus is truly in your heart because there are no answers for you out there. There are no answers for any of us to find,' the old monk irately stammered, his lower lip shaking as he spoke emotively, stepping toward Magda. 'In fact, it's interesting that they visited us on your return.'

'What do you mean by that?' grunted Magda. The old monk fell quiet, fearing he had voiced too much. Magda's searching glare angered him.

'This all started when you arrived here. Now you leave us and, on your return, these demons appear at our door!' the monk said.

'Do you think I'll be judged by you? You're scared. A scared old man, looking for an answer you cannot find. Open your eyes!' Magda shouted.

'We must remain calm. We have to work together. We must not fight amongst each other. We must pray that our brother recovers and we must find a way forward from here,' Boyan said.

-Chapter 54-

The MagJet containing Captain Wren was re-entering the atmosphere, recalled by an automated signal emanating from the Future Logic Facility. The atmospheric regulators pumped heated air into the cockpit, warming the deactivated android.

The jet's autopilot plotted a course for the facility. After half an hour, Wren's core temperature had risen enough for the emergency reactivation protocol to kick in. His eyes twitched as his systems came online. After a few more moments, he was able to move his arms and right his head, which had slumped to the side.

Already approaching the runway at the facility, he tried to alter the course of the MagJet but was unable to deploy the flight controls or affect the course of the craft. Zooming in on the runway ahead with the front camera, he saw the expanse of white covering the ground. The runway itself, no longer visible. Typing in the override code, which was accepted, the flight controls still did not present themselves.

Sitting straight back in the flight chair, he braced himself for the autopilot landing. The wheels touched down on six centimetres of white powder as the powerful jet engines sucked up the powder and kicked up the material in the swirling wake of the aircraft. Coming to a standstill halfway down the runway, the engines disengaged automatically.

The human forms guarding the perimeter of the base turned and moved toward the MagJet at speed. As the powder settled around the craft, Captain Wren observed the shadows of the human forms that surrounded him from all sides. Looking down at the control panel, he reset the flight systems completely. As the screens went blank, he saw a woman approaching with a small girl. The human forms stood aside as they came closer and he was able to see them in better detail.

Olivia had activated code 713. He could not be captured and should not have returned to the facility. A face blank of expression, Captain Wren looked at the screens displaying the Argo Industries logo. Considering his options rapidly, he knew that the MagJet contained no explosive payload. His preferred option.

The white dust cleared as the woman and small girl stood back. The remaining human forms moved a step closer, raising their arms toward the MagJet. An invisible energy pushed the MagJet down on its landing gears. Looking around, Captain Wren registered that the MagJet was hunkering down toward the ground. The craft had squatted almost as far as it was able on its landing gear, before the airframe began to groan.

'All systems, nominal,' the computerised voice promised, as the flight controls presented themselves before Captain Wren. He hit the ignition and the engines whistled back to life. Enormous heat expelled from the afterburner, blowing two human forms standing directly behind the MagJet, away in flames. Those standing in front were able to jump out of the way just before the craft belted down the runway. Still under the influence of the unknown downward force, Captain Wren engaged full thrust and tried to take off.

The end of the runway approaching, there was no lift. The three wheels were still on the ground. Reaching a speed much higher than usually necessary for take-off, the nose lifted and the MagJet took off. Veering to the right slightly to avoid a watchtower, the craft caught the tops of several trees before gaining altitude and speeding into the distance. Taryn and the remaining human forms watched as the lights on the wings flashed, until they could no longer be seen in the late afternoon dusk.

Taryn continued to stare in the direction of the mechanised unit that had made its escape. She wore the comfortable grey body suit, given to her by the human forms. Somehow, its softness and warmth provided some relief from the gnawing pain that tormented her. The innocence of her childlike expression had faded within a short time. Skin tightened over her cheekbones and remaining features. Her bones hurt, as though being rearranged. Fine, silky, jet-black hair had started to grow on her head. She had seldom thought of her father, Jerome Docherty or her mother and brother during waking hours, but at night she would remember them. Like a distant memory, painfully buried.

'I want to fly in a machine like that,' Taryn softly suggested to Samara as the injured human forms were carried silently into the facility.

'You will have anything you desire. Anything you need. First, you have a lot to learn,' Samara replied. She had started to take on the appearance of somebody that Taryn knew well.

The pleasant evening sounds of the surrounding jungle were all that could be heard. Leaving Samara's side, Taryn crossed the runway and headed toward the perimeter fence. As she walked, white powder levitated from the ground in a fine haze that shrouded her ankles. Samara followed closely behind. A small monkey could be seen through the metal fence, cowering behind a bush in the jungle beyond. The undergrowth and shrubs were covered in the white powdery material. The jungle, affected by the Sift, was thickening, with some of the plants and trees taking on strange new colours and leaf formations.

Taryn kneeled down to look at the monkey. Red and sore, the primate's eyes stared back. It hissed loudly before disappearing into the undergrowth and up one of the nearby trees. Human forms scrambled fleet-footedly up behind Samara and Taryn. An immediate sense of danger engulfed them both as they stepped back away from the fence, turned and ran toward the facility. Two human forms shielded them physically as gunfire rang out from within the thick jungle. Bullets whistled through the air past Samara and Taryn as they ran, striking the ground at their feet. One bullet tore through Samara's calf, bringing her to the ground with a thud. Taryn stopped and ran back, lying on the ground beside her as the two human forms threw themselves on top. Distracted by the arrival of the MagJet containing Captain Wren, the human forms had been unaware of the hostile approach. Now repurposed to develop the Galadron ranks, the Pebble no longer affected or monitored the remaining human population of the planet Earth. The Galadron's abilities, whilst substantial, were still not honed or precise.

The gunfire stopped as the attackers watched the human forms swarming out of the gate and dispersing into the jungle beyond. The shadows of great warriors and sentries from the past chased the party of ten confused local survivors who had armed themselves with AK47s and come to look for the cause of the white powder, but now fled. They had found what they were looking for, but soon would wish they hadn't.

The fading light reflected dimly from the white powder coating the jungle. The wide receptive eyes of the human forms were able to spot movement ahead through the foliage. The attackers heard movement over the ambient noise of the jungle all around. They had already been exposed to a lethal dose of radiation by coming into contact with the Sift. The attackers stopped running, backing into a circle and looking frantically outwards in all directions. Unable to see a target, they breathed heavily, pointing their weapons at the still and terrifying jungle.

The human forms surrounded them slowly. Kneeling behind cover, the Galadron sentries closed their eyes and bowed their heads.

One of the terrified men involuntarily pulled the trigger of his gun, letting out an agonising scream as his body spun in a dazed stupor. The automatic gunfire chattered as he was rendered unconscious. Bullets ripped through the legs of three of the other attackers, sending them to the ground in anguish. Screaming at each other in confusion, the remainder of the men started to fire their weapons wildly in all directions.

The sentries stayed hidden as bullets struck the cover they hid behind. Another two of the attackers fell to the ground unconscious. The remainder looked at them and then at one another with unbelieving and terrified eyes, before their world turned black.

The three men laying on the ground with gunshot wounds to the legs had lost too much blood already, too weak and full of terror to attempt to lift their assault rifles. As the human forms approached from all sides, they looked down at the irradiated bodies of the unconscious men on the jungle floor. With keen and piercing precision, they gazed into the eyes of the three injured men.

A pistol whipped round from behind the back of one of the attackers and two shots rang out. The second passed straight through the neck of a Galadron, who crumpled to the floor instantly. The remaining three men were instantly rendered unconscious by the combined minds of the remaining human forms.

Looking at the fallen sentry, the human forms turned and squinted in anger at the sight of the unconscious attackers. As the first of them regained consciousness, their screams were muffled by their weakness. Waking to the dreadful sound, the remaining men shrieked in pain, their minds flooded with unbearable phantom pain. Their final punishment was short-lived as the Galadron ended the lives of the attackers without mercy.

Sliding long fingers into the mouths of the twisted dead faces, the human forms began to drag the bodies of the men back into the facility by their hard palates.

Samara stood to her feet with Taryn. Dark-red blood leaked from her leg. The white powder was soft between their toes as another swathe of Sift wafted through the trees toward them. Engulfed by the cloud, appearing grey and stormy in the darkness of dusk, Taryn stepped forward and threw her arms around Samara's waist.

-Chapter 55-

Seventy-two hours since the crash landing at the Exodus Base, both Science Officer Morgan Reeves and Flight Engineer Laurence Havering were unconscious. In chemically induced comas, both patients were strapped to beds in the medical room. Data transmitted by the Nanoblood indicated spinal injuries, ruptured blood vessels and broken bones in them both. Olivia knew any involuntary movement before full healing might cause paralysis or death.

Nanoblood and Boon supplements were introduced intravenously through drips. Morgan and Laurence's blood was purified and doped by a type of universally accepted synthetic blood, bursting with just the right amount of oxygen. Only time would tell what permanent damage had been caused by their injuries.

There was nothing more Olivia could do for them. Their chance of survival increased exponentially with each passing hour as the Nanoblood fused bone, repaired tissue and reconnected nerve fibres, the miniature robots themselves becoming the conduits of nerve impulses.

She had already been distracted from her primary objective for too long. Disconnecting her link to the Veil spacecraft, Olivia hit the pressure pad to leave the medical room. Hugh immediately detected the disconnect and hailed Commander Mortimer to the bridge.

Returning to the smashed shuttle, Olivia saw that only the shell remained since the automatons had picked it apart. The stowage compartments were still sealed. She accessed the storage space where she had secreted the rucksack brought from the Future Logic Facility.

Throwing the bag over one shoulder, she hastily made her way toward the MarsLab1 on the shores of the underground lake. Standing patiently in the lift, Olivia waited as it dropped her down to sub-level 2. The lift doors opened and the breeze that flooded her senses smelt crisp and clean. Walking down a long, gently lit corridor past numerous doors, Olivia reached MarsLab1. Gaining access to the lab just before Hugh was able to follow Commander Mortimer's instructions to cut off her access to all areas within the base, Olivia strolled in and placed the rucksack on top of a metal counter.

Not all of the equipment had been set up but one particular machine had been rendered operational as soon as it was installed. The subroutine of the automatons, programmed to ensure its viability as soon as practicable. Olivia awoke the system from its sleep before opening the rucksack and removing the case. Flipping it open, a small cloud of vapour spilled from all sides of the frozen interior, dissipating quickly.

Picking the first of the glass containers out of its foam support, Olivia raised it to the light and could see nothing inside. Placing the container in the first slot, a metal shutter closed as soon as it detected her hand move away. An orange flashing light indicated the gentle warming of the container.

Taking the remaining containers one by one, Olivia filled all forty-two available slots. The metal shutters closed and flashed orange. She stood with crossed arms and watched as the lights started to change. Eventually, all lights were green and the system asked for the execution code to be entered. Olivia typed in the six-digit code and hit 'Execute'.

A gentle hum emanated from the large machine as Olivia waited patiently. Genetic material was extracted from each bio-sample within the glass containers. Transmitted into separate freshly thawed bovine eggs, from which the nuclei had been removed, the ova were subject to mild electric current before being deposited into individual culture sacs.

Objective complete, Olivia's attention was drawn to the view from the concave ground-to-ceiling window that looked out over the underground lake garden. Several acres of land sprawled out on the downward incline to the water. A variety of plants and young trees basked in the light of powerful, full-spectrum bulbs suspended from the rocky roof above. Powered by the excess of solar electricity produced by the planetary network of PoleGuard units.

Beyond the garden, the full-spectrum bulbs illuminated an expanse of still water that went on as far as the eye could see. Olivia's observations were interrupted by the beeping of the machine, indicating the successful completion of phase one.

Hastily returning up to the medical room without hindrance, she reconnected to the Veil spacecraft as Hugh and Commander Lacey Mortimer saw the unconscious Morgan and Laurence lying strapped to the beds on their monitor.

'Olivia, what happened?' asked Lacey searchingly.

'A temporary disconnection. I have re-established the link,' Olivia responded.

'You have one chance to tell me why you accessed MarsLab1,' Lacey impatiently said, clenching her fist. Silence ensued. Hugh had monitored Olivia's actions up to her access to the labs, but the lab itself was free of cameras. 'Tell me now!'

'I am following mission directives,' Olivia responded calmly.

'I give you mission directives! I'm in command here!' fumed Commander Mortimer, met with a brief pause from the other side.

'My directives are set by Mike Argo,' replied Olivia, a warm smile on her face, running a finger down the side of Morgan's face and tracing round the side of her oxygen mask.

'Mike Argo is dead! You will tell me what you were doing in MarsLab1!'

'Commencing the cloning protocol,' Olivia conceded as her smile spread wider. Commander Mortimer looked at Hugh in confusion. Neither was aware that such technology had been either constructed or brought down to the Exodus Base.

'Who are you cloning?' Lacey's tone quivered in angry anticipation.

'Mike Argo, Bob Meertens, Josephine Hancock, Jerome Docherty, Vincent Madden, Henrietta Rekman, Isabel Fuentes, Katsu Otani...' Olivia began to list the names of employees of Argo Industries, members of Onyx and others. As the list grew longer, Lacey Mortimer looked to Hugh, who returned a blank stare.

'Is this what it's all been about? From the beginning? Was this the plan?' Lacey interrupted, mouthing the words 'lock her in,' to Hugh.

As the pressure pads at the doors of the medical room locked and turned red, Olivia carried on looking at Morgan's resting eyes.

'No, the cloning protocol was only intended to be used in case of mass decimation of the Onyx leadership. What are your intentions?' asked Olivia as Hugh activated the GridWatch droids.

'My intentions? My intentions are to keep you guarded in that medical room until I can come down there and personally rip your fucking head off!' shouted Commander Mortimer.

'Mr Argo would have been very disappointed in you, Commander. He spoke highly of you. When the time comes, he will know the truth,' Olivia said monotonously, as Commander Mortimer burst out in a torrent of laughter.

'Disappointed in me? You have no idea, do you? When the time comes, you will be the disappointed one!' shouted Lacey Mortimer.

Olivia severed the connection to the irate commander as she heard several GridWatch droids arrive outside the medical room. Approaching a control console, Olivia entered the Exodus Base control override code and gained instant access to the base and all systems.

'She has gained full access to Exodus Base systems!' said Hugh with alarm.

Entering a sequence of letters and numbers into the comms system, Olivia's finger hovered over pressing 'Send'. Pushing down, the sequence was transmitted to the Veil, instantly activating the explosive charges on the ship. Within a split second, the Veil was decimated. Shattered into billions of pieces in the silence of space.

THE END

30707820R00170

Printed in Poland
by Amazon Fulfillment
Poland Sp. z o.o., Wrocław